The Lost Story

Amit Goyal
Sudhanshu Gupta

GRAPEVINE INDIA

Grapevine India Publishers Pvt. Ltd.
Plot No. 4, First Floor,
Pandav Nagar,
Opposite Shadipur Metro Station,
Patel Nagar,
New Delhi - 110008
India
grapevineindiapublishers@gmail.com
contact@grapevineindia.in

First published in India by Grapevine India Publishers in 2012

Copyright © Amit Goyal & Sudhanshu Gupta, 2012

Typeset and layout design: A & D. Co.

All rights reserved

For sale in India only

Printed and bounded in New Delhi

This book is sold subjected to the condition that it shall not, by way of trade or otherwise, be lent, resold, hired out, or otherwise circulated without the publisher's prior written consent in any form of binding or cover other than that in which it is published and without a similar condition including this condition being imposed on the subsequent purchaser and without limiting the rights under copyright reserved above, no part of this publication may be reproduced, stored in or introduced into a retrieval system, or transmitted in any form or by any means (electronic, mechanical, photocopying, recording or otherwise), without the prior written permission of both, the copyright owner and the above mentioned publishers of this book.

Acknowledgements

I never imagined I would write a book. When Vidya Subramanian, a close friend, told me many years ago that I would do that one day, I brushed the comment aside and never thought about it again. So my first and biggest thank you goes out to Vidya, for believing in me even before I did. And for the fact that this book would not read half as well as it does right now if it wasn't for her editing effort.

I would also like to thank both my parents and my sister, Divya, for their love and support. A very special thank you to Shweta Chandan and G Arjun – for all the encouragement and the good times we've spent together.

Thanks also to Ash Roy, G Force, Ashwin and Arjun Vagale of Jalebee Cartel – if I had to retrace my steps to where it all began, it has to be the day when you brought a few simple lines I wrote to life with *Mirrors*. To Sameer Desai, the editor for indianvideogamer.com, for giving me an opportunity to write for his website, further bolstering my confidence, my heartfelt thanks. He has also agreed to read this book, which will be the first work of fiction he has ever read of his own free will. This has to be some kind of historic milestone.

Thanks are also due to Dev Bhatia, for helping us out so much with the promotion of the book; to Tamagna Ghosh, for a fantastic cover design; and to Grapevine India, for all the helpful inputs and feedback that went into making the book better.

And finally, a big thank you to all our readers and friends. We hope you enjoy reading this book as much as we have enjoyed writing it.

Oh, and Mohit Malani, I *did* write about it. How about that?

— **Amit Goyal**

Everything has a beginning. The first time that I was ever encouraged to write was in third grade by my English teacher (whose name I cannot remember). She gave me a 10 on 10 in my essay on "The Autobiography of a Horse". That was the first and the last time that I ever scored so much in anything academic. A sincere thank you goes out to her... for giving me a 10 on 10.

In more recent times, I would like to thank Divya Rai and Saurabh Garg for their unstinting support and encouragement. I still think you guys pull my leg with all the kind words – but I shall not complain.

I thank my parents – for their love and support even when my endeavours are not convincing enough.

To Bethune Velamati for his three great ideas for short stories – all of which revolved around a bar, a bunch of guys, a (few) beautiful girls and a bet. Thankfully, none of those stories made it into the book.

A Jupiter sized thank you to Vidya Subramanian, G Arjun, Dev Bhatia and Tamagna Ghosh. Words are not enough to list down the reasons for thanking you all – so please imagine that there is another Jupiter out there in the Solar System with a big 'Thank You' engraved around it.

Lastly, thank you to the readers. Hope you enjoy reading the book.

— **Sudhanshu Gupta**

Contents

"What is it about stories that fascinates you?"   *9*

Chapter 1: The Hunt   *17*

"It's not yours yet."   *31*

Chapter 2: Happy New Year   *37*

"How do we hide on an empty dance floor?"   *52*

Chapter 3: The Long Journey Home   *56*

"You can always change their fate with a stroke of your pen."   *89*

Chapter 4: Fearless   *94*

"Aren't you even a little afraid to open the door?"   *116*

Chapter 5: Love At First Sight   *125*

"You will need the key. That is the only way."   *141*

Chapter 6: Re-entry   *147*

"These are not my memories."   *164*

Chapter 7: The Broken Bottle   *174*

"Are you here to steal from my house?"   *193*

Chapter 8: The Annoying Old Man   *203*

"You love playing God, don't you?"   *215*

Chapter 9: Wish You Were Here   *223*

"The fact that they end."   *245*

Chapter 10: The Lost Story   *248*

"What is it about stories that fascinates you?"

"So, what is it about stories that fascinates you?"

Sandy snapped back to attention as he heard the words. His heart was beating quicker than normal, and he still hadn't quite wrapped his head around the fact that he was sitting in Saleem Afzal's drawing room.

The frail old man, Mr Afzal – in the flesh! – waited patiently for an answer to his question.

Saleem Afzal. Winner of The Booker Prize... His house! His drawing room! His couch!

"Listen, son. Spacing out suits me much better than it does you. So how about an answer right about now?" Saleem Afzal repeated.

"Could you repeat the question?"

Could you repeat the question? You know perfectly well what he asked you, you idiot. Of all the people in front of whom I could make a fool of myself, I had to do it in front of Saleem Afzal.

"What is it about stories that fascinates you?"

There was a hint of exasperation in Saleem's voice. Sandy didn't want to keep him waiting for an answer, so he blurted out a response before he had fully articulated it inside his head.

"The fact that they end, sir."

"Excuse me?"

"Uh... it's because they come to an end. You know, like how there's always an ending to a story. It doesn't go on and on forever even after the 'story' part is over..."

Sandy trailed off and fell silent. Saleem frowned.

"You didn't think it through, did you?"

"No sir... I didn't," Sandy admitted dejectedly. *This is not going well at all.*

"Can you please stop calling me that?"

"What, sir?"

"Sir."

"Oh... okay, sir."

Saleem sighed and closed his eyes. Sandy took the opportunity to survey his surroundings; and from what he could see, it was quite evident that Saleem spent a lot of his time in the drawing room. A blanket lay crumpled at one end of the couch that he was sitting on, as if Saleem had slipped out of it just before Sandy arrived. The glass top of the table in front of him had rings left behind by the countless mugs that had been placed on it, a couple of used plates with dried gravy on them stared patiently through the glass top, and the rest of the table had newspapers and magazines strewn all over it. *Are We At the Brink of Another World War?* screamed the newspaper closest to him. The TV remote lay right next to Saleem on the couch. The dining table beyond the sitting area had nothing more than a few empty glasses on it, presumably left there by Saleem after a quick drink of water. Cobwebs on the corners of the walls collected dust, tempting a forgotten broom somewhere in the deep recesses of the house.

This house needs a good cleaning.

"What was your name again?"

"Sandy, sir."

"Okay, Sandy Sir... I can see that stimulating conversations are obviously not your area of expertise. So I'll get straight to the point. I have a proposition for you. Something I'm sure you'll like. But sustaining a conversation from one end can be really tiring. How about this... come back tomorrow and we'll discuss it?"

The not-so-subtle jibe was swept aside by the elation that Sandy felt at that point.

A proposition, he thought to himself. He wanted to jump and scream, run outside and kiss the first person he came across. But he figured that such a reaction would probably startle the old man to death. He controlled his impulse, and stood up calmly.

"I'll see you tomorrow, sir," he said in a shaky voice.

"Close the door on your way out."

Sandy started to walk towards the door.

"...and make sure you erase the word 'sir' from your vocabulary before you come next time."

Sandy nodded and opened the door to walk out of the apartment.

"And kid... one more thing – I really liked the story you sent me."

Sandy's heart swelled with joy once again, but he couldn't quite find the words that he wanted to say. Instead, he just blushed, nodded sheepishly, and closed the door behind him. He had to muster all of his self-control to not break into a jig as he walked down the stairs.

"Can you believe it, Tara? The great Saleem Afzal! The one and only! He really liked my story. That's what he said... 'I really liked the story you sent me.' Those words. *Really. Liked.* I never quite appreciated the beautiful melody these two words create when put together."

Sandy raised his glass of juice and tipped it slightly towards Tara before taking a sip. He was intoxicated with joy. Everything felt unreal, almost like a dream. He was a big fan of Saleem

Afzal's, having read all of his books multiple times. In fact, Sandy attributed his desire to be a writer to Afzal, wanting to follow in the footsteps of the celebrated writer. He had come across his email address in the library database, and had finally mustered the courage to write to him and send him the story that he thought was his best work, asking for feedback and guidance. He had not really expected a reply. When he found that he had actually received one, Sandy had almost fallen off his chair. And when he found that Saleem Afzal actually wanted to meet him, he finally did.

"I don't think life could have been any better!" he said happily, gulping down the remainder of his juice in one go.

Tara smiled weakly. Her father had been made the Global Marketing Head at the MNC he worked at. Things were still in process, but they would be moving to Singapore in two or three months. She was going to tell Sandy today, which was why she had asked him to this dinner, but Sandy was so happy when he got back from meeting Saleem Afzal, that she didn't have the heart to break it to him. Just the prospect of meeting his idol had had him hopping like a bunny on steroids for the past week... and this was so much more.

Sandy did not notice Tara's consternation and went on.

"You know what he said? He said he had a proposition for me. Wow! What could it be, Tara? Maybe he's writing another book. I know he hasn't written anything for the past 23 years, but who's to say? Maybe he needs some help with that and wants to hire me as a research assistant. How great would that be!"

Tara nodded her head. Sandy's gestures were even more animated than his voice. The chicken dumplings on her plate looked delicious, but she wasn't feeling hungry at all. Sandy, however, did not miss a step.

"He is so old, Tara… nothing like how he looked on the covers of his book. Of course, it's been so many years… and they haven't been kind to him. And he lives alone… seemed kind of sad and lonely. Nobody should have to see such days. Certainly not someone as extraordinary as Saleem Afzal," Sandy said.

"Doesn't he have a wife… or children?" Tara asked.

"Never got married. I wonder why. I mean, girls must have been lining up for him back in the day. Tara, I can't wait for tomorrow! Oh… by the way, you said you wanted to talk about something when we spoke yesterday. What is it?"

"Nothing… I've forgotten what it was. Let's eat."

"So here's the deal, kid – considering you are such a huge fan, you would know that I haven't written anything in years."

Sandy nodded his head. Saleem was talking through the biryani in his mouth that Sandy had brought him.

"This biryani is delicious, by the way. Get some more for me tomorrow. Anyway, the point is that I haven't written anything for a very long time but I want to. And I can't do it alone."

"I don't get it," Sandy said, holding his breath for Saleem's response.

"It's not that I can't write a story… I just can't write all of it. It just stopped happening abruptly after I wrote *Lighthouse*. I tried and tried but…" He left the sentence hanging and sighed. He stole a glance at the door on his right. The room was locked. "Anyway. This is where you come in."

Sandy's eyes were wide open. He could see where this was heading, and it seemed too good to be true.

"This is going to be my last book. And you are going to

write it with me. I don't care how it turns out, but I want that rush of flipping through the pages of my creation one more time. It's been far too long. Publishing it shouldn't be a problem either. I might be a has-been, but my name still commands some respect."

"What exactly do you mean when you say that I'm going to write it with you?" asked Sandy in a trembling voice. His head was swimming.

"We're going to collaborate, kid, and this is how it's going to work – One of us starts a story and takes it up to a point, from where the other person continues. While the first person works on the first half, he cannot tell the other what he's working on. Not even the slightest of hints. When the second person receives the first half, he has to take it forward without any inputs from the first person. Understood?"

"Yes!" Sandy was breathless. He had goosebumps. It sounded a bit unconventional, but he was not complaining. His name was going to appear alongside the great Saleem Afzal's on a book! He always wanted to be a writer, but such a start to his career was beyond his wildest fantasies!

"So my final book is going to be a book of short stories..." said Saleem to himself as much as to Sandy.

"Makes sense, doesn't it?" said Sandy, not realizing that the thought had tumbled out of his mouth. Saleem raised an eyebrow.

"I... I mean..." stammered Sandy, "...it's been so long since you wrote anything... I bet you must be bursting with stories to tell. Why tell just one, right?" Sandy chuckled nervously, but Saleem just stared back at him. "No offence, sir," he added hurriedly and fell silent.

Saleem continued to stare at Sandy for a while, his thoughts indiscernible. Then, his features relaxed.

"None taken. Lets get started. I've already emailed you the first half of our first story. Don't come back before you finish it."

Good kid, thought Saleem as Sandy closed the door behind him on his way out.

He got up gingerly and walked to the window. It wasn't much of a view – the rear wall of the neighbouring building. Saleem drew the curtains. The room instantly went dark. He walked back slowly to the couch, sat down, and leaned back.

I hope you are happy now, thought Saleem. He was angry and bitter about his situation, his condition, about himself. He had no control over things any longer... he had lost all control 23 years ago. Ever since that fateful day when everything had changed.

Saleem turned his head and stared at the lock on the door.

"Go easy on him. He is a good kid," he said out loud to the emptiness of his house.

Sandy ran up the stairs of his apartment building. He couldn't wait to see what Saleem had sent him.

I'll be the first person to see something the great Saleem Afzal has written in 23 years! God, I hope this is not just a dream.

His mother opened the door. He greeted her with a quick 'hi' and made his way to his room.

"What's the big rush, Sandy? Come for dinner," his mom called after him.

"Not hungry, mom. Leave it in the fridge for me... I'll eat later."

"Why don't you come and eat with me and your father?"

"You know Sandhya, I think I'm forgetting what our son looks like," his father called out in a lighthearted tone from the dining room.

"Very funny, dad! I'll catch you guys later," he shouted and shut the door behind him.

Sandy opened his email and saw Saleem's mail. The document was called *Untitled 01*. Sandy downloaded it, while simultaneously trying to take off his shoes and jeans, and pulling up his shorts. He took about 30 seconds to change, and then sat down in front of his laptop on the desk. The document had been downloaded.

Sandy could feel the hair on his arms stand up in anticipation. He took a deep breath, and double-clicked on the document.

CHAPTER 1

The Hunt

Sujit walked slowly along the cycle path. The calmness of the lake on his left was in sharp contrast to the passive belligerence of the small trees and bushes that lined the face of the hill on his right. They threatened to reclaim the path should the opportunity present itself. The invisible insects that made these trees their home added to the effect, their cacophony lending their hosts a continuous guttural; the kind that insects make when darkness slowly begins to creep in. But to Sujit it seemed almost orchestral, and he felt oddly soothed by it. *Order out of chaos*, he thought and chuckled to himself. From a distance, he would have seemed like a man walking in a trance. But in fact, he was very aware, taking in these sounds and sights, and the fresh mountain air, as he walked further along the lake in the picturesque town of Bhimtal. The sky was overcast, and he preferred it that way. The forests that covered the face of the surrounding mountains looked lush and sombre, as if they held a million secrets.

It was a peaceful little town, with most pesky tourists making their way to the more popular Nanital, further up on the mountain range in front of him. At night, the shops, hotels, and houses of Nanital came together in an elaborate arrangement of lights, giving an impression of an alien ship looming ominously, poised to strike with whatever evil it brought along from the far reaches of the universe.

The world, he thought, *is always tipped at the edge of an accident waiting to happen.*

Fahid wouldn't have agreed, thought Sujit. He shuddered, trying to push the thought away, only to drift over to a much more disturbing one.

He heard the screams, and the frantic shuffling of feet, as his fearsome foe came for Sujit after marking him for his next prey. He ran down the corridor into the door leading to the staircase. He ran up the stairs till he was out of breath, feeling the presence of the terror bearing down on him. His chest was exploding. Soon he was on all fours, struggling up what seemed to be an endless flight of stairs. The exit was guarded by two gargoyles, staring down at him with manic grins on their faces. He could hear the heavy breathing of the monster behind him, and the sinister incantations. It was poised to strike, and there was nowhere left to run. The gargoyles at the top of the staircase began to shake, and then crack apart, and the grin on their faces widened to a leer in the fiery red glow of the sky. He had to face him. He had to turn around.

But he didn't want to.

Sujit stopped and turned to face the lake, instead. He let its tranquility wash over the chaos created by the flashes from his past. He continued to push it away, allowing himself to believe that when we look the other way, the monsters stop chasing us. In a world tipped precariously at the edge of chaos, he held on to the notion that time was on his side. He stood rooted to his spot, staring intently at the stillness of the lake. He then went down to the edge and unwound the fishing line.

The hotel had been kind enough to lend him one of theirs, and suggested pointedly that he might want to take a local fisherman along. It was a half-hearted attempt, dictated by hotel policy. They had been wary of him, having sensed that something was not quite right about Sujit. They probably ruled out delinquency pretty early, or else he would have been evacuated unceremoniously as he was during his stay in Salsburg. Perhaps it was his demeanor, distant and foreboding, and it worked out just fine for Sujit. For his part, he didn't particularly mind Chandra. In fact, Chandra was one of the very few people he liked talking to. He knew the most interesting stories about the city, even if they seemed a bit far-fetched, and he was always smiling, which eased the burden that Sujit always carried with him. But he knew Chandra had gone to his village, and Sujit wanted to be left alone. He turned down the hotel's suggestion firmly, and they did not insist again.

What they didn't know was that Sujit was an expert at handling a fishing rod. In his training days in the First Order, he often spent a lot of time on the banks of the Crystal Lake, with his mentor, Fahid. He remembered his booming voice and the twinkle in his eyes when they discussed irrelevant topics such as balance in the universe, and the purpose of the Order. Mostly, he remembered the skin peeling off his face as he was consumed before his eyes. He remembered the screams.

He had to face him. He had to turn around.

Sujit pushed away the returning thoughts by focusing on the surroundings. He could see a bunch of tourists on a distant bank, and could hear the ringing of bells for the evening prayer at the temple behind him. He then settled in on a dry spot at the edge of the lake, and threw in the line.

Prayer and temples were the first things he turned to after the horrible events during the hunt. He had never been a religious man, and neither was he sure of God's existence. But for some reason, he had always felt drawn to the repose within the walls of temples.

"You may find it strange that most of us readily believe in the concept of a higher power that has never been directly perceived," Fahid had said, "but people do find peace in it. And that is what matters."

Sujit had never admitted the fact to anybody that for some reason, temples made him feel at peace. He would sit in a temple and watch people pray. He felt as though he could feel their tranquility and steadfast devotion and he would almost feel that divine presence that Fahid spoke of so lovingly. Almost.

Which is why he spent a lot of time at temples after Fahid's death, hoping to get closer to God, to be able to talk to Him and gain from His wisdom, and mostly to find peace. Instead, all he found were memories, the screams, the incantations, and the grin on the faces of the gargoyles.

He had to turn around.

When prayer didn't work, he turned to the next best thing – Heroin.

Unlike temples, it worked like a charm. With the drug flowing through his veins, disconnected flashes from happier times followed the initial euphoria. And among them, he felt at peace. In most of them, he returned to the Crystal Lake and the many conversations with Fahid.

'Had we known that time was so short, had our conversations been different?' Sujit often wondered.

Eventually, the drug would wear off... and all that he would be left with were a filthy room, a filthy bed and a woman he had no recollection of. The edge of the chaos on which our world tethers would return with reality, and he would no longer be able to drown out the screams till the next hit.

With no help coming from any quarters, Sujit began to travel. He would pick places that were small, sparsely populated, and had a 'static' feel to them. He would never stay in one place for more than two weeks – no friends, no baggage.

He had to turn around… but was he ready?

His time in Bhimtal was almost up, and just as he was figuring out his next destination, he felt a mighty tug on the line. He had caught something!

At first, he was taken aback by the effort his prey was making to break free. His first reaction was to let go, but an old fire suddenly flared inside him. He did not know why, but he wasn't going to give up. He came out of his stupor and the world around him filled with sound and colour. He pulled hard at the line, and the desire to triumph over his prey overtook everything else he was feeling. Somehow, in that moment, there was only hunter and game—nothing else mattered.

He was not going to let go, and he gave the line another tug, just as the screams returned inside his head.

"So? Do you have something for me?" asked Saleem.

"Umm… yes." Sandy leaned forward and extended a few sheets of paper. His hands were shaking with nervousness. Saleem looked at the sheets in front of him, and then leaned back and put his hands behind his head without taking them.

"Read it out to me," he said, and settled deeper into the couch.

Sujit tugged so hard at the rod that the line snapped. "Must've been a really big one," he sighed to himself.

He sat back down and took out the little packet from his

pocket—the one that he always carried with him. He carefully lined up the tools: the curved head of a silver spoon, a zippo, a syringe, fresh needles and a small plastic bottle of heroin. He attached the fresh needle to the syringe and emptied a carefully measured quantity of the white salvation on the spoon. He didn't need anything to weigh it on. Like an addict, he could look at the fine crystals and know their weight. He drew some water from the lake into the syringe and squirted it over the crystals. Clicking open the zippo, he lit it in one quick gesture of the thumb, kept it under the base of the spoon and watched as the damp crystals slowly melted into a white liquid. Drawing the heroin into the syringe, he held it upside down to make sure there was no air trapped in it. Without a flinch, he inserted the needle into the median cephalic vein at the crook of his left elbow. As a last measure to avoid any air, he drew some blood out, and finally pushed the now reddish elixir slowly and steadily all the way until the last drop.

Headrush.

The lake became absolutely still. The breeze slowed down. The chatter of the tourists at the other side now seemed even more distant. The green of the trees started to blend with the blue of the sky. The screams and the incantations started to dissipate.

Peace.

His mind floated into the past.

He saw himself standing at the banks of the Ganga at Haridwar. His parents had just been cremated. They said somebody had slipped into the house at night and murdered them in their sleep. They talked in hushed voices about the state of the bodies, the missing parts, the bites. They talked in even quieter voices of the monster that some of them had seen fleeing the house.

Sujit was in a state of shock. He had been orphaned. He was eight years old.

His thoughts then wandered to the training camp of the First Order. He had been adopted by Fahid from the orphanage a year after his parents' death. For the next decade, every single day, he trained to be a killer. He trained in martial arts, to use everything from a kitchen knife to a .50 caliber Barrett sniper as weapons. He mastered stealth and silence, grit and patience. In another life, at 19, he would have probably been studying economics or history or arts and chasing girls. However, in this life, he studied guns, and could assemble and disassemble an M-16 rifle in less than 35 seconds and could hunt and kill any animal to walk the planet with his bare hands.

He was always Fahid's favourite. "You shall be the best amongst us," Fahid told him. "And as a member of First Order, you will protect humanity from the forces of darkness. That is as God willed and that is how it shall be."

By the time Sujit was 19, Fahid had taken him under his wing completely. Within the next few years, they had become partners. It was a First Order policy to hunt in pairs. It made operations swifter, efficient, and fail-safe.

Fahid would spend four hours each morning praying by the Crystal Lake.

"Why do you pray so much?" Sujit would ask him.

"We are all children of God. But the members of the First Order have been bestowed with the task of carrying out His work with our own hands. We must thank Him for this honor each day of our lives. Besides, it helps one retain focus, something that you must learn to do. You can accomplish more with your mind than you will ever get out of muscle and ammunition," Fahid would say before going back to praying.

Sujit, not being a believer, would argue with Fahid, "If your

God is the almighty, then why does he create evil to begin with? Is he toying with us? And if he is so almighty then why doesn't he eliminate evil once and for all? Why does he leave us humans to clean up after him?" He believed monsters were simply freaks and a manifestation of the human mind. All very mortal. All very fallible.

"You won't understand right now, Sujit. There has to be a balance to things. A balance to the universe," Fahid would comment.

They would frequently get into this debate about balance and order in the universe.

"Balance! The world is constantly tipped at the edge of disaster waiting to happen and you sit by this lake and call it balance? This does not make any sense."

"Now now, Sujit. This is merely a way of looking at things. What you see as tipping at the edge of disaster, I see as perched finely in balance. Besides, the universe always tries to balance and stabilize itself."

Sujit would eventually walk off.

It didn't take him long to become obsessed with the idea of closure. Sujit grew impatient for revenge, now that he had the tools and means to pursue his parents' killer. He justified his desire for revenge with a misplaced sense of justice. He believed if he could slay The One, the evil that commanded all darkness, that he would be able to end this for good. He had begun his search for The One and his lair. He began pulling out and interrogating his minions and parasites from the dark alleys night after night and slaying them. This led to the leaders of the First Order becoming more and more concerned. He was upsetting the balance. He was pulling out too many monsters. Asking too many questions. This had started a chain reaction. The Dark Side retaliated. More knights of the First Order perished. The world had started to shake and stumble on the edge of disaster.

One day, by the lake, Sujit told Fahid that it was time. He had finally located The One and was going after him. He was going for the final hunt. By the time Fahid could turn around and say anything, he was gone.

His thoughts drifted to the grand mansion in front of which he stood that fateful night. The air was completely still. No moon. No sound. No activity. For some reason, the mansion was completely unguarded. Sujit had not met any resistance. Not even a foot soldier. *They would never leave their mansion unguarded like this.*

It was a trap and he knew it. But his thirst for revenge drove him to take the risk. He opened the heavy double doors and stood in the middle of the great hall. *The architect of this mansion must have a thing for gargoyles*, he thought to himself. He drew his twin Desert Eagles and made his way up the staircase that led up from the hall.

Pain. Panic. Fear. Flashes.

Sujit heard the screams, and the frantic shuffling of feet, as his fearsome foe came for him after marking him for his next prey. He ran down the corridor into the staircase. He ran up the stairs till he was out of breath, feeling the presence of the terror bearing down on him. His chest was exploding. Soon, he was on all fours, struggling up what seemed to be an endless flight of stairs, even though he could see the end of it up ahead. The exit was guarded by two gargoyles, staring down at him with manic grins on their faces. He could hear the heavy breathing of the monster behind him, and the sinister incantations. It was poised to strike, and there was no where left to run. The gargoyles at the top of the staircase began to shake, and then crack apart, and the grin on their faces widened to a leer in the fiery red glow of the sky. He had to face him... he had to turn around...

Fahid had followed him to the mansion knowing Sujit could not fight The One alone. He had come to his rescue, and now, Fahid was dead. Sujit blacked out.

His thoughts meandered back to the quarters next to the Crystal Lake where he had awakened after the hunt. He couldn't move. It felt like a mountain had collapsed on him, pinning every part of his anatomy down to the bed. His memory was completely blank and he had no recollection of what had happened. He was told that Fahid was dead and, for some reason, The One had spared him. Despite all the painkillers and the medication, visions of Fahid's gory death came back to his head. He couldn't sleep. He spent countless nights wondering why The One hadn't kill him as well. He mourned the death of Fahid, the only person who had ever come close to being a father to him. He held himself responsible for his death. Anger and guilt, compounded by questions of why he had been spared accumulated within his mind.

The day he got better, and could walk, Sujit was cast out of the First Order.

"There is no place for people who cannot respect God and his balance in the First Order," he was told.

A loud shriek woke Sujit from his trance.

He looked around. He was back at the lake in Bhimtal. It had become dark. He had completely lost track of time in his drug-induced reverie. He took in a deep breath of the cool mountain air. His eyes traced the dark outline that the hills around him drew against the deeper, darker sky. The lake seemed to have an eerie stillness about it.

Ever since he had been caste out of the First Order seventeen years ago, he had wandered. It wasn't just aversion to human attachment that kept him loose. It was also the tails. For the last seventeen years he had had not one, but two tails. He had noticed them for the first time in Gdansk. Sitting by the pier at night, staring down at the endless ocean, he had spotted a figure from the corner of his eye. While he had not looked at it directly, he had become aware of the pair of eyes locked on him. On his way back, he had felt another shadow bearing down upon his own. Both the First Order and the Dark Side were keeping an eye on him.

He detested the First Order for casting him away and not understanding his actions. He had devoted most of his life to the service of the First Order only to be thrown out. He thought they were weak and blind in the faith of God, who really didn't care about what happened to them. None of them had understood his quest to end the conflict and rid the world of evil. "Where there is good, there must be evil," they would say. *Spineless fools*, he thought.

And of course he hated the Dark Side for being responsible for the death of his parents, the death of Fahid and for everything wrong that had ever happened to him. Isolated and alienated, he harboured his hatred for everybody. He was preparing himself for the inevitable, which would come one day. Which side would attack first? He didn't know.

Sujit scanned the trees and bushes in the distance to his left. That is where the shriek had come from. His eyes had adjusted well to the moonless night and the heroin had drained out of his system by now. His eyes darted to the right, as he stood up and did a quick survey. One of his tails, the fair, brown haired kid was gone. He had obviously been a new recruit in the First Order. But the absence of the fair tail was not what struck him. It was the multiple pairs of eyes he spotted in the growth all around him. Soon, they started emerging. They crept slowly towards him from all directions. He was surrounded on all sides. The monsters were countless and were filling up the space between the bank of the lake and the tree line. They crept towards Sujit as he prepared himself for what he knew was going to be his last fight.

His whole life – this tale of loss and hatred – was finally in its last chapter. As the vile creatures inched closer to him, Sujit thought of the First Order and what he now considered to be their betrayal. His heart was exploding with anger. *"They have left me here to die."*

The monsters stopped converging ten feet away from him. They encircled him as they continued to growl and gnaw at the air towards him. Their necks snapped with horrible sounds.

"What's the matter? Let's go!" Sujit screamed at them in desperate anger.

But they didn't make a move. They stood back at an ominous distance, surrounding him. Sujit screamed back at the ring of evil around him.

Slowly, from behind the monsters, The One emerged and stopped a few feet away from him. Hatred and anger exploded in the two pairs of eyes that were now sizing each other up for the second time, as the howls of the hordes surrounding them got even nastier. A dark, thick cloud descended upon this gathering in the valley as a cold wind howled through the tall pine and deodar trees around the lake.

What ensued was an epic battle. Teeth sunk into flesh. Nails scratched through skin and tore at bones. The two bodies twisted and were broken with a fury driven by pure hatred. Pain endured led to more pain delivered. They twisted and slammed each other in ways unimaginable by the sickest of imaginations. The wind turned into a gale as the trees around them howled and bent in pain. All this while, the monsters stood and screamed at the perverse display in front of them.

Finally, it came to an end. The monster lay face down on the ground. Sujit stood on his back, crushing him further down. He held the monster's head, and with one quick pull, ripped it out of its body. Sujit held the monster's head up high and let out a victorious scream, even as blood from the severed head gushed down his raised arms and on to his face.

It's over. It's finally over.

Sujit sank to the ground as the monsters began kneeling in front of him. They started chanting the incantations he had heard in The One's mansion that night.

He had done it. He had finally slayed The One who commanded all darkness. The quest he had begun eighteen years ago had finally come to an end. He felt a sense of joy. However, that elation was quickly overrun by anger, yet again. *The First Order.* They had not listened to him. They had ridiculed him. They had abandoned him. Admonished him. *Had they acted earlier, Fahid might have still been alive,* he thought. He now blamed the First Order for Fahid's death.

The minions picked him up and took him to the lake as the first rays of dawn broke through the horizon. Bells and chimes rang in the temple in the distance and filled the silence that had been created once the monsters stopped screaming and the wind stopped howling. He crawled up to the edge of the lake on all fours. He looked at his reflection in the water. It wasn't the Sujit he once knew in the reflection anymore. Years of hatred, isolation, heroin, killing, and carrying revenge in his heart had turned him into something else entirely.

Fahid's face looked back at him through the reflection. "Chaos is as much an illusion as order. Balance alone is final. If you upset the order of the universe, it will conspire in mysterious ways to balance it again."

Sujit covered his face with his hands. He wept as the monsters gathered around his feet. "Don't worry, my children! I will take care of you now," he said. And he wept some more.

Sandy stared at Saleem intently. He had a peculiar expression on his face, halfway between anger and pain. The silence in the room was deafening.

"Leave."

Saleem spoke with such finality that Sandy could not bring himself to protest or ask why he was being ejected so unceremoniously. He could feel the tears welling up in the corners of his eyes.

I think I've just messed everything up. I've disappointed Saleem Afzal.

Sandy got up and walked quickly to the door. He stopped when he heard Saleem's voice behind him just as he was getting out of the door.

"I'm working on something else.... something different.... I will mail it across to you by tomorrow."

Sandy let out a sigh of relief. "Thank you, sir. I won't let you down next time."

"You haven't let me down this time."

"Then...?"

"I just want to be by myself right now."

Sandy wanted to ask a million more questions, but it was evident that it would be of no use. He got up and left.

"It's not yours yet."

Saleem watched the whole fight unfold in front of him from the shadows. He felt nothing... it didn't matter who eventually won. It was a surreal sight, though – the ring of minions around the two fighters screaming and howling rabidly... The stars soon began to vanish into nothingness as sunlight slowly crept up on them. The mountains watched with stony silence. The lake watched with icy calm. Perhaps they knew and understood the futility of the battle too...

As the first rays of light broke over the mountain, the fight finally came to an end amidst the cacophony of the raging monsters and temple bells. With a cry that sounded as if it ripped his soul apart, Sujit tore the head off his defeated foe with his bare hands.

Saleem watched as the monsters carried off their new master, leaving the body of The One behind to rot. Dust to dust.

Saleem came out of his hiding spot, and walked up to the edge of the lake where the body of the demon lay. Blood from the headless body trickled into the lake, giving the water a reddish, muddy tinge. Saleem sank to his knees, feeling very thirsty all of sudden. He cupped his hands together, and drank from the tainted waters.

"No!"

Saleem woke up with a start. He looked around to find himself in familiar territory.

I must have dozed off while reading the story again.

In the dim light of the table lamp, he saw sheets of paper strewn around all over the room. Saleem got up, cursing the ceiling fan, his joints aching more than usual, as if admonishing him for not using his bed to sleep.

He walked painfully around the room, collecting each sheet of paper. One sheet had slipped partly under the doors of the locked room. Saleem pulling at it, but it wouldn't budge – as though something was holding it from the inside.

"Let it go! It's not yours...." Saleem stopped abruptly in the middle of the sentence. The sheet gave way and Saleem put them all together neatly in a stack on the side table, placing the lamp on top of them. The unspoken word rang in his ears, filling his mind with fear and apprehension.

Let it go! It's not yours yet.

In his mind, he could hear the sound of laughter. It wasn't a figment of his imagination.

"Any particular reason you're taking so much interest in Saleem Afzal, mister...?"

"Sandeep Gupta. But my friends call me Sandy," Sandy spoke brightly with a broad smile on his face. Perhaps a little too brightly to come across as genuine.

"We are not friends yet, are we Mr Gupta?"

Sandy's face fell. *This guy's not going to be easy.*

"I guess not," he said.

Sandy was in Khan Market, one of the more popular stomping grounds for the young, eager, and extravagant of Delhi. He had been sitting in the Jainson Bookstore for the last three hours, passing his time by reading Neil Gaiman's *Neverwhere*. Saleem had spoken very highly of the writer, and had asked Sandy to read both his books and his graphic novels, especially the *Sandman* series, which he would not stop raving about.

But that was not why he had come to the bookstore. He had come to meet the owner, Ashok Jain, a well known publishing agent, who had launched many famous authors. One of the authors associated with the *Jainson* name in their early days was Saleem Afzal.

"I'll have you know Mr Gupta that I did not deal with Saleem Afzal. I was too young when he was in action. My father, Brijnath Jain, dealt with him."

"Can I speak to him then?" Sandy asked.

"No, you can't."

Ashok did not offer an explanation as to why he couldn't speak to his father. Sandy was at a loss for things to say. The silence, broken only by the steady creaking of the ceiling fan, was becoming uncomfortable. Sandy decided to give it another shot, not willing to let his whole afternoon go waste.

"You must be what? 40 max?" he asked.

"Are you going somewhere with that?" Ashok said, clearly irritated.

"Yes. Saleem quit writing at his peak... about 23 years ago. You must have been in your teens back then. I was just wondering if your dad spoke about him to you?"

Ashok gave Sandy a piercing look. Maybe he sensed that Sandy was not going to relent.

"I don't need much... just a little bit of info about Saleem," Sandy persisted.

"What for?" Ashok asked.

"My college project."

"What's your project about?"

"Writer's block," Sandy lied smoothly.

"So you are going to ask me the question everyone asks?"

Sandy pulled out his winning smile. "Actually, no... I want to ask you something entirely different."

"And that is?"

"Saleem's love life. I know he never got married... but maybe a girlfriend? Or maybe his whole outlook towards relationships and stuff."

Ashok burst out laughing. He continued laughing for a whole minute before he stopped. And then he started again. Sandy felt a burst of irritation.

What's so funny? I hope he is not going to tell me that Saleem is gay.

"So you decided to ask me the second question that everyone asks." Ashok began shaking with laughter again. Sandy was very surprised because Ashok didn't come across as the kind of person who ever laughed out loud. With his sharp eyes, thin moustache, and a business-like demeanour, he seemed like the kind of person who could read through a P.G. Wodehouse novel with a straight face, constantly analyzing its saleability.

"No kid, he did not have a girlfriend... not that I know of."

Sandy was visibly disappointed. Ashok noticed, and decided to give him something to go on. He seemed harmless and genuine enough.

"Listen... I've met Saleem only a few times, maybe four or five. But my father did talk a lot about him. He had quite an imagination... always lost in a world of his own, even when he wasn't writing. He never mentioned a girl in his life, though. In fact, the only woman even remotely associated with Saleem was that editor woman... I can't remember her name but that was strictly professional. If there was something, dad would have known. Saleem told him everything. They were thick as thieves. But let me tell you something that might help you understand another aspect of your project's subject.'

Finally something worthwhile. Sandy leaned forward.

"Saleem's block probably didn't have anything to do with

emotional trauma. But physical trauma... that could well be the culprit."

Ashok paused dramatically in an attempt to build anticipation for what he was about to say next.

"Two months before the release of his last book – *The Lighthouse* – Saleem was in a major road accident. I know what you're thinking... that's the sort of thing that would have made the headlines, considering he was such a high profile personality. But it was swept under the rug primarily because Saleem came out unscathed. A drunk truck driver had crashed his lorry into his car on the highway. The truck was driving at almost 60, and Saleem was going much faster. The accident should have killed him. But it didn't even leave a scratch... just knocked him unconscious for three days."

"But wait... it gets stranger. While he was in the hospital, my dad went to see him and took me along. Saleem was unconscious, but I guess he was having nightmares... because kept saying strange things out loud."

"What kind of things?" Sandy asked.

"I don't remember for sure... but I think he was blabbering something about something that needed to be locked away and what not... it was very disturbing. The doctors said he was hallucinating. The more creative the person, the more creative the hallucination, they said. Made sense too. When he woke up, he didn't remember anything. The doctors kept him under observation for a couple of days, but they didn't detect any brain damage or internal injuries, so they let him go. And he seemed fine too... but he didn't write after that."

There was silence again. For some unfathomable reason, Sandy was afraid. He thought hard about the times he had spent with Saleem so far, trying to analyse their meetings for strange behaviour. His thoughts were interrupted by Ashok.

"Listen, I think you should leave now. I've given you enough food for thought, and I have this writer coming in... one of those MBA turned authors... they sell like hot cakes... Oh and, you cannot quote me on any of this. If any of this comes out, I'll deny it, and it is all outlandish enough for you to look like a fool, considering you have no credibility to your name," Ashok said.

"Definitely. Thank you for your time, sir." Sandy got up to leave.

"Are you going to buy anything for wasting so much of my time?" said Ashok, reverting to his usual curt manner of speaking.

"Yes. A couple of Neil Gaimans. Do you have any of his graphic novels, by any chance?"

Ashok made a face. "Comics are for children."

CHAPTER 2

Happy New Year

"So how was your meeting with that publishing agent?"

Tara and Sandy sat at their usual spot in the coffee shop. Sandy wasn't talking much. He appeared to be focussing all his energies on doodling on the newspaper on the table. *Civil Unrest at an all-time high in Argentina*, read the headline.

"Hello! I'm talking to you!" Tara repeated.

Sandy snapped out of his reverie. "It was interesting... but I didn't get what I was looking for."

"And what was it that you were looking for?"

"Some information about his love life, relationships... stuff like that."

"Uh-huh. And why did you need that?" Tara asked.

"Why don't you read this?"

Sandy held out a few sheets of paper, and went back to doodling on the newspaper.

To this day, Rahul doesn't know what made him do it. New Year's Eve always got a little out of hand, with the mad rush of parties and endless alcohol in a grand send off to the year gone by.

'What exactly do we celebrate?' thought Rahul, as he drove to his friend Suresh's place. That was where the festivities were scheduled to begin. *'What does the end of another year mean in the grand scheme of things? The clock ticks over from one moment to another on a planet celebrating alone among eight other lifeless rocks, circling around a ball of fire. And all of these lie ignored in some remote corner of one among the infinite galaxies of countless such systems. What is this moment worth in the grand scheme of things?'*

Of course, no one really wanted to listen to this nonsense, especially on New Year's Eve.

The radio reminded him to not drink and drive, just as a car full of screaming college students zoomed by. He carried on, then took a look at himself in the rear-view mirror and said out loud: *'Fuck it!'*

He took a U-turn at the next signal and switched off his cell phone after sending a message to Suresh that something had come up and he won't be able to make it to the party. He then drove back home.

No one was there, of course. His family had gone off to be part of a larger gathering of the extended family, which had the potential to get as crazy as it did in many of the hottest clubs in the city. As he thought of morning after hangovers and tired feet, Rahul felt good about his sudden decision to give it a rest this year.

He turned on his laptop and logged into Facebook. Though he wasn't averse to technology, or unfamiliar with Facebook, it still felt alien to him. He browsed through his news feed. Most of it announced where his friends and the rest of the people in his friends list were celebrating that night, there were a handful of new year resolutions, some flowery gibberish about all the promises and prosperity that the new year would bring, just like any other new year, and a few photographs from the family get-together two days ago.

He chuckled at a funny advertisement for a video game that wasn't half as good as the video, and then typed in her name in the search box.

To this day, Rahul doesn't know what made him do it. And he immediately regretted it.

She looked absolutely stunning in her new profile picture. He felt his gut clench, and for a nanosecond he was lost in that beautiful smile. '*I still love her.*' The thought blind-sided the left side of his brain for a split-second before better sense could dismiss it as a knee jerk reaction.

In that smile, he re-imagined a million moments. He remembered their first date, and how nervous he had been. It was his first ever date. She had told him how no movie is ever complete without popcorn. Rahul hated popcorn, but he shared popcorn with her in every movie they watched together.

Another movie, a few dates in. He spent the first half not watching the movie at all, instead contemplating whether to take her hand or not. In the second half, he did… and botched it up by landing up in a fairly messy tangle of arms. She laughed and untangled them, but did not let go of his hand.

Their first kiss… he still didn't know how he had summoned the courage to suggest it. She said no. He kissed her anyway. She didn't back off. He didn't know if he was doing it right. Then an arm wrapped around his neck. And then the other.

Taking a walk together, their fingers playing with each other's. He was half listening to her, and half in a daze. He loved her so much. The world couldn't have been more right.

He remembered the day he met her after spending six

months apart. He waited for her across the road. She saw him from the other side. And smiled her widest smile.

That smile, he thought, *I still love her.*

He had spent a very long time telling himself that he had moved on, but memories of her always surprised him with the intensity and ease with which they pervaded his mind. His mind would spring into denial at these moments, ignoring everything that followed the happy days and constructing a fairy tale of a future that could never happen. It was intoxicating, and he would allow his mind to run amok till he was rudely brought back to reality.

That wasn't happening tonight though. His mind insisted on going all the way through the troubled times that followed. The distance, never acknowledged yet painfully obvious, and always swept under the carpet. And finally, the break up.

'The roller-coaster and the house of horrors are often side by side,' he announced to the empty house, before finally giving in.

He remembered the phone call, the finality and determination in her voice. He couldn't believe that the same voice that had told him how much she loved him so often was telling him that it was all over. He remembered waking up the next morning, hoping against hope that it was all a horrible nightmare, and the shattering realization that it was not. The morning was so much worse than the night before, and the tears that he had held back amidst all the begging and pleading finally gave way.

He remembered meeting her a few days later to continue his desperate bid to turn things around. He had got her a gift. It was in his pocket. He kept thinking if it would be a good idea to pull it out. They talked, drank coffee and left. The gift remained in his pocket.

He remembered having crawled into a shell. His mind asked the same question again and again: '*Why?*' He didn't even know whom to ask. He stopped caring, but didn't stop feeling. Each day it became harder to wake up and go through the motions of the day, but he did anyway. He remembered his hollow smiles, and trying to drown himself in work, which went well, atleast for a little while.

He wrote to her a few times, but never got a response. He would stare at the only picture he had of the two of them for hours. Later, he buried it deep inside his drawer, but never threw it away. He stopped going to the places they had visited together, for fear of nostalgia. He stopped listening to the songs she loved. He tried to remove her from every aspect of his life, only to realize – after two long years – that he couldn't. She would forever be a part of his life.

Six years of his life had flashed through his mind in less than six minutes.

It was still five minutes to midnight. He felt better, but her smile stubbornly refused to leave him. He logged into his email account, and typed out a mail to her.

'*Happy New Year. Hope each passing year brings you success and joy.*'

Before he could press *send*, his mind sprang into action again. He imagined her waiting breathlessly for his email in front of her computer screen. Years of distance, and a string of short-term relationships only making her realize what she had lost. Then, a reply: *Let's meet.*

He imagined meeting her the very same night, away from the commotion of parties and celebrations in a quiet coffee shop. They look at each other, and finally do what they had stopped doing in the final days of their relationship. They talk. *Really* talk. They both work out what went wrong. And with that understanding comes the possibility of a future together. It is not spoken of, but it lingers in both minds.

He drives her back home. She gets out of the car and smiles. *'I'll call you tomorrow'*, she says. *That smile.*

A planet celebrating alone among eight other lifeless rocks, circling around a ball of fire. And all of these lie ignored in some remote corner of one among the infinite galaxies of countless such systems. What is this moment worth in the grand scheme of things?

Rahul laughed. He laughed his way into the New Year.

Just as Rahul was about to press *send*, the doorbell rang.

'Who could that be?' he wondered.

"Hmmm... makes you think if there might be something in his head. Doesn't it ?" said Tara.

Sandy nodded. Tara's eyes were darting between the sheets of paper she was holding and Sandy's face, almost as if the words in front of her had seized her and weren't quite ready to let go.

"Seems so real," she said softly.

"EXACTLY!" shouted Sandy, startling the three girls sitting at the adjacent table. "Which is why I need to know about his past life."

Tara raised her left eyebrow. Sandy always found her irresistibly sexy when she did that.

"I don't get it, Sandy. You'll have to be a little less cryptic."

Sandy leaned forward and took a deep breath.

"Tara, I can't disappoint him. I need to get this story right. And for that, I need a point of reference from his life... to get some clues about what might work and what might not—for him. This is the biggest thing that has ever happened to me, and probably the biggest thing that will ever happen to me. I can't afford to let him down."

There was a fire in him... of the kind Tara had never seen. He had always been passionate about everything, from his assignments and projects, to the debating society and the literary club he had co-founded in college. This, however, was something else. This bordered on desperation.

"You sound obsessed," she said.

"It's not that... It's just..." Sandy was grasping for words, shuffling his feet under the table, and looking nervous. "It's just that he's my role model, Tara. I want to be able to write like him. The way he wrote... writes... his books... they speak to me like no one else's work. And if he likes what I write, then that is the first step in that direction."

"So let me get this straight, Sandy. You plan to impress the guy by telling him a story straight out of his own life? Don't you think he'll want to be surprised by you?"

"But what if he doesn't like what I do with it?" Sandy asked.

"Then you move on and put this one aside. He wants to work with you so you can tell your own stories, Sandy. He wouldn't want you to write like him. He would want you to write like you. You'll be letting him and yourself down by trying to tailor it to his preference. He's telling his stories. You tell yours."

Sandy kept quiet for a while. Then he got up all of a sudden.

"You're right, Tara... I'm going to go home and finish it. Thanks a tonne! Don't know what I'd do without you."

Sandy kissed her on the cheek and left. Tara stared after him with sad eyes. She still hadn't told him about her imminent move to Singapore.

"You'll find out soon enough, sweetheart," she said softly.

Rahul looked at the clock in the system tray on his desktop. 12:10 AM, 1st January 2011.

Hmm. Can't be my folks already, he thought to himself.

Before he could get up, the doorbell rang again, and again, and again for the fourth time.

"I'm coming! Hold on!" he shouted at the door.

The bell rang twice again in the 8 seconds it took Rahul to get to the door.

Irritated, Rahul reached for the door knob shouting "God! What's the hur... Suresh?"

Rahul stood at the door wearing a bemused look and stared at the man who had been his closest friend for the last eight years. Before he could say anything, Suresh hugged him and picked him up a few inches above the ground.

"Hhhaappy Neeww Yeear, my friend," Suresh slurred as he hugged Rahul.

Rahul wriggled in the big man's grasp, trying to break free and said. "Happy new year to you too, you bloody giant. Now put me down. Will you?"

Suresh put him down and stumbled inside the house.

"What are you doing here, Suresh? I thought you'd be partying, getting drunk, and sweet-talking some woman in one of those super-expensive clubs.

Suresh was a well-known playboy among his friends. He was 28, lived alone and had a reputation of never having been in a relationship for more than three weeks at a stretch, and never having been single for more than three days at a stretch.

His friends were perpetually jealous of his popularity with women.

He dropped heavily down on the couch, rattling the large bronze figurine of the elephant-headed Ganesha that stood next to it.

"Yeah well I wasss. But after you sssent me that SssMsssS and sswitched off your phone, I knew you had decided to come home and ssulk over what'ss her name... yes... that Sspriha again."

"Of course not! I just didn't feel like starting the New Year getting wasted and waking up with a hangover the next day and... you know...?" Rahul fumbled for a logical explanation. Suresh, for his part, looked completely uninterested in what he was saying.

"Oh, don't give me that! That'ss what it wass and you know it." Suresh waved his right hand in the general direction of Rahul.

Rahul responded with a sheepish expression on his face, "Well I am mostly over her now... I think."

"Rahul. Rahul. My friend," Suresh had some trouble picking himself up, but he managed it after a few seconds of contorted flailing.

He walked up to Rahul and put his hands on his shoulders. "I've known you for what... eight yearss now?"

Rahul nodded.

"That makess it how long that you've known me?"

"Eight, I would guess," Rahul shrugged.

"Sso eight years we've known each other and the last three yearss you've been acting like a complete losser. I mean she'ss been gone for sso long. And you're sstill burying yourself deeper and deeper in... in... what are you burying yourself in?"

Rahul said nothing, hoping Suresh would forget the current topic of discussion before the next sentence formed inside his head.

"Nevvvaaaaar Mind... I've decided that I'm not going to let you do thiss to yourself anymore. I can't let my best friend wallow in hiss own sself induced misery forever." Suresh waved an unsteady index finger in Rahul's face. "Tonight, my friend, we're going to change all that. We're going to sstart thiss new year with a bang." He winked at the last word, in an attempt to emphasise the pun.

Rahul walked to his father's minibar in the room. "Come on, Suresh. You know I'd rather not. Here, shall I fix you a drink?"

Suresh followed him. "Nonssensse! And of course we're going to have a drink! But I'm going to make it... move!"

Suresh reached for the Smirnoff at the back of the shelf, knocking down a bottle of Jack Daniel's in front and, not noticing, turned towards Rahul.

"Pluss, you remember what Shakespeare said, don't you? He said, the best way to get over one woman, is to get another one! Seriously, what a guy! I'm always amazed at the truth he packed into simple words... Where are the shot glasses?"

Rahul smiled. "No, he didn't say that. And they're behind you on the second shelf."

Rahul wasn't going to labour the point. This was a discussion they had had multiple times and Suresh always won, especially when he was drunk.

Suresh poured two shots of vodka and handed one over to Rahul. Suresh raised his shot glass and his voice. "Let'sssss kickstart tonight, sssshall we?"

They gulped the vodka down.

"Now, get dressed. Quickly. I've got a car waiting downstairs with a group of friends and we're going out to party. There're ssome nice girlss in there and we're going to introduce you to some of them." Suresh pulled out his Dunhills and lit one with his Zippo embossed with a playboy bunny.

"Alright. I'll just put on a jacket and some shoes." Rahul knew Suresh was not going to leave without him.

"Yeah yeah, whatever. Just do it already." Suresh was already pouring another round of shots.

Rahul came back in a couple of minutes and Suresh handed him a refilled shot glass. "Let's go, buddy. Here'ss to a happy new year. And remember what Shakespeare said."

Two shots down, Rahul walked down the two floors with Suresh to his Honda City in an almost upbeat mood. The car was already full. There was another guy and three girls sitting inside already. The party was already in full swing: drinks were being poured sloppily into plastic glasses and Bob Sinclair was loudly imploring the world to hold on.

"Grab a seat next to those women in the back," Suresh winked at him again as he eased in behind the wheel.

Rahul squeezed in and introduced himself. They smiled and wished him a Happy New Year.

He smiled back at them. The two vodka shots had helped him leave some of his inhibitions and baggage back upstairs. "Well, I hope so, ladies. I sure hope so."

The drive was not going to be too long. Rahul was squeezed in next to a girl who had introduced herself as Neha. She was pleasant and pretty. Unlike most Delhi girls on New Year's Eve, she chose elegance over flamboyance in her dressing, wearing a blue coat over a simple yet tasteful black dress. Apart from some lipstick and some blue eye shadow to go with her coat, she was not wearing much make up. Rahul wondered if the alcohol made her more likeable. Rahul downed two vodka-cokes in quick succession. Their arms brushed each other's every now and then. He imagined Spriha's soft skin, the way it felt as he would draw fictitious figures on her back with his fingers. The way her smooth hair felt around his fingers, as he would tuck a stray lock behind her ears as they lay together looking into each other's eyes for hours. Neha's charms drowned in his two very potent vices: Alcohol and Spriha.

"Rahul! Hope you've met Neha! She's Ssssingle," Suresh yelled above the Black Eyed Peas' I have a feeling".

"And Neha! Hope you've met Rahul. He too… is sssssingle". He laughed loudly, as though he had said something incredibly funny. Rahul looked shyly at Neha who smiled back at him and hit Suresh playfully on his left shoulder. Rahul thought of Spriha smiling.

"We're here!" Suresh announced. "*The Warehouse*. Best place to party in town. I have a table reserved. Just walk up and mention my name." Suresh pulled up in front of the waiting valet.

The group walked into the club through the heavy door from the chill outside. Inside, it was as dark as the music was loud. Lights danced around in pre-programmed chaos. Bodies jumped and jived in the flashes of the strobe lights. '*It's like watching a movie at thirty frames per minute*' Rahul thought to himself.

To him, walking into a nightclub always felt like walking through two different dimensions. One moment you are freezing in the cold streetlights. A couple of steps, and you are standing in an immensely loud room, on a wooden floor with no room to stand.

Rahul stood in one corner of the twelve-foot bar and scanned the crowd through the crazy lights. He imagined he saw her, Spriha, dancing at the center of the crowd. He imagined walking up to her and holding her in his arms without saying anything. He imagined kissing her. Nightclubs are no places to hold meaningful conversations anyway.

Suresh grabbed him by his left arm.

"Hey! Quit gawking and let's get a drink"

"What?" Rahul screamed back.

Suresh came within inches of his ears and shouted, "I SAID – QUIT FOOLING AROUND AND LET'S GET A DRINK."

Nightclubs are no places to hold not-so-meaningful conversations either.

The two joined the rest of the group at their table. Suresh made his way to the middle of the semi circular couch and squeezed in. Neha waved Rahul into the spot next to her. He sat down and looked across at Suresh who was uncorking a Dom Perignon and pouring it into everybody's champagne glasses.

A few songs and a couple of drinks later, everybody settled down as the alcohol settled in them. Rahul was surprised by the fact that he was having a good time. Neha was laughing at his jokes, and her eyes were playfully flirting with his. Rahul thought about how it used to be with Spriha. They would spend hours at nightclubs holding each other close and dancing. It would feel like they were the only ones in the club.

For some reason, he felt the same way right now. Except that he was alone and there was no Spriha.

"Lost-in-trance-boy!" Suresh shook his left shoulder.

Rahul looked up at Suresh who was standing beside him. "What happened?"

"You passed out! Come on! Let's go! Everybody's on the dance floor! Neha's missing you!" Suresh grabbed him by his arms and picked him up.

Rahul took a few seconds to find the ground with his feet. "You go ahead... I need to get to a washroom first"

"Alright! But don't take too long or Neha will get bored," Suresh winked. "And no more drinks for you tonight!" Suresh disappeared into the crowd.

Rahul washed his face with cold water and looked at himself in the mirror. He missed Spriha. He regretted the fact that he missed her. He was annoyed at himself for not being able to move on even as another year passed him by.

He thought of what Suresh had told him Shakespeare had said; and then thought of Neha. *Yes. It was time to move on.* He straightened his shirt and jacket, and walked back to the dance floor wading through the crowds, with more conviction and a spring in his step.

Just then, he saw her.

There she was... a couple of feet away, in a short green dress, looking as gorgeous as ever. Rahul could not believe his eyes. The music died down to a dull thump as their eyes met. Everything faded to nothingness; and those short seconds in which their eyes met seemed as long as millennia. The song changed to "You're beautiful" by James Blunt. It was her favourite song, and she smiled.

Rahul realized he had been holding his breath all this while, and he slowly let go, trying to compose himself. Spriha closed her eyes, and started to move slowly to the song. She raised her arms above her shoulders and clasped them together, moving slowly to every note. She opened her eyes for just one second, with a look in her eyes that held untold promises.

Rahul walked up and danced with her. He put his hands on her hips, just as she wrapped hers around his neck. They moved together to James Blunt as he sang about her. No words were spoken. No words were needed.

Her face was inches from his. He could smell the familiar faint smell of *Romance*, her favourite perfume. Everything was perfect. Rahul closed his eyes just as she moved closer and whispered in his ear.

"Not that I mind, but don't you think these moves would work better on a slower song?"

Rahul almost jumped with surprise. The nightclub, the sea of people, the noise, and the hard-hitting electronic music materialized around him, and he looked in disbelief at the girl he was holding in his arms.

"Is something wrong?" asked Neha.

"No... no..." The fragrance of *Romance* lingered in Rahul's mind. "I think I've had too much to drink. Is that *Romance* you're wearing?"

She smiled, with both pleasure and relief. Her eyes were playful. "Yes! Lets go sit somewhere. Or do you want to go somewhere else?"

Rahul took Neha's hand. Her fingers closed around his fingers one at a time, noticed Rahul, and he felt himself helplessly drawn to her in that moment.

What is this moment worth in the grand scheme of things, Rahul thought to himself, as they walked out of the club.

"How do we hide on an empty dance floor?"

A smile played on Saleem's lips.

"What?" asked Sandy. They were sitting in their usual spot in Saleem's drawing room. Saleem had just finished reading the story, and Sandy was hoping to get some real feedback this time.

"Nothing," said Saleem, his voice rife with amusement. "For a guy who is fascinated by the fact that stories end, it is a bit ironic that you've ended a story with a beginning."

"Do you like it?"

"Doesn't matter if I like it... I'm more interested in this contradiction of yours."

"Well... even if it ends with a beginning... the bottom line is that the 'story' is over, even if their life isn't." Sandy gestured with his finger.

"Go on."

"Who's to say that Rahul didn't relapse? Wasting away his life pining for Spriha.... or maybe Rahul and Neha... or for that matter, some other girl, got together, and lived a fairly unremarkable life. You know... got married, had kids, put them through school, married them off, died and were forgotten. Life can be a real downer, you know... with only a few events worth being called stories... and even if they end in the beginning of another chapter, they do end.

"That's a thought," Saleem mused, "But you've surprised me. You always came across as carefree and jovial, and not to a mention, a little silly at times. But you have your share of cynicism. I always thought it to be the vice of the weary and the aged."

"Well... life is full of surprises," said Sandy with a smile.

Saleem suddenly looked serious. "Yes… it is."

Bloody hell… he's on the verge of a mood swing again… Damn!

"Okay!" said Saleem, shaking off the storm Sandy's words had stirred up in his mind for no apparent reason. "Let's switch this time around… you write the first half… and I'll finish the story."

"Cool… I actually have an idea too… mind if I sit and write here?" Sandy asked.

"As long as you don't think out loud."

"So you don't get a hint of the story?"

"That… plus I want to take a nap," Saleem replied.

She danced alone on the middle of the floor. There was absolutely no one else in the club. Saleem was mesmerized by her movements. So graceful. So angelic. He walked up to her, confident and sure.

"May I have this dance?"

"You may."

Saleem took her hand in his, and placed his other hand on her back. They started moving and turning slowly to the music.

"We don't have too long, though," she said.

"Doesn't matter."

"Let's hide. They'll take longer to find us."

"How do we hide on an empty dance floor?" Saleem asked.

She moved a step back and smiled an enigmatic smile. There was mischief all over her face. Saleem was falling in love. She raised both her hands, did an elaborate twirl of the fingers, and said – 'Abracadabra.'

Suddenly, the dance floor was full of people, dancing all around them.

"Let them find us now," she laughed and moved closer to him.

And they danced. They danced till they lost sense of time. Days passed and years went by and they kept dancing, lost completely in each other. Finally, she moved her lips to his ears and said, "What is your name?"

Saleem didn't want to answer. He held her close and kept dancing.

"What is your name?"

It wasn't her voice this time. It was a masculine voice... authoritative, sharp and loud. One that sent chills down Saleem's spine. He opened his eyes with a start.

He was standing alone in the middle of the dance floor. The people were gone. The music had faded. She wasn't there, either. He stood in the middle, surrounded by swirling tornadoes revolving around him. He counted four of them. Saleem wasn't in unfamiliar territory.

Thoughts. Dreams. Unstable streams of consciousness imploding violently, taking the form of tornadoes.

"It's been a long time, hasn't it, Saleem...? Isn't that what you are calling yourself these days?" came a voice from the sky. They all looked identical, fierce and unforgiving.

"What do you want from me?" screamed Saleem.

"You already know the answer to that question"

"Maybe he's forgotten," chipped in a different voice

"He'll remember soon enough. Won't you, Saleem?"

"REMEMBER WHAT?" shouted Saleem. His frustration at not knowing was growing. It felt as though it was just out of grasp... like when a person sometimes forgets where his wallet is moments after putting it down. Saleem thought hard, but drew a blank.

"Be patient. You'll remember in time."

"But how?"

"There are still stories left to tell. He's good, you know… the kid. He understands."

"What does he understand?" Saleem asked.

"That stories need to end."

The tornadoes began to close in on Saleem. He could feel them pulling him in different directions. He felt dizzy. He was breathless and his vision was blurred.

"Don't go near him," he almost pleaded.

"We didn't go to him, Saleem. You brought him to us."

"STAY AWAY FROM HIM!" screamed Saleem.

CHAPTER 3

The Long Journey Home

"Stay away from whom?" inquired Sandy.

"Huh?"

Saleem rubbed his eyes and looked around. He had been dreaming again. He looked at Sandy and saw a concerned look on his face.

"Was I talking in my sleep?" asked Saleem in a matter-of-face voice.

"Uh, yes... and just before you woke up, you screamed 'stay away from him.' You talk in your sleep a lot?"

"All the time," Saleem lied.

Sandy nodded, and then his face broke into a smile.

"I've emailed you the first half of my story. You want to read it now?"

"Yes... but not with you breathing down my neck. Go home now. Come back tomorrow. Same time."

Sandy slung his bag over his shoulder.

"Sure thing, old timer!" he said cheerfully. He waved at Saleem and left.

Nitin stood in the small balcony of his guesthouse and looked at the dark landscape around him. Shades of black, grey and blue. He sipped hot tea from a bone china cup and glanced at his TAG Heuer.

5:38 AM. Any minute now.

He took another sip of tea.

Too much sugar.

Over the last 12 days, he had told the caretaker atleast twice everyday to put less sugar in the tea. It had not worked as well as he would have liked, but atleast what had been concentrated sugar syrup on day one had now come down to what can be described as 'very sweet' tea.

These mountain people, they like tea in sugar instead of sugar in tea. Nitin found himself smiling at the thought of the caretaker – Pratap. A humble man, Pratap had lived all his life in the mountains around Maraur, got married and raised his kids here who were also living their whole lives in the same mountains just like their father.

Some light finally broke over the mountain to his left. He watched in amazement as nature's sunrise orchestra began its performance all around him. He imagined a section of the orchestra light up and musicians softly strike the triangular chimes just as the sky over the mountain began to be illuminated with a soft, warm glow. The flutes joined in as the now orange glow filled the rest of the sky in front of him. The dark mountain ranges around him seemed to suddenly take shape as light fell on them. The violins and the cellos added melody to the mesmerizing score as spectacular mixtures of yellow and fiery red lit up the sky behind the mountains in the east. The instruments picked up pace, building up to a grand finale. Nitin could almost hear the rising crescendo of the drums, snares and trumpets as the majestic sun rose in the east. The music played on as sunlight filled the valley, illuminating each contour and reflecting off the million dew drops on the leaves. The whole valley shimmered and gleamed in front of Nitin as the music gradually faded in his imagination. He closed his eyes and let the warm sunlight wash over him, and felt a warmth in his heart, even as the music of the imaginary orchestra faded away.

He took his wallet out of his back pocket and pulled out a photograph. He smiled as he held it in his hands, and felt the warmth of his heart run though his arms, all the way to his fingertips. He ran his fingers over Naina's face in the photograph and the smile grew wider on his face. He was going back. Back to Naina. The next day was their first wedding anniversary.

He tucked the photograph back into the wallet and took one last glance at the glittering valley before turning back towards the room.

Pratap was knocking at the door.

"Saheb, the cab is here. Are you ready to leave?"

Nitin opened the door and saw the servile caretaker with his hands clasped in his usual way.

"Yes. My bags are lying on the bed. Please take them to the car. I have to make a phone call."

He walked up to the hall and picked up the receiver of an old telephone and dialled Naina's cell phone. Mobile phones didn't work in Maraur. Telecom companies had not expanded their networks to this part of the world for lack of critical consumer density in the area.

The phone rang at the other end a couple of times before Naina picked up.

"Hello..." she murmured lazily.

Nitin felt his heart melt. "Good morning, sweetie," he said "Hey... what time is it?"

"It's 5:47. I just called to say I'm leaving now, and I'll see you tonight." He imagined her stretch and turn slowly under the sheets.

"Alright, honey. Have a safe trip."

"I will. Now you get back to sleep and I love you." It occurred to him that he would never get tired of saying those last few words.

"Love you too."

Nitin replaced the receiver and walked out on the porch of the guest house where Pratap was loading the luggage into the boot of the Tata Indica. The driver was wiping the windows of the car with a cloth.

"All done, Saheb. I've also kept yesterday's newspaper on that seat as you had requested."

Nitin pulled out a hundred rupee note from his wallet and handed it to Pratap who took it with both hands.

"Thank you, Saheb. I wish you a safe and pleasant journey. Please don't forget to say 'Om Gana Ganapathaye Namah' for good luck."

"I will, Pratap. Thank you." Nitin turned and walked towards the car where the driver was standing with the back door open.

The higher you go up the mountains, he thought, *the stronger the superstition levels get.*

"Namaskaar Saheb, my name is Rahu," said the driver as he held open the door.

Rahu was dark, skinny and obviously not from the hills. He had a big, bushy moustache and large eyes. The kind that blink lesser than you think they should.

"Namaskaar. Is it Rahu or *Rahul*?" Nitin checked as slid into the car.

"No Saheb. It's Rahu. My father named me Rahu and my

twin brother Ketu. He said our mother died *because* she gave birth to us."

Rahu shut the door, got behind the wheel, and rolled the car into first gear.

Nitin took a few minutes to digest the names of the two brothers.

Rahu and Ketu were two ominous characters in Hindu mythology. It is said that once as the gods and demons fought against each other, the gods were on the verge of losing. Lord Brahma suggested that the gods churn the ocean, which would yield an elixir and make them invincible. However, the gods could not do it alone. They asked the demons to help them churn the ocean and take part of the elixir.

Thus began the great churning which brought forth many things from the ocean including a poison that almost destroyed the worlds. Finally, when the pot of elixir came forth, a greedy struggle began between the gods and demons to possess all of it. Lord Vishnu then disguised himself as the beautiful Mohini and offered to serve the elixir to both- the gods and the demons. She made the gods and demons sit in two separate rows went from one to the other, serving the elixir equally to both. Cleverly, she served elixir to the gods and plain water to the demons until Svarabhanu, one of the demons, spotted this deceit. Svarabhanu quietly disguised himself as a god and moved into the gods' row and receive the elixir. Just as he began to drink, his neighbours – the Sun god, Surya, and the Moon god, Chandra, realized that he was actually a demon and raised an alarm. Swarabhanu's mischief enraged Lord Vishnu who beheaded the demon immediately. However, since he had already swallowed some of the elixir, he had become immortal. The severed head thus became *Rahu* while the rest of the body became *Ketu*.

It is believed that Rahu now traversed the heavens, in search for revenge, on his eight horsed chariot to devour the Sun and the Moon for having denounced him. Whenever Rahu succeeds, an eclipse occurs.

Rahu and Ketu are hence believed to be inauspicious. According to Hindu astrology, people born under the celestial influence of Rahu and Ketu, find no peace in life. They are believed to be exposed to their enemies and their wisdom, children, and riches are destined to be destroyed.

Great, Nitin thought to himself, *just great.*

Even though Nitin was not a superstitious man, Rahu's eyes and his name had sent a slight shiver down his spine.

He looked at his watch.

6:30 AM

I should be home by 10 tonight, he figured, since Maraur to Chandigarh was usually a 13-hour journey.

The car squeaked and honked through the narrow streets of the Maraur market. Maraur was a small mountain town with a population of about 15,000 and nothing more than farms all around.

He stared at the commotion outside and wondered how humans are able to populate even the most difficult of terrains such as mountain slopes. It never ceased to amaze him. Bustling markets, narrow yet traversable motor passes at the highest altitudes, farms cut into mountains. All these seemed nothing less than magical to him.

"Human will-power and ingenuity," he would often say, "are what make miracles happen."

He looked at Rahu's reflection in the rear view mirror. There was something about him that had been bothering him. The unblinking eyes made his throat go dry.

Rahu sat very stiffly as he drove the car out of the market

and onto the highway. There was something else that bothered him about Rahu, but he just couldn't put a finger on it.

"So Rahu, what does Ketu do?"

"I don't know Saheb. He disappeared after he strangled our father," Rahu replied without blinking.

"Oh…"

Disconcerted, Nitin decided it was probably best to not engage in conversation with Rahu for the remainder of the trip, unless it was extremely important. He slid down in his seat and looked out of the window as the majestic mountain range slowly rolled past him. He decided to think about more pleasant things and pulled out the picture from his wallet again. He allowed his thoughts to drift towards Naina.

He had proposed to her within the first week of college, and she had said yes. They had a perfect love story throughout college; after which Nitin got a job in a logistics firm based out of Chandigarh and Naina had got a job in a software firm in Bangalore. They got married in couple of years and Naina had quit her job to settle down with Nitin in Chandigarh. The wedding had been a short and sweet affair, attended only by close friends and family.

That was exactly one year ago from tomorrow, he thought to himself.

Rahul had been sent on a critical month-long project to oversee the setting up of an important warehousing center for his company at Maraur. He had requested his boss to take four days off in the middle, to celebrate his first wedding anniversary with his wife back in Chandigarh.

His boss had simply said an "OK" in reply.

Nitin was planning to take her down to Sukhna Lake and have a candle light dinner by the lake. They didn't need anything more elaborate than that to make the evening special.

BANG!

A loud noise jolted Nitin back to the present. He saw Rahu turn the wheel wildly to the right in a bid to bring the car back to the road. Nitin grabbed the front passenger seat in panic and screamed. "RAHU! WATCH OUT!"

The car spun out of control and the wheels shrieked. It finally came to a halt, 60 feet from where they had started spinning. Thankfully, there had been enough straight road to prevent them from falling off the cliff. Nobody in the car spoke.

Nitin sighed, releasing the panic that had choked his throat. He looked at Rahu, who was staring at the abyss that lay below them, his eyes, wider than ever before. Nitin thought he saw a maniacal grin on his face, but it could be his mind playing tricks...

"What just happened?"

"A tyre burst, Saheb. The right one in the rear. Just as we were turning around the last bend. Then we spun out of control. It happens." Rahu stepped out of the car to inspect the burst tire.

"It happens! *It happens?* You almost got us killed back there! Do you even know how to drive?" Nitin was fuming.

"You should be thanking me, Saheb. I saved our lives," Rahu was already raising the jack under the car.

"Saved my life, my foot!" Nitin kicked a stone down the cliff and pulled back his hair with both hands. He stood a foot away from the edge of the road and tried to calm himself down. He stared at the small river that flowed at the bottom of mountain and wondered how many days or months it would have taken for the authorities to discover them, if at all. He imagined tears rolling down Naina's cheeks as she was told about it. He took several deep breaths. He realized his mistake and immediately felt sorry about it. He knew Rahu had actually saved their lives and he had shouted at him in a rush of adrenaline. He decided not to apologise to Rahu though.

"Saheb. I've changed the tyre. Let's go."

Nitin turned as Rahu tightened the last bolt. He decided not to look Rahu in the eyes and got in the car.

"We'll need to get the puncture fixed in the next town, Saheb. Just in case…"

"Yes. I know. And *please* drive safely." He looked at his watch. *9:42 AM.*

About half an hour of a thankfully uneventful drive, Rahu pulled the car into a small garage at a small nondescript village on the way. He pulled out the punctured tire from the boot and rolled it over to the man smoking a *bidi*, who finished it and then got to work on the tire.

Rahu came to Nitin's window and knocked at the glass with his knuckles.

"It's going to take half an hour, Saheb. You might want to stretch your legs till then."

Nitin was irritated as he emerged from the car.

"Alright. But ask him to hurry up." He slammed the door and walked towards the few scattered shops he could see down the road.

He stopped at a grocery store and picked up a Fanta. He looked around at an assortment of local biscuits and confectionary that decorated the store.

In today's age, you know you are in a different world altogether, he noted to himself, *when you don't find your regular brands of chips, biscuits and confectionary in the grocery store.*

He walked further down the road looking at houses on the slopes. He looked at his watch every now and then.

10:53 AM.

Rahu pulled up in the taxi next to Nitin and honked.

"Let's go, Saheb. Puncture's fixed."

"Let's go. We're already late". Nitin got back into the car, and they drove out of the village.

Nitin resisted the urge to tell Rahu to drive faster. He knew it was not wise to rush while driving in the hills. He had already seen a few Border Roads Organization signs fly past them.

It's better to be late than never, one of them had said.

The early start, coupled with the adrenaline rush of the burst tyre and the wait at the village had made him drowsy. He decided to get some sleep. He had always been a deep sleeper. The sharp turns of the mountain roads didn't trouble him. He slept.

When he woke, the sun was on him, and the heat was making him uncomfortable. He opened his eyes and looked around. The car was not moving. It had been parked at a clearing on the side of the road. The bonnet was open and he could hear sounds of metal hitting metal. He looked at his watch.

1:37 PM.

Nitin was irritated.

What now?

He stepped out and saw Rahu bent over the engine, hitting at some part with a pair of pliers. The sight made Nitin regret his decision to graduate with a civil engineering degree.

"What's happened now?"

"I don't know, Saheb. There seems to a problem with the engine. It suddenly began to sputter, and finally died. I think there might be a problem with the spark plug here."

"You think? But you don't know for sure? How then will you fix it?" Nitin couldn't believe his luck.

"I'm a driver, Saheb. I can fix a flat tyre and a few basic things. I'm not a mechanic."

"Great! What do we do now? Wait here for a mechanic to appear magically and fix the car?"

"We will have to wait, Saheb. Not for a mechanic to appear though. I'll hitchhike to the town that is about 45 minutes downhill from here, get the plug fixed, and then hitchhike back. You will have to stay with the car," Rahu said.

"What? You mean I'll have to wait for another two hours here? Listen, Rahu. We are already running late, thanks to that bloody burst tyre back there. We should already have been in Bidouli by now. And now you're telling me that I'll have to wait here for two hours? I have to reach Chandigarh tonight, it's my first wedding anniversary tomorrow." Nitin resisted the urge to grab Rahu by his collar and shake him up.

"Saheb, what can I do? What happens, happens. We can't plan for these things. This is all God's doing"

Nitin swore under his breath and sat down on a milestone that read *Bidouli – 70 kms.*

A mini-truck soon pulled up and stopped next to their car. Rahu walked up to the driver and spoke to him in an incomprehensible language, probably the local vernacular. They stole glances at Nitin.

Nitin was not bothered. He just wanted to reach home, *on time*.

Rahu waved to Nitin as he jumped in the back of the mini-truck and it sped away. Nitin sat on the milestone and watched it till it disappeared around the mountain.

I should have left yesterday, in a different car and with a better driver.

He picked up the previous day's newspaper that was lying in the car and spread it on the bonnet. He considered himself lucky that the day's newspaper arrived by evening in Maraur. There were places in the interiors that received newspapers two days late, and then there were places that didn't receive newspapers at all.

In obscure places high up in the mountains where it takes you three days to walk to the nearest grocery store, you probably don't care about what's happening in the world. And the world doesn't care about what's happening to you.

He read every article in the *Himachal Herald*. He read through the regular national political news, and other major news on the first four pages. He then learned about the state politicians bickering and slinging mud on each other for the next four pages. He then read about the happenings in the smaller districts. He read about a footbridge collapsing in a town, killing two people. He read about a child being carried away and eaten by a leopard in another village.

One article in particular caught his eye. It was about a blind old man in Maraur district who had reportedly had an otherworldly experience about two weeks back. It said that the man was sleeping in his hut one night when somebody had knocked on his door. He had opened the door to the familiar sounding voice that had requested to come in. This other man came in, made tea for both of them and talked about God and His miracles. The man had then tucked the old man in bed. The article then went on to say that the old man was surprised when he woke up because he could miraculously see again. Not just that, the old man could reportedly move objects with his mind now. People from surrounding villages were flocking to the old man's village to meet him. The article quoted the old man preaching about God and claiming that he was going to attempt to teleport himself to Haridwar. "If you focus your mind on something, and want desperately for it to happen, then sometimes the mind materializes it for you," the article quoted the old man.

He stared at a black and white picture of the old man in the newspaper. His eyes had an unsettling glare about them.

Nitin folded the paper and put it back in the car. He found the article rather amusing. He thought about the old man and his sudden transformation into a messiah, fed by the superstitions of the uneducated masses.

He thought about it a little more and wondered at the idea of having the power to move objects with his mind. He looked at his watch again.

3:31 PM.

Where the hell is that Rahu. It's been almost 2 hours now and no sign of him.

He took out his cellphone but there was still no network. He cursed the telecom operators.

With nothing else to do except curse, he decided to go to sleep again. He dozed off quickly.

He dreamt of having powers like the old man he had just read about in the article. He dreamt of standing at his site in Maraur and erecting a warehouse just by thinking about it and his bosses giving him a promotion for such an achievement. He dreamt of doing all of Naina's chores at home by simply thinking about them.

His dreams gradually turned into nightmares. He dreamt of coming home one day, opening the door and being struck by a wave of fear and panic. The living room was in a mess, as if it had been ransacked and a struggle had taken place in the room. The lampshades and magazines were strewn across the floor. The furniture was all upside down. The window panes were broken. He ran up the stairs to their bedroom and heard Naina scream. He broke through the bedroom door and saw Naina crucified on the ceiling and screaming for her life. There was blood all over the room. Even the walls and the ceiling had splashes of blood. Naina's blood. He saw the old man from the article sitting on the bed and staring at him with those unnerving eyes and all the small objects in their bedroom swirling around him like in a tornado. He yelled at the old man, "What are you doing? Let her go! LET HER GO!"

"Saheb!"

"Saheb!"

Nitin opened his eyes. Rahu was shaking his left shoulder through the window.

"Saheb, are you alright?"

Nitin realized he had been having a nightmare. He was sweating profusely.

"Saheb, I just reached here and saw you sleeping in the car. But then I realized you were shivering and shouting. Did you have a bad dream?"

Nitin looked at his watch.

7:54 PM. It was dark outside. He was still recovering from the nightmare.

"Yes I did. Why did you take so long?"

"I tried to get it fixed, Saheb. But it just wouldn't work. Finally we had to look around town for a new one. Anyway, it's dark now… we should stay in Bidouli tonight and leave tomorrow morning. The hills become more dangerous in a moonless night such as tonight."

Nitin smelt a strong stench of whiskey under Rahu's breath.

"A new one, huh? You fucking liar! You were not searching for a new plug. You were getting drunk! Don't you know I have to get home to my wife tonight? It is our anniversary tomorrow."

Nitin was fuming. The day's events had been building up inside him and were now ready to explode through his fists on Rahu's face.

"There, there, saheb. I only had two pegs because it was getting cold. You're getting mad at me for no reason."

Nitin tried very hard to calm down. He wished the day had started differently. He wished he had had a different driver. He wished there was some way he could reach Chandigarh that night. He remembered the old man from this nightmare and thought about his special abilities. He wished they were true and he had them. He wished, and he really wished hard, he could teleport himself to his house right at that moment.

"Get me to the nearest town with a phone." Nitin knew there was nothing much he could do at the point. Rahu was right about not driving on the route at night.

Rahu drove to the first lodge he saw in Bidouli.

The board read *Cedar Lodge*.

Nitin looked at his watch.

10:15 PM.

Exhausted, Nitin got off the car and headed for to the STD booth next to the lodge.

He called Naina's cell.

No Answer.

He called her again.

No Answer.

He called her a few more times again. There was still no answer.

He guessed she might have probably dozed off, waiting for him. He decided to grab some dinner at the lodge, freshen up, and then try to call her again.

The room was small with just enough space for one person to walk around the bed. There was no TV. No fan. It was just a bed and four walls. Yet, to Nitin, the bed looked inviting.

I'll just straighten my back for 10 minutes and then order some food.

He imagined Naina's disappointment, and felt his back relax as he lay down on the bed. He imagined having those special powers again and teleporting himself to his house. He imagined kissing Naina and assuring her he was there. He imagined sleeping with her in his arms.

He slept.

The beeper alarm in his watch woke him up.

Nitin woke up in panic. He looked at his watch.

6:30 AM.

SHIT. SHIT. SHIT. He realized he'd fallen asleep and not even called Naina again. She must have tried his number a hundred times and would be worried sick by now.

He ran down to the STD booth from where he had tried calling her the previous night.

He punched in Naina's number and heard it ring.

"Hello."

"Honey, I'm ssoooo Sorry. I'm ssoo very sorry. I had such a fucked up trip yesterday with a flat tyre and a bad spark plug and the worst driver... We even almost had an accident... I'm very sorry, but I tried calling you last night and you didn't pick up and then I thought I'd call again but then I was so exhausted that I dozed off... and I just woke up... I rushed to call you... but don't worry, I'm leaving right now and I'll be there by noon and..."

"Hello? Who's this?"

Nitin paused. "Honey. It's me. Nitin. I was just saying that I'm leaving right now and..."

"Who Nitin?"

Nitin suddenly felt a sharp pain at the back of his neck. "Naina. Sweetheart. Nitin. Your husband, Nitin. Look I understand you are angry but I'm..."

"You're not my husband Nitin. My husband came back

home last night at about 11 PM. In fact, he's sleeping here right next to me."

The pain at the back of Nitin's neck exploded and spread through his head like a forest fire. He felt as if the mountains around him were erupting.

The receiver fell from his hands.

And then he fainted.

'What is it about stories that fascinates you?'
'Because they end, sir.'

Something had stirred within Saleem when he had first heard Sandy say that. It wasn't pleasant, and it wasn't entirely unfamiliar either. Something had been happening ever since he had started working on the book. Something beyond the realm of his comprehension, maybe even reality.

His first instinct was to laugh at these thoughts. But he wasn't sure anymore. It all seemed a bit too sinister, and Saleem considered putting an end to all of it. He looked around and saw the sad old apartment which had rotted away for 23 years. His life which had rotted away for 23 years.

Things were changing... whether for good or bad, Saleem didn't know. But he could do with change, and hope for the best.

He was finally telling stories again, and that was good. And right now, he had a story to finish.

Nitin looked in amazement as the light broke over the mountains to his left. Watching the sun peek out from behind the hills was an amazing sight to behold. The orchestra behind him rose to a crescendo, as the sun began its majestic rise to its throne in the sky.

Suddenly, the sun exploded in a blinding flash of light, forcing Nitin to turn away. Bewildered, Nitin turned his head and carefully squinted in the direction of the flash. A chariot approached slowly from where the sun had exploded.

Nitin watched with his mouth agape as the chariot, drawn by four majestic horses and resplendent in pure gold, came down next to him. The Sun God emerged from his chariot and smiled at him.

"Let's go, brother. It's almost time," he said to Nitin, and began walking towards the dispersing orchestra behind them. Nitin began to follow him, almost in a trance, when a voice erupted out of nowhere in his ear.

"Lets go, Saheb! Your wife must be waiting at home."

Nitin sat up with a start. He had been lying on the sofa at the reception of Cedar Lodge. The caretaker, a frail old man wrapped in a worn out shawl and a monkey cap, was staring curiously at him. He kept a respectful distance which would atleast give him a chance to escape, should Nitin decide to jump out of the sofa in a bid to bite him.

Rahu was bent over him, his eyes full of a concern that the rest of his face and voice could not express. There was another man next to him, whom Nitin didn't recognize.

"What happened Saheb? Babu here told me that you fainted while trying to make a phone call from his STD booth."

Nitin's senses sprang back to life. The mention of the phone call brought it all back to him.

"My wife... my Naina," spluttered Nitin.

"What happened to your wife Saheb?" asked Rahu.

"Rahu. Get the car out... we have to get back to Chandigarh immediately."

Nitin sprang out of the sofa and pulled out his wallet. He took a thousand rupee note and waved it at the caretaker, who did not take it, fearing that whatever had come over Nitin might be contagious.

There was no time to waste. Nitin thrust the note into the hand of the caretaker, and turned towards Babu, pulling out a fifty this time.

"And this should take care of the phone call. Rahu... let's go! And for the love of everything you hold dear – no more accidents, all right? We have absolutely no time to waste."

Everyone continued to stare at Nitin, not moving a muscle. The fifty-rupee note was still in his hand.

Nitin, already in a state of panic, exploded.

"WHAT IS WRONG WITH YOU PEOPLE?! WHY AREN'T YOU TAKING THE MONEY? I NEED TO GO NOW!!!"

Babu finally spoke up in a timid voice, "You don't owe me any money, Saheb. You fainted before your phone call could go through."

Shock, followed by a wave of relief. Nitin almost didn't want to believe him.

"The call didn't go through?" asked Nitin slowly. Telling himself as much as asking Babu.

"No Saheb. All lines have been down in the town since last night. Probably because of the rain. It happens a lot here. I was coming out to tell you that when you were dialing the number. But before I could tell you, you fainted. You can come and check."

"No... that's all right... but I'm pretty sure I spoke to my wife," said Nitin, trying very hard to remember if the conversation had really happened. He wasn't sure anymore.

We can always find out.

Nitin pulled out his cellphone. There was still no signal.

If the hard lines are down, the cell phone network stands a snowball's chance in hell, thought Nitin.

He stood rooted to his spot, confused and unsure about what to do next. He desperately needed to get in touch with Naina. She must be worried sick about him. Rahu spoke up to break the silence.

"Let's go, Saheb. It will only take about six hours to reach Chandigarh from here. It's not even eight in the morning... you'll be home to your wife by lunch time."

"Yes, you're right. Let's just get out of here," said Nitin. "We'll probably get a cell phone signal once we get lower down. You go to the car, I'll get my bag from the room."

"I got it for you, Saheb. It's already in the car." Nitin felt a small burst of appreciation for Rahu.

"Thanks, Rahu. Let's go."

They stepped out in the morning chill. The sky was overcast, and the damp smell of the rain was in the air.

"Let's hope it doesn't rain," said Rahu.

"Yeah..." Nitin suddenly remembered Pratap. He looked up to the sky and spoke out softly, "Om Gana Ganapathaye Namah." Rahu glanced at him as he said the words, but didn't say anything. They both got in the car and drove away.

Nitin's mind kept going back to his imaginary phone-call with Naina. From a purely logical point of view, it made absolutely no sense, and the thought comforted him. He was here, and there was no way that phone-call could be real. This wasn't some science-fiction movie starring Arnold Schwarzenegger.

"The guy can barely speak clearly! How he managed to become such a successful actor, and then the Governor of California is beyond me!" Nitin teased her, knowing full well that she'll retaliate.

They had just finished with watching *Terminator 2: Judgement Day* on their brand new home theatre system. It was one of Naina's favourite movies. Unlike most girls he knew, Naina relished action movies, and she could go on and on about how Terminator 2 was the greatest action movie of all time.

"Who cares about his acting, Nitin? He's an uncaring, unfeeling robot in the movie. Suits him well... doesn't it? And he has the physique to die for. You're just jealous."

He jumped as Naina pinched him sharply, and ran for the bedroom.

"OWWW! Why you little... you think you can hide from me in there?" said Nitin, rubbing his shoulder.

Naina stuck her head out of the bedroom door. "Who wants to hide, big boy?" she said, in the sexiest imaginable voice.

Sitting in the taxi, Nitin smiled to himself. He looked at his watch.

9.00 AM

He looked at his cell phone. Still no signal. Nitin wanted to scream in frustration. The fear lingered within him. *What if that phone-call really happened?* Nitin imagined reaching home and ringing the door bell. The man who opens the door looks exactly like him. Speechless and horrified, Nitin continues to stare at him as Naina joins the man. She shows no signs of recognizing him. *Yes? How can we help you?*

Nitn pushed the thought away. He reminded himself that

something like that was simply impossible. With nothing else to do, Nitin picked up the copy of the Himachal Herald lying in the car since the previous day and began flipping through it without reading. He stopped at the article about the old man, and stared at his picture. *Now is the time when I really need the power you claim to have, old man.*

"Don't worry, Saheb," said Rahu looking at him in his rear-view mirror, "I'll get you home in no time."

If only to distract himself, Nitin decided to strike up a conversation with Rahu.

"You know about this old man, Rahu? The one who claims he's got these amazing powers now by divine intervention."

"Yes, Saheb. Everyone in these parts know about him. People are flocking to his town for his blessings. Even I plan to go there soon for his blessings. Maybe he can dispel the curse that has hung over me since the day I was born."

Nitin felt a wave of irritation sweep over him.

"Why are you people so damn superstitious? A chap makes up fantastic stories, and takes all of you for a ride. There is a reason the government takes so many measures to make education accessible to everyone. So that people can free their minds, and look at the world for what it really is, instead of believing in such nonsense."

"Do you believe in God, saheb?" said Rahu.

"What?"

"Do you think God exists? Do you pray to Him? When you got into the car in the morning, you spoke a short prayer to Lord Ganesha."

"What does me believing in God have to do with anything?"

"Because if you can believe in God, then why is it so hard to believe in his miracles? You city folk are very quick to dismiss the signs and omens from a higher being as superstition, never realizing how superstitious you yourselves are. You just assumed that because I'm a driver, I have had no education. But in fact, I know how to read, write, and speak English. I know how to use a computer and even the Internet. Even though Ketu and I were never allowed to go to school in our village, we always wanted to learn. So we would steal books from other kids and read them. When those books were no longer enough, we would go to the library in the town nearby to read even more books. I still read in my free time, and I'm sure that I'm more educated than all the kids in my village... combined."

Nitin was taken aback by this revelation. He had not seen that coming. Rahu went on.

"Coming back to superstitions – irrespective of whether they are real or not, the truth is that they cannot be ignored. We live by these omens from the day we are born to the day we die. It's not easy to ignore them when they become the basis of our lives, and in many cases like Ketu and mine, go on to define who we are. Christians worship *Issa*, who was heralded as the saviour of mankind because of a prophecy even before he was born. Wasn't that superstition? Yet millions bow down to him without question.

"Similarly, Ketu and I were born with a curse. A curse that killed our mother. A curse that drove my brother to murder his own father. A curse that proclaimed us to be monsters. When everyone around you lives with a superstition without question, it ceases to be a superstition. It becomes your reality. We found that out the hard way."

Nitin was left speechless. For the moment, Naina and his apprehensions were driven out of his mind by the monologue from this supposed simpleton driving the car.

What is someone capable of such intelligent conversation doing driving a taxi? Curiosity got the better of Nitin. He leaned forward and touched Rahu's shoulder.

"Tell me about your brother. And yourself."

Rahu glanced at Nitin again in the rear view mirror. Then, he began talking.

"Ketu and I were born in a small village called Arwaad in Bihar. You wouldn't have heard of it, Saheb. It has nothing worth hearing about. Just another small little settlement close to the town of Badhia. Like I told you, our mother died while giving birth to us. Our father took that as a sign of some evil within us, and named us Rahu and Ketu. It was just a pathetic attempt to shrug off the responsibility of raising two children. He paid off the village *pandit* to declare that we had been born under the influence of the devil, and our fate was sealed by those words.

We owe our lives to our *maasi* – our mothers sister – who raised us despite the protests of the rest of the village. She chose to be shunned by the rest of the village rather than let us die. When we were five years old, *maasi* passed away. And we went back to live with our father, who grudgingly took us in. After all, there was all sorts of work to be done around the house, and our father saw two capable servants in us.

We grew up being beaten up regularly and lived amidst constant reminders of how we killed our mother and *maasi*, how we were like the devil, and how we deserved much worse than the lives we had right now. The rest of the village followed suit. Anyone we touched, even by accident, had to be cleansed at the temple before he could come back into the village. We were too young to understand this, and it felt like a game to us. We would touch someone simply for the fun of seeing him run frantically towards the temple. It was worth the thrashing we got for it night after night.

When we saw other kids in the village go to school, we wanted to go too. Our father refused to send us. The headmaster refused to take us. It became another game. We would hide outside classrooms and learn what the other kids were learning. Being treated as inferiors can either destroy your morale, or drive you to do better, Saheb. Ketu and I were driven. We learned. We stole books, notebooks and pencils; and hid them in the fields where we would study and teach each other to read and write. During the day, we would go to the nearby town and do odd jobs. With the money we earned, we would buy books to teach ourselves. We never let our father know about this. He would just take our money and spend it on alcohol.

Unlike the rest of the boys in the village, we wanted to make something of our lives. We believed there was a place for us in the world, away from the superstitions and the persecution of the villagers. Once we had collected enough money, we enrolled ourselves in a school in the town where no one knew who we were. We read many books about religion and philosophy, looking for answers that would redeem us from the damnation that our village had condemned us to. For a while, it seemed as if we were on our way to brighter days.

But destiny caught up with us. When we were sixteen, an epidemic struck our village, killing many. Almost everyone in the village suffered to some degree, except the two of us. So, they blamed us for it. The unrest built up in the village until one fateful night – the night of the *chandra grahan*, a lunar eclipse – the son of the *mukhiya* succumbed to the disease.

Ketu woke me up at three in the morning. We heard people shouting outside, and by the sound of it, it seemed as though the entire village had gathered in front of our door. We didn't dare open the door, but the noise was enough to even shake our father out of his drunken slumber. He went outside, and closed the door behind him. Minutes, which seemed like hours, passed until our father entered the house again. walked towards us, and we knew what was going on. They had come to get rid of us, and our father had obviously decided to comply. We were too grown up for him to beat us up, and only returned home well after he had passed out from his drinking. We were of no use to him anymore.

I didn't know what to do. I was paralysed with fear. But Ketu was ready. All I saw was the flash of a knife's blade. I watched in horror as our father collapsed, his eyes wide with surprise and his throat slashed. Blood flowed all over the floor. I can't remember exactly what happened after that, but I remember Ketu dragging me over the back wall. I remember us hiding in the fields all night. The villagers didn't dare look for us. To them, evil was up and about that night.

When I woke up the next morning, Ketu was gone. Our dreams had been shattered. I made my way out of the village, took up a job with a contractor who supplied labour to construction companies. A few years later, I began driving taxis. And that is how I got here."

Nitin did not speak for a while. He stared outside the window of the cab as they drove on in silence. It had started raining heavily, and they drove slowly through the driving rain.

He felt guilty for treating Rahu the way he had all this while. Rahu was right. Superstition was a way of life. Every one lived with superstitions of their own, and scoffed at those of others. He glanced at his cell phone again. There was still no signal. For some reason, Nitin no longer felt the urgency that had been driving him that morning. Naina, his anniversary, and his ridiculous notions about the events of the morning felt far away.

Nitin snapped out of his reverie when the car came to a halt. He could see other cars in front of them, and none were moving. It had stopped raining. Rahu went out to see what the problem was.

"There has been an accident up ahead, Saheb. The road is too narrow for any vehicle to pass. I'm sorry but it looks like we will have to wait."

Nitin looked at his watch.

2.00 PM.

A few hours ago, Nitin would have cursed at his run of bad luck. But right now, he just felt drained and hollow. He nodded at Rahu, slid low on the seat, and shut his eyes.

"Let's go, brother. It's almost time," the sun god said to Nitin. Nitin followed him past the massive orchestra, through the ornate hallways in the clouds to an open courtyard. They took their seats among the other gods.

The sun god leaned towards him and spoke, "You see that bunch over there on the other side? They are the demon horde. Illiterate and superstitious, they denounce the age of glory and knowledge we want to lead the world into."

Nitin turned to follow the pointing finger of the sun god. Except for their rustic and unkempt appearance, they didn't seem all that different from the gods.

"The *manthan* was an unprecedented success. We almost

lost the world to the poison, but we're safe from it thanks to Lord Shiva, who will henceforth be known as *Neelkanth*. We now possess the elixir of life, but as per our… *arrangement*, we have to share it with the demons."

The sun god turned his head towards Nitin, and mistook his confused expression for distress.

"Don't look so despondent, brother," he said heartily. "Lord Vishnu has a plan. Under the pretext of serving elixir to both the gods and demons, he will transform into a gorgeous *apsara* to distract the demon fools. And then, he will cleverly serve them plain water, and the gods shall be invincible by the power of the elixir. We will then crush them and lead the world into an era of harmony and peace."

The sun god sat back looking very pleased. The light slowly dimmed over the courtyard, till Nitin could only make out silhouettes. The murmurs slowly died down as the dark sky above came to life with stars that appeared one by one, till the whole courtyard was illuminated by their soft, ethereal glow.

A figure began to descend from the sky. Dressed in white, the beautiful curves of her body glowed in the light of the stars. Music filled the courtyard, and every note seemed to emanate from inside Nitin. Every chord tugged at his heartstrings, and the harmony played with his senses. Nitin looked at the *apsara* who had now completed her descent from the sky.

Naina stood at the centre of the courtyard. He stared at her, unable to blink, unable to breathe, unable to speak. He, like everyone else in that courtyard, was utterly lost in her beauty, which glowed brighter than any star in the sky. Their eyes met. A hint of a smile on her lips. Nitin closed his eyes.

When he opened them again, she was dancing. Gracefully. Vigorously. Sensually. Every now and then, she would serve the elixir to the demons and the gods, never breaking a step, deftly intertwining the two acts. Nitin was mesmerized by the dance, till he was distracted by a sudden movement to his left. He turned, but could see nothing out of ordinary... but he was was sure he had seen something.

He watched as Naina poured the elixir in the glass of one of the gods sitting a few seats away from him. He was old, and Nitin thought he looked familiar. Unlike everyone else whose eyes never left Naina, this god's gaze was fixed on the elixir. Just as he raised his glass triumphantly to his lips, comprehension dawned on Nitin.

He turned to the sun god. "That man... I know him! He's the man I saw in the newspaper! That's how he got those divine powers... he drank the elixir of life. He's not a god... he's a demon!

The sun god stood up and erupted in a furious flash of light. "DONT LET HIM DRINK THE ELIXIR! HE'S A DEMON!"

A look of pure fury contorted Naina's beautiful face. In front of his eyes, she transformed into the most glorious of gods, Lord Vishnu. He cut the old man's head off with his *chakra*. The head and the body of the old man disintegrated into ashes, as the gathering stared aghast at the scene in deathly silence. Lord Vishnu turned towards the other demons, his chakra now revolving on his right index finger, still dripping blood. There was murder in his eyes, and the demons felt the force of the elixir of life that coursed through his veins. They slowly backed away from the courtyard. Suddenly, the ashes of the old man seemed to erupt, and two little boys emerged from the haze. They began to run out of the courtyard.

"Don't let them get away!" screamed Nitin. He was gripped by panic. "They are the spawn of evil. They will bring a curse upon all of us. DONT LET THEM GET AWAY!"

Just then, the whole courtyard began to shake.

"Wake up, Saheb! We've reached!"

Nitin looked at Rahu uncomprehendingly. It was dark outside, and it took him a moment to figure out where he was.

That was quite a fantastic dream.

"Saheb! We've reached your house in Chandigarh. It's 8 o'clock. You're a deep sleeper, Saheb. It took me quite a while to wake you up.

His senses still dull from his nap, Nitin looked outside to see the the familiar sight of his porch. The lights in the living room were on. Nitin thought of Naina, and smiled. His first impulse was to run to the house and sweep Naina off her feet. But he controlled that urge.

Nitin got out of the car, and turned to Rahu. He pulled out his business card and handed it over to him.

"You are a good man, Rahu. And you deserve much more than what life has given you. But circumstances can always change. Call me next week on that number, and I'll hook you up with my local sales team. From there, you can work your way up."

Rahu stared at the business card for a few seconds, and then for the first time in two days, he smiled. He looked at Nitin, his eyes full of gratitude.

"Thank you, Saheb. You will definitely hear from me again."

Rahu got into the car and drove away.

She must be worried sick, and she'll be furious! But once I tell her the story of these two days, she'll be fine. I'll make it up to her for missing our anniversary.

Nitin froze in his tracks 10 meters from his house. "Something isn't right," he said out loud to the silence around him. He turned to look behind him. Rahu had gone. He began to walk slowly towards the house again, trying to figure out what was nagging him. Just as he reached for the doorknob, comprehension dawned on his face, and suddenly Nitin was very, very scared.

How did he know my address? I never gave it to him.

The door was unlocked. Nitin dropped his bag and rushed inside. The living room was in a mess, as if it had been ransacked and a struggle had taken place in the room. The lampshades and magazines were strewn across the floor. The furniture was all upside down. The window panes were broken. He ran up the stairs to their bedroom, his heart in his mouth.

He burst through the door and saw a sight that made him die a million deaths in that moment. Naina lay on the floor. Not moving. Not breathing. Her eyes were wide open, her beautiful face scratched and bleeding, and her clothes ripped. Nitin dropped to his knees, and stared at her without touching her. His mind went blank.

"She put up quite a fight. But after a couple of blows to the head, I had my way with her."

Nitin looked up slowly. The mocking voice had come from the far corner of the room. A man emerged from the shadows, with a lecherous grin on his face. He slowly made his way towards Nitin.

In that moment, Nitin was filled with fury. He let out a scream of anger, and charged at the man in front of him, driving his shoulder with full force into his stomach and bringing him down. The man, surprised by the sudden attack, could not counter. Nitin rolled his fingers into a fist, and smashed it across the face of the man. He did it again. And again. And again. The man had been completely blindsided by the attack, and the series of hard punches to the face had rendered him powerless. He turned his face slowly towards Nitin, and Nitin remembered who he was.

"You're that truck driver who gave Rahu a lift to *Bidouli*. Why did you do this to my beautiful Naina? What have we done to you? How did you know where we live? ANSWER ME, YOU SON OF A BITCH!" screamed Nitin as tears ran down his cheeks.

A strong arm suddenly gripped Nitin around his neck.

"Good evening, Saheb," said a familiar voice. "I see you've met my brother Ketu."

Nitin felt a sharp pain in the back of his head, followed by darkness.

Nitin opened his eyes slowly, and saw the dead body of his wife lying next to him. Her eyes were still open, staring blankly at the ceiling. He couldn't move, and his head hurt. Rahu and Ketu stood in front of him. The children of the devil, in all their glory. Rahu held a sledgehammer to his shoulder.

In pain and misery, Nitin could only utter one word. "Why?"

Rahu laughed. "Why? Maybe destiny brought you to us. Or perhaps you were born under the wrong stars like us... born under the shadow of evil and condemned for an act we had nothing to do with."

"But... I thought you were a good man." The pain in the back of his head intensified, and tears streamed down his eyes. *Naina was dead.*

"There are no good or bad men, Saheb. Just men and the

purpose for which they are born. Ketu and I were naïve to think that we could control our destiny and determine our path. But everyone was right about us from the beginning. The night we killed our father, we finally stopped running away, and accepted who we were, and what we had been sent to do. We were born under the sign of evil, sent to do the devil's work."

Rahu's words made no sense to Nitin. He could only think of Naina.

"But how…?"

"Come on!" said Ketu. He was fidgety. "Lets kill him and leave."

"Wait Ketu! Saheb here has been much nicer to me than the others. We can take a few moments to answer him, as a repayment of his kindness." Rahu turned to Nitin, "We only needed a touch of chloroform while you were sleeping. From there, it was as simple as pulling out your wallet. Everything we needed was there. Usually we do not wait this long, but then Ketu saw the picture of your beautiful wife. He wanted her, and I wouldn't deny my brother anything. The world has done that enough."

"So, that phone-call…?"

Ketu interrupted before Nitin could finish. "Your wife loved you a lot, Saheb. All I had to do was tell her that my brother will kill you if she didn't say what I told her to," he mocked.

Rahu raised his sledgehammer.

"It's time to end your suffering, Saheb."

Nitin closed his eyes. He remembered the sound of Naina laughing. The pain at the back of his head eased up a little. Then, he waited for the final blow.

"You can always change their fate with a stroke of your pen."

Saleem looked around the empty courtyard – it had all the telltale signs of a recently concluded party. Scattered mugs, confetti shots, psychedelic lighting, and tissue paper strewn around. The occupants – both the gods and the demons – were long gone, though.

"One helluva show! Too bad it had to end in tragedy," muttered Saleem to himself.

The captivating performance by Naina still lingered in Saleem's mind. "She danced just like her," he thought.

The clouds moved through the courtyard. He could smell rain in them. A vision flashed across his mind – walking in the rain, crying, the tears blending into the water streaming down his face. The images faded away as quickly as they had come.

"Let's move out of here before it starts raining. There's nothing that can be done now, anyway," he heard a voice speak out behind him.

A man dressed in white robes was walking towards him. His face was impassive, but kind. The sun god gestured to Saleem to follow him into an arched hallway. The hallway ended in a valley. He could see a castle up in the mountains to his left. There was a lake in front of them, with water so pure and clean that it glistened in the light of the sun.

"The Crystal Lake," said Saleem.

"Yes… I reckon you would recognize those two out there as well."

Saleem saw a boy sitting next to a young man holding a fishing rod and talking to him. The boy was captivated by whatever the man appeared to be saying.

"Fahid and Sujit?" said Saleem.

"Yes," replied the sun god. He looked at Saleem. There was sadness in Saleem's eyes, as he pondered what fate had in store for them.

"Don't look so sad. It's just a story. You can always change their fate with a stroke of your pen."

"No... their story is done."

"But there are others in need of doing."

The sun god stopped, and looked intently at Saleem. It was a piercing gaze... one that made Saleem feel squeamish.

"I have no idea what you are talking about."

"So you have absolutely no recollection of The Lost Story?"

The words stirred something deep within Saleem... something that he could not remember, or did not want to... He suddenly felt a sharp pain shoot up in his chest.

"It seems you've locked up more than just the manuscript in that room of yours, Saleem. But it won't stay locked up for long. Every story must be finished."

The pain in Saleem's chest was getting sharper. Saleem sank to his knees. The sun god seemed oblivious to Saleem's deteriorating condition.

"We'll get to it in due time. For now, I have a gift for you." The Sun-God reached in his robe and pulled out a syringe. Saleem was fading.

"The elixir of life," he said, and plunged the needle into Saleem's chest.

"Epinephrine administered. OT is ready, Doctor."

The ward boys rushed Saleem into the operation theatre, followed by the doctor and two nurses. Sandy's heart was beating fast.

Sandy stood frozen outside the door.

He had found Saleem writhing on the floor of his drawing room, next to the locked door. Had Sandy not forgotten to pick up his cell phone when he left, it might have been too late.

It might be too late as it is.

Sandy pushed those thoughts away. He called up his parents and told them what had happened. They had offered to come down, but he declined. He wondered what Saleem meant by the words he had spoken just before he was rushed into the ER.

The Lost Story.

Before Sandy could think anymore, the doctor emerged.

"He'll be fine. He suffered a heart attack, but nothing we couldn't handle. You did well by not panicking. Have you informed his relatives?"

"I don't think he has any."

The doctor raised his eyebrows.

"Why don't you come back to check on him later, then?" said the doctor, and left.

Tragedy averted, Sandy's mind returned to Saleem's words. There was terror in Saleem's eyes. Even as he was fading, his eyes would not leave the lock on the door he was sprawled in front of. Sandy had seen him steal glances at the door many times before too.

Something isn't right here.

Sandy decided to go to Saleem's house first thing in the morning.

Sandy could not shake off the guilt of entering Saleem's house without informing him. He stood at the door of what was undoubtedly Saleem's bedroom.

He peeked in without entering, as if the doorway represented a moral threshold. It was humble and meagre, much like the rest of the house. The dusty bed, neatly made, with a single brown pillow looked like it had not been slept in for months. There was a side table next to the bed, and a cupboard built into the wall facing it. The curtains were drawn on the right side of the bed.

Still not willing to step inside, Sandy weighed his decision. *I've already intruded on his private space by stepping into his house without permission. Might as well go all the way.*

Sandy stepped in. He immediately felt shivers run up his back, and thought he heard whispers. Sandy spun around, his eyes moving automatically to the locked door in the living room.

"Just my imagination," said Sandy out aloud. "Let's get this over with!"

He turned around again and walked slowly towards the cupboard door and wrapped his fingers around the door knob. It felt cold and unyielding in his fingers.

I suspect it will be locked, but no harm in trying.

He turned the knob but it didn't budge.

Expected. Sandy decided to move on.

"Now if only the side table drawer is locked as well, I can leave with a bit of my conscience intact," he said. Sandy was spooked, and talking to himself eased his mind.

The drawer opened. It was empty but for a photograph. Sandy picked it up. It looked like it was taken at a hill station resort. Sandy could see a lake behind the two figures. One of them was undoubtedly a much younger Saleem, who looked delighted at being photographed next to whoever the other person was.

After some deliberation, Sandy put the photograph in his

pocket. Just as he was turning to leave, his eye caught the edge of a thin object peeking out of the base of the bed. It looked like a photo frame.

"Another photograph?" said Sandy.

He bent down on his knees to pick it up, the irrational side of his mind urging him to look under the bed and discover the horrors beneath. Suddenly, Sandy was very scared.

He finally stole a look. "Nothing but dust," he said, followed by relieved laughter.

He pulled out the frame from the bed. There was another old photograph in it. It was four people in front of a fairly ordinary looking building.

"They all look like college kids," said Sandy. He paused and then burst out laughing. *I'm talking as if I'm 50 years old.*

Sandy reckoned that one of these kids must be Saleem Afzal. He took the photo out of the frame, and stuffed the frame back where he picked it up from. He put the photo in his pocket, this time with less inhibition.

"Research time," said Sandy out loud, and left the room.

CHAPTER 4
Fearless

"I trust the week-long vacation was welcome," said Saleem, by way of greeting.

He was sitting up in his hospital bed, looking visibly healthier. His progress had been nothing short of remarkable, surprising even the doctors. But they wanted to keep him under observation for a few more days as a precautionary measure. Saleem had asked Sandy to bring him his laptop.

"Well... I had a couple of project submissions so it hasn't exactly been a walk on the beach."

"Done with your Masters?" Saleem asked.

"In two months," Sandy replied.

"And after that?"

"Well... considering I'm collaborating with you on a book, I am seriously considering writing as a career option. I've always loved telling stories."

"I suppose writing can be a high for someone like you," said Saleem, not sounding very pleased. "It is an opportunity to re-create the world as you see it," he went on, as if talking about something else entirely, "Uninhibited. Unshackled... Maybe I should thank you."

Sandy was taken by surprise. "Thank me?"

"Yes… I wouldn't be writing stories again if it wasn't for you."

Sandy didn't know what to say to that, so he just reached into his bag and pulled out a few sheets of paper.

"I've started another story while you were out. So why don't you read it while I read *this*."

Sandy showed Saleem his copy of Neil Gaiman's *Neverwhere*.

Saleem nodded at Sandy, who had been expecting a much warmer response, and then busied himself with the story.

The young woman settled into the plush arm chair in front of him. She adjusted her collar mic until it was hidden perfectly under the neck of her blouse with just the small clip visible. Abhay watched patiently as the make-up lady applied a bit of last minute make-up to the twenty-something anchorwoman's cheeks. The cameraman had finished preparing the frame, and was adjusting the curtain to ensure that the light was optimal for the shot.

Abhay's small living room had been transformed into a makeshift studio over the past month. The patchy colour on the walls was gone, done up with a brand new coat of paint to make a better background for television. The decrepit old sofa had been replaced with a new plush couch and big, kingly cushions. Two comfortable arm chairs sat in the far corner of the room, facing each other diagonally. Two ornate lamps had been placed next to them to adequately illuminate the faces of the occupants.

The anchorwoman signalled to the cameraman that she was ready, the make-up-lady shuffled out of the camera's frame, and the cameraman finally said, "We're rolling."

"Good evening, ladies and gentlemen. Tonight in this special feature we bring you an exclusive interview with the man who has become a symbol of bravery. He embodies the nation's resolve to take terrorism head-on, and defeat it. He has managed to single-handedly infuse courage and confidence into each and every Indian, inspiring us to look terrorists in the eye and let them know that we are not afraid of them anymore! And that we will not bow down to them. Ladies and gentlemen, Mr Abhay Arora."

Abhay heard the camera whirr as it zoomed in on him.

"Thank you, Pratibha. You are very kind, and it is a pleasure."

"So tell us Abhay, how does it feel to be awarded with a Bharat Ratna?"

"It feels like an out-of-body experience. This whole... everything in fact, since that day... feels... like... out of this world. But I must say that I have only done what any Indian in my position would have done."

Abhay spoke the words mechanically. He had said this to umpteen journalists in the past month. He wondered if the number of 'exclusive' interviews he had been in this past month was closer to 30 or 40. He couldn't remember.

"Abhay, you killed an armed and trained terrorist and saved a woman's life! That is no ordinary thing!" The young anchor waved her hands animatedly while her perfectly straight hair stayed completely still.

"Not really, Prathibha. After all, I'm a simple insurance salesman and not a trained soldier. I was merely in the right place at the right time..."

Abhay's mind replayed the incident, even as he spoke. It was a regular house sales call in the life of a regular struggling insurance salesman. He remembered the feeling of self pity as he sat in the small living room of Mrs Smita's small house. The room was smaller than even his tiny living room. The old threadbare sofa he sat on smelt of years of poverty and neglect. The table at the center creaked and swayed under the pressure of his hands as he lay out a brochure on it to explain to her the various products that his company had to offer. He hated selling life insurance policies. He hated his job, his boss, and his whole sad and meaningless existence. He could see that Mrs Smita was too poor to be able to buy any of the confusing schemes he was trying to explain to her. He had still decided to go on with the whole thing since he had already started.

Pratibha interjected his thoughts.

"So, Abhay, could you please tell our viewers what really happened that night and how did you manage to bring the terrorist down?"

"Sure," Abhay began his well rehearsed story. "So... I was sitting in Mrs Smita's house, explaining to her all the helpful products my company, Alliance Life Insurance Corporation, has to offer..." An image of a cheque for 30 lakh rupees flashed through his mind. His company had paid him that much for mentioning its name in every interview he gave. They had also given him a double promotion since that night.

"Suddenly, this man wearing a mask and carrying a large gun barged into the room. Of course, I didn't know who he was at that time."

The image of the masked man came back to him. He recalled the paralyzing fear that he had felt as the man waved his AK-47 at him. Mrs Smita's loud shrieking as the terrorist grabbed her by her hair and dragged her away from the sofa also came back to him.

"This man then grabbed Mrs Smita, who had started

shouting, and threw her on the floor and pointed the gun at her head. He repeatedly asked her to stop shouting."

The strange feeling of urinating in his own pants came back to him. He had done so as the man pointed the gun at the woman's head. She was making too much noise for his patience.

At that point, he had remembered his mother's advice that she often gave him if he wanted to go stop the neighbour from beating up his wife, or help a sick old man on the road and take him to the hospital.

"Middle class people like us should not get involved in other people's affairs, son. It's better to turn a blind eye to other people's suffering. You never know what kind of mess your act of bravery or kindness may get you into," she would tell him.

"Since Mrs Smita couldn't stop shouting, the man finally hit her on the head with the butt of the gun. She fell down... unconscious... and then he pointed the gun at me."

"Wow! How did it feel to have a gun pointed at you?"

Pratibha's eyes glimmered with excitement.

Abhay recalled dropping down to the floor and holding the masked man's feet with his hands. He had begged and pleaded with the man to spare his life and even suggested that if the man let him go he would leave quietly and not mention a word about this to anybody.

"I am not a part of this. I don't care about what you want from this woman. Please just let me go. I promise I will not say a word of this to anybody. Please, just let me go. Please... I beg you. Please!" he had wailed.

The man had tried to kick him away repeatedly. He remembered feeling absolutely helpless, as he watched his tears trickle down the man's dirty brown shoes.

"...I felt a rush of adrenaline take over me," he said to the anchorwoman with practiced calm, "but my mind kept telling me to keep cool. I sat there calmly and told him that he didn't scare me." Abhay had said this line so often, he could say it in his sleep.

"I sat there for about five minutes while the man locked the doors and windows of the room. The television in the room was still on and the live news report was talking about a terrorist attack in our part of the city. It said that terrorists had attacked a popular tourist destination and had then split up while the police was hunting them down. It also advised everybody to lock their doors and windows. That's when I realized the gravity of the situation."

The terrorist had actually smashed the TV after they had heard the piece. Abhay's fears had multiplied. His grovelling and pleading had intensified as mortal fear welled up in his heart.

"The terrorist paced back and forth in the room while I sat there, waiting for my chance to strike him. I figured he was trying to think of his next move. I also realized we had become his hostages. I knew I had to do something quick. Suddenly, there was a loud knock at the door. It was a police officer who was shouting for us to open the door. Mrs Smita's screaming had worked. After knocking a few times and a little shouting, the brave police officer broke the door and barged in..."

Abhay remembered the relief that he had felt as the policeman had broken in. The ruthless cold-blooded terrorist, however, had been ready and had fired his AK-47. The policeman had fired his revolver almost at the same instant as the terrorist. Abhay had watched in horror as bullets were fired in both directions and blood splattered across the walls of the small room. The wounded policeman had then thrown himself at the terrorist, who fell backwards on the smashed TV set. A bloody brawl had ensued as Abhay stayed down on the floor, paralyzed with fear, not even daring to look up. The apathy that had been ingrained in him had kept him pinned to the floor. He had felt castrated, unable to help a dying man. He had been trained to be a mute spectator to crime.

The two men threw punches at each other and rolled on the floor while the policeman shouted at Abhay to pick up the gun and shoot the terrorist. Abhay had been unable to move. He had watched as the policeman, who had been badly wounded, was eventually overpowered by the terrorist. The terrorist pushed the policeman to the ground, and sat on his stomach trying to strangle him. The policeman had mumbled desperately, in choked whispers, "shoot him!" as the terrorist tightened his grip around the officer's neck.

"...The terrorist had been ready and shot the brave police officer who then fell on the floor. The mad man jumped on the officer and tried to strangle him. I knew this was my chance so I jumped on him and choked him with my arm while he was bent over. I told him to let go of the officer's neck. Finally, with all my strength, I threw him at the TV set. While he picked himself up, I grabbed the officer's revolver and shot him. It was only later that I found out that I had been too late to save the officer's life." Abhay sensed a palpable intensity in the room as the television crew seemed to be hanging on Abhay's every word.

He remembered the deathly silence in the room as the policeman stopped struggling, and the terrorist collapsed on top of him. It was then that he had realized that the terrorist had also been mortally wounded; and had fallen — exhausted from the officer's dying attempts to capture him. A few moments after that, Abhay had quietly stood up and picked up the officer's gun which had been lying on the floor all along. He remembered the shiver that had gone through his spine as he pointed the gun at the back of the terrorist's head. He had closed his eyes and pulled the trigger.

"...Finally as the terrorist fell down, he begged and pleaded with me to spare him. But I knew that he was still a threat to us. A wounded tiger is always more dangerous. I shot him in the head."

Abhay felt the intensity in the room reach a crescendo.

He remembered opening his eyes and seeing the limp body of the terrorist lying at his feet with its head split open. As he had stood rooted to the spot, shocked at his own actions, Mrs Smita had regained consciousness. What she then saw was a visibly shaken Abhay bent over the dead terrorist with the revolver in his hand. Sobbing with relief, she had run to him, embraced him and thanked him for saving their lives.

"What happened after that?" Pratibha felt her excitement subside a little.

"...Then Mrs Smita became conscious and thanked me for saving her. Soon, more police officers arrived along with journalists... and from there on, you all know what has happened."

Abhay had tried telling Mrs Smita that it was really the policeman who had saved them. However, this woman, who was crying on his shoulder and kept thanking him for having saved her, gave him a whole other perspective on the incident. At that moment, his apathy and fear struck him again. His mother's words came back to him. *"You never know what kind of mess your act of bravery or kindness may get you into."* He wondered if he would be held guilty for shooting a wounded terrorist who had already been neutralized. He imagined being called a coward for not having saved the brave policeman.

It struck him that instead of telling the whole truth about the incident, it might be a better idea to twist a few facts... just a little bit. It could, at least, save him from all the dire consequences he had imagined. He decided to relate his part in the incident as an act of bravery. After all, he had convinced himself, it was he who had fired the fatal shot at the terrorist and saved everyone, anyway. And moreover, he reasoned with his conscience, there wouldn't be any negative consequences of this lie for anybody.

By the time the police arrived, he had made up the story of his bravery and narrated it to them. He figured that irrespective of how the truth was told, the dead policeman would, in any case, have received a posthumous medal, and his family, some compensation. Mrs Smita was convinced that he had saved their lives. Her gushing testimony had only strengthened his stand.

"We are proud to have a brave citizen like you amongst us," said Pratibha, who was now sitting up with her back straight. "So how has your life changed for you since that fateful day?"

"I am still the same Abhay... just the world around me has changed a little." He smiled warmly as he thought of how drastically his fortunes had turned since that day: A double promotion and an endorsement deal from his own company, a few other product endorsement deals which were in the making, cash rewards by a few Indian companies, and the numerous marriage proposals.

"One last question, Abhay. Is there anything that you wished you had done differently that day?"

He thought of the dead policeman's body. His feeble, desperate, dying cries echoed in his mind. The officer's widow and their four year old daughter, who he had met later at the funeral, had stood in front of him and cried. He told himself that it was fear that had paralyzed him. He reminded himself that if he had done anything in that state, it would probably have led to all their deaths.

He said, "Not really... Things always happen for a reason. Although, I do wish that the brave officer could have been saved..."

The interview ended soon after. The news crew left as quickly as it had arrived. Abhay ordered dinner from a nearby restaurant, ate it by himself, as he watched the news, and decided to call it a day. He thought about those 30 minutes that changed his life a month ago as he switched off the light.

"Sandy!"

Sandy was lost in *Neverwhere*. He was at the part where Richard Mayhew was facing the prospect of crossing Night's Bridge. A horrid and fatal manifestation of his deepest fears and dreams, known and unknown, lay ahead of him, silently calling him through the darkness. Sandy was wondering what he would see on Night's Bridge.

"SANDY!" Saleem repeated loudly.

"Yes? Sorry... I was a bit lost in *Neverwhere*..."

"It tends to do that."

Sandy nodded. His mind had still not returned completely from Night's Bridge. Saleem went on, regardless.

"Anyway... I need you to do something. Give me a sheet of paper. I'm putting down this address for you. It's in Daryaganj. I want you to go to this place and meet Vidya Shankar. Tell her I sent you."

"What's this for?"

"I reckon we should start talking to a publisher," Saleem said.

"Oh! She's a publisher?"

"A very good one. She's a damn fine editor too."

"Did she handle your books?" Sandy asked.

Sandy suspected this was the same editor Ashok Jain spoke of. Saleem did not say anything.

"All right... I'll go see her tomorrow. I think I'll make a move now, while you work on this," Sandy said.

"It should be done by tomorrow."

"Excellent! See you soon. Hopefully at your place." Sandy got up to leave.

"Sandy, we should step on it. I'm not sure if I'll survive another one of these," he pointed at his heart.

"Come on! We both have to attend our first book signing together," said Sandy, but only with a half-hearted smile.

"Hmmm," mumbled Saleem, and turned away.

Abhay woke up to the ringing of his phone. His first impulse was to disconnect the call.

Who calls so damn early in the morning?

He squinted at the alarm clock on the side table. The time was 9.30 AM. Abhay jumped out of bed in a flash.

Shit! I'm late! I can't believe I forget to set the alarm again last night. Sanjay is going to have my head on a platter for this.

Sanjay was his boss. Ex-boss, Abhay reminded himself, and smiled at the thought that he had now been promoted to a position above Sanjay. His current boss never came into work before lunch. Knowing that he could get away with it, Abhay eased up and stretched out his arms. He then reached for the phone. It was his Mom.

'Hi Mamma!'

'Why did you take so long to pick up the phone?' His mom seemed irritated.

'I was asleep, Mamma. The phone woke me up.'

'Sleeping at 9.30? Aren't you getting late for work?'

'*Haan*... but I have taken the first half off for some bank work. It has to be done today,' Abhay lied to his mother. He didn't want her to launch into a monologue about sincerity towards work, which would then lead to the topic of living a simple and healthy lifestyle; since she would naturally assume that he was up late last night. Eventually, it would come down to his smoking, which she utterly despised.

'Still... you should not take work lightly, Abhay. You may be a national hero, but your company won't pay you after a point of time if you slack off from work.'

'Mamma! It's not like that! I said it's important. Why would you think I'm slacking off from work? Anyway. Never mind. Tell me why you called.' Abhay was irritated by his mother's tone of voice.

'Arre baba! Don't get angry! Listen... I met Mrs Singh in the morning on my way to the temple. She was telling me about this girl in her family. I had even met her once at Mrs Singh's house. She's very beautiful, Abhay... just like a fairy. Very fair, slim, and just the right height for you. Plus she works for the... uhhh... some human something department... I don't quite remember.'

'Human Resources. It's the department of a company that does recruitments.' Abhay always sounded disinterested when his mother brought up marriage proposals. In truth, he was always keen to know the specifics of the proposals that came for him. The worth of a man lies in the kind of marriage proposals he gets, Abhay always thought. And his worth had certainly gone up ever since his fortunes had turned.

'*Haaaaaaaannn*! Human Resources department of a very reputed company in Delhi only. She's perfect for you, Abhay!

Even the family is great! If you want, maybe I can set up a meeting for the two of you in the next couple of days...?'

'Sure, Mamma. Set it up,' said Abhay as nonchalantly as he could, but his heart was beating faster at the prospect of meeting a girl who looked like a fairy.

'Excellent! I'll call Mrs Singh right now.'

'Sure Mamma. I should get moving too. It's getting really late, now. You take care, and let me know. Bye.'

Abhay hung up the phone.

Abhay walked into office at 11.30 and walked straight to his brand new cabin, after a quick look at the attendance register. Sure enough, his boss wasn't in yet.

He switched on his new laptop, and downloaded his emails. He didn't particularly feel like working, but went through the grind of reading, replying and deleting emails. He decided to work on the presentation for the upcoming regional meet at Kaziranga on 'Devising new and innovative techniques on motivating the sales-force.'

He was thrilled at the prospect of being a part of a meet that was exclusively for management. I am one of them now, Abhay reminded himself. Abhay daydreamed about fast-tracking up the corporate ladder, when he was shaken out of his reverie by the ringing of his phone.

"Mr Abhay Arora?" a female voice said from the other side of the phone.

"Yes?"

"Hi! This is Pratibha Shikhavat from News Now. I interviewed you yesterday."

"Oh yes! Hi Pratibha! How are you?" Abhay asked.

"I just wanted a quick comment from you on the reports from this morning. Are you worried about this rather disturbing development?"

"Uhh... what reports?"

"You don't know?" Pratibha seemed surprised.

"No... not really. Actually, I woke up late today morning and had to rush to work. Have been quite busy here too... so didn't quite get the time to read the newspaper. Can you tell me what's going on?"

Abhay felt a slight inkling of fear. *Had they somehow found out the truth?* was the first thought that crossed his mind. He didn't even want to imagine the repercussions of that.

Pratibha spoke in a hushed, fearful tone. "Abhay, the organization that the terrorist you killed belonged to, has issued a *fatwa,* calling for your death."

Abhay felt the ground beneath his feet give way. Fear gripped his body, and he found himself at a complete loss of words. With great difficulty, he tried to focus on what Pratibha was saying.

"...tan Times picked it up from the transmission on Emzoor TV in Afghanistan. Apparently, the leader of the organization has issued the edict, calling all believers to bring you to death for murdering a warrior who fought for freedom. We're trying to source the actual tape itself. For now, we just wanted a comment from you for the evening news. Hello? Abhay?"

"Yea... yeah, Pratibha... I'm here! Listen... this is all a bit too much to absorb. I don't want to give any comments for now. I'll talk to you later."

"Wait! Abhay!"

Abhay hung up the phone. It immediately rang again, and he disconnected the call without answering it. He stared at his phone for a good two minutes, fighting with himself, not wanting to absorb the information he had just received.

The phone began to ring again. Abhay disconnected the call, and switched off his phone.

"Hello? Commissioner Govardhan?"

"Abhay! What can I do for the man with balls of steel today?"

Abhay had met Commissioner Govardhan at the policeman's funeral. He had congratulated Abhay, and had said that terrorism is not defeated by countermeasures, but the will and defiance of men such as him. He had given Abhay his number, and told him to call if he ever needed anything.

"Sir. I need police protection."

"Police protection? Why on earth does the bravest civilian in India need police protection?"

"Sir, haven't you heard the news? The terrorist organization has issued a *fatwa* for my death."

Abhay had expected any of a range of reactions from Govardhan. Laughter was the last of them

"Abhay, Abhay, Abhay! Do you even know what a *fatwa* is? They come a dime a dozen. You don't need to worry about it."

Panic joined fear, and Abhay felt the sensation of being full up to the brim.

"What are you saying, sir? The leader of one of the biggest terrorist organizations has called on his brothers to kill me. They can come from anywhere. They can be plotting against me right now. I'm completely exposed and unprotected. You cannot take this lightly."

"Abhay, I've studied *fatwa*s in great detail. What you need to understand about them is that they are not the word of law, even in a fundamentalist state. There have been such *fatwa*s against famous writers like Salman Rushdie and Taslima Nasreen. That doesn't mean they stay holed up in their homes for the fear of their lives! In fact, *fatwa*s have even been issued that deem terrorism and the killing of innocents as forbidden. Does that stop the terrorists? No. Don't fall for the dramatics of these news reporters. *Fatwa*s have been misconstruted as death warrants by the ignorant, and these reporters only fuel the fire. They just need a news story to latch on to, however irrelevant it may be. If they can turn the search for a politician's dog into breaking news, then you can well imagine how much they will hype up such an edict. Trust me, you don't have anything to worry about. Our information network has tightened after the last attack. It is not easy for terrorists to enter our country. The moment you are actually in danger, we will be the first ones to know, and we will take the necessary precautions then. You can relax for now."

But Abhay could not relax. He remembered the cold, merciless eyes behind the mask. He imagined the terrorist gunning him down in cold blood.

"I see your point, sir, but what's the harm in taking precautions? I'm requesting you to consider this."

"I don't understand this at all!" Govardhan seemed annoyed now. "You were fearless in the face of a terrorist standing two feet away from you. How can a mere proclamation from thousands of kilometers away get you so agitated?"

In that moment, Abhay contemplated telling Commissioner Govardhan the truth. *"Because I never did it! I did not kill the terrorist... your officer did! All I did was urinate in my pants, fall to his feet, beg him for mercy, and not save the life of your officer when I had the chance! I didn't do anything... and I don't deserve death threats for something I haven't done!"*

Abhay took a moment to consider the disastrous

consequences that such a confession would have. He would be disgraced by the media and the country. Not only would he lose his promotion, but also his job. All the marriage proposals, the endorsement deals, and the life full of promises ahead would disappear as quickly as they had come. And his mother... her friends would ridicule her to no end.

The last thought gave him an idea.

"It's my mother, Sir. She... she is coming into town tomorrow or day after, and I don't want to take a chance when she is around. I am willing to face any terrorist again, but I wouldn't be able to bear her coming in harm's way, even if it's a thousand to one possibility. For her sake, please give me police protection," Abhay pleaded.

"Fine. All right. I'll send an armed constable to be posted outside your house tomorrow evening."

"Can't you send him today?"

"No I can't, Abhay. I need the time to get this sanctioned. Good bye, and for God's sake – stop panicking!" the Commissioner said.

Abhay trudged slowly towards his bike. The rest of the day had passed in a haze. He had called his superior and taken the rest of the day off. However, he did not want to go back to an empty house, and the prospect of being among people felt safer. He had gone back to his office, locked the door of his cabin, and stared at the screensaver on the laptop monitor till he noticed that it was dark outside.

He realised that he had been sitting inside his cabin for hours. It certainly hadn't seemed that way. He couldn't remember what he had been thinking about in all this time.

All he could feel now was a strange numbness, and intermittent throbs of fear in his gut. He decided to not stay in office any longer, especially after it was dark and almost everyone had gone home.

Abhay felt helpless as he walked towards his motorcycle parked in the basement. He was a sitting duck for trained terrorists, who could come out of anywhere, kill him and disappear in the blink of an eye. His looked suspiciously from one dark corner to another, as he tried to spot a man who wasn't there in the shadows, his ears cocked to catch the imaginary sound of approaching footsteps.

He quickened his pace towards his bike. *What stops them from coming out from behind that car and shooting me? Or from waiting for me at the exit of the parking lot and kidnapping me?*

Or from planting a bomb on my bike.

He stopped a few meters from his bike. The dull throbbing sense of panic had amplified and completely immobilized him. Abhay took a few deep breaths, and then began to circle his bike, keeping his distance. He tried to look for anything that did not belong to the bike on or around it.

"Nothing here," thought Abhay, "but what's the harm in playing it safe? I'll just call a cab and go home. I can always take the bike tomorrow. For all I know, they could follow me by tracking my bike. This will throw them off."

Abhay called the cab service and waited for it by loitering around in the lobby of the building, always keeping himself within sight of the security guard at the door.

Just as the taxi pulled up outside the building, another possibility presented itself to Abhay.

What if they pre-empted this, and sent a terrorist in disguise? Besides, if they've seen me, they can always take the cab down. I'll be all alone in it. This is too dangerous!

His phone began to ring.

"Unknown number. Probably the cab driver."

Abhay switched off his phone again, and walked out of the building towards the bus stop nearby.

The paranoia refused to leave Abhay even inside a crowded bus. He refused to take a seat, opting to stand close to the exit instead, ready to make a quick getaway at the sign of anything out of ordinary. He got off at the bus stop near his apartment complex, and walked towards it as fast as he could, just stopping short of running. He rushed to the elevator, and as the doors closed in front of him, Abhay finally breathed out.

What if they're waiting for me at home?

Abhay stopped short of putting the key in the lock. He scanned the silent, empty hallway, looking left, then right.

Abhay contemplated knocking on his neighbour's door and asking him to stand guard while Abhay checked out the apartment.

"But why? What reason am I supposed to give them? That I am on the run from trained terrorists and that they may be waiting with AK-47s inside my house? Is there an end to this?"

Abhay was scared and tired. With no other option, he turned the key in the lock, and slowly opened the door. All the lights inside the house were off. Abhay left the door ajar behind him, and then turned on the lights in each and every room, checked every corner and cupboard till he was absolutely sure that he was alone in the house.

Abhay heaved a huge sigh of relief. He walked up to the open door and peeked outside without stepping out of the door. First left, then right, and then straight across.

Lying in bed, he weighed his options.

He could confess the truth, but would a life of disgrace be any better than being killed now in cold blood? He cursed the moment he had decided to tell his own version of events. Humility. Honesty. Sincerity. Hard work. Words that his mother spoke often. Words that had never held any meaning to him. He had taken every shortcut life had thrown at him, and it was finally one too many.

He tried to take comfort in Govardhan's words... but the eyes of the terrorist, and the muzzle of the gun kept coming back to him every time to neutralize it.

"Can I go to the police with the truth? No, they would probably arrest me for twisting the facts or something. Or do even worse."

The media? They would mock him.

The terrorists? Even if I could reach them without them putting a bullet in my head, they wouldn't believe me.

Mamma? Her heart would break.

Abhay did not know what to do. He wished he could go back in time.

KNOCK! KNOCK! KNOCK! KNOCK!

Abhay sat up with a start. He looked at his table clock. It was half an hour past midnight. 'Who could it be at this hour?'

The knocking on the door intensified, louder and more frantic now.

'Wh... Wh... Who is it?'

No answer. Just more knocking.

Abhay walked slowly to the door. He could see the shadows underneath his door of shuffling feet.

"Who is it?"

More knocking. It seemed as though the people outside were ready to bring the door down.

He hunted for his phone in his pockets and bedside. It was nowhere to be found. The sinking realization hit him that he had probably dropped the phone in the bus or while rushing to the apartment building.

This is it. So much for Govardhan's assumption.

He could clearly see those cold, merciless eyes in his mind. Numbness washed over Abhay, to the extent that he completely lost sensation. The world dimmed around him, and the sound of frantic knocking became dull.

Fear. Desperation. Panic. Everything that had assailed him since that afternoon peaked to a level beyond cognition...

Unable to think, Abhay did the only thing he could. He opened the door.

It was the security guard. He was holding out Abhay's mobile phone.

"Abhay sir, you dropped your phone at the gate. It must have been lying there for so long. But thank God no one took it."

The guard was smiling earnestly. Abhay took the phone and tried to thank the guard, only to realize that he couldn't find his voice. The relief that had washed over him had rendered him speechless. Instead, he just nodded at the guard and closed the door. As he heard the footsteps of the guard fade away, Abhay slid down slowly to the floor along the wall and burst into tears.

The two children wrestled playfully in the garden with each other, laughing and screaming.

"Careful boys!" said their grandfather, keeping an eye on them above his newspaper. He was reading the editorial prompted by the recent wave of terrorist attacks across the country.

"…over the years, their guns may have become better, their bombs more lethal, and their plans bolder. But their weapon is still the same. Fear. Until we realise that living in fear is a choice rather than compulsion, the terrorists have won without firing even a single shot." The editorial had concluded.

The children came running over to him.

"Dadaji! Please tell us the story of how you single-handedly defeated a scary terrorist and saved the wounded lady!"

The cold, merciless eyes. The muzzle of the gun. The images of that day's event twenty seven years ago were still etched in his mind as if they had happened yesterday. Abhay shuddered.

"Dadaji! Tell us, na!"

"But you've heard that story a million times!" He didn't want to revisit that day. Not today.

"Just once more!"

"Yes… last time."

"Please."

"Please."

"Please."

"Please."

Abhay conceded. "All right, but only after you both finish eating lunch."

"YAAAYYY!" The two kids happily ran inside, and Abhay followed them in. Before closing the door, he did his usual routine, a ritual that had turned into a habit over the years. He peeked outside without stepping out. First left, then right and then straight across.

"Aren't you even a little afraid to open the door?"

The door rattled relentlessly, as if five people were inside trying to break out. Saleem was surprised that the lock had not broken and fallen off by now.

"Don't open it." The voice was full of terror. Saleem turned his head to find Abhay standing behind to him. His eyes were wide open, and he was sweating profusely.

"Don't open it," he said again, "you don't know what's in there."

"Actually, I do."

"Really? What is it?"

"The Lost Story."

"Uh-huh. I wonder what's in it." Abhay walked away and sat on the sofa, where he tucked his arms between his knees and began rocking back and forth.

"That's what I have to find out." Saleem reached out and took hold of the lock. The door stopped rattling immediately. Abhay sat down.

"Aren't you even a little afraid to open the door?" he asked, helplessly.

"I am," said Saleem calmly. His fear of the door, the voices, and the uncertainty still gnawed at him, but there was an undeniable sense of clarity about what needed to be done.

"Then why are you doing this?" Abhay almost cried.

"Because the alternative is to lead a life like you did."

Abhay opened his mouth as if to say something, but no words came out. His shoulders dropped, and he hung his head.

"Fear is not good for storytelling," said Saleem and turned his attention to the lock.

"Now if only I could figure out where I kept the blasted key to this thing!"

"So this is the Mecca of the publishing industry in India," said Sandy out loud.

He was walking down a road which was probably twelve feet wide, and looked ready to explode with the sheer number of vehicles on it. Cars aside, Sandy had never seen so many cycle-rickshaws at the same time in his life. They looked like an endless centipede of metal and tyres.

There was no respite on the pavement – or that which qualified as the pavement – on either side of the road. The whole thing was lined with shops, predominantly bookstores. A sea of people moved in and out of these shops and into the thin lanes that cut the main road every hundred feet or so. Sandy was looking for the office of the Meta Publishing House on one such lane.

The office turned out to be one of several decrepit buildings deep inside a narrow lane, up three narrow flights of stairs that did not have enough room for two people walking shoulder to shoulder. Thankfully, Sandy did not have to face this problem, and he entered the office of Meta Publishing House, feeling very exhausted, parched, and underwhelmed by the true face of the business of publishing.

"What do you want?" said a man who happened to be in the room, quite rudely. He wore a plain shirt and trousers, had a bald patch on his head and a pencil moustache. Sandy guessed he must be in his forties.

He was taking out manuscripts from a cardboard box and throwing them carelessly on one of the desks lining the left side of the room.

"I'm here to meet Ms Vidya Shankar," said Sandy.

"Do you have an appointment with madam?"

"Ummm... no."

"Then you can't meet her," said the man, and went back to dealing with the manuscripts.

"Listen! I've come from very far," Sandy persisted.

"How far?"

Sandy was taken aback by both the question and the suddenness with which it was posed at him. But he recovered immediately.

"Greater Kailash in South Delhi," said Sandy, raising his eyebrows and wiping the sweat off his forehead theatrically. The man laughed.

"This morning, a man came from Coimbatore wanting to meet madam, and couldn't. She's very busy. If you have a manuscript, just give it to me. And give your address and phone number to that lady over there."

"Listen! Can you at least tell her that Saleem Afzal has sent me? She might agree to meet me."

The man looked at Sandy as if he was a rodent.

"If I disturb madam, she will shout at me. What's in it for me to get shouted at?"

Sandy sighed. *Of course. There had to be something in it for him.* Sandy pulled out a crumpled hundred rupee note from his pocket and stuffed it in the man's shirt pocket. The man continued to stare at Sandy. Sandy pulled out another hundred and stuffed it next to the first one. When the man still refused to budge, Sandy finally spoke up.

"Look... I only have one hundred rupees left, and I need that to get back home. So can you please tell Ms Shankar that Saleem Afzal has sent someone to meet her?"

The man, convinced that he could not milk more money

out of Sandy, turned around to make his way to the door at the end of the room. Just as he was entering, Sandy shouted out,

"Don't forget the name. SALEEM AFZAL."

"So, how do you know Saleem?"

Her voice was disinterested and aloof, much like her demeanour.

"Well, I am a huge fan of his work. So I wrote this story, and dug out his email address and e-mailed it to him. Next thing you know, I get an email from him with an address asking to meet. I could not believe my luck... So I went, and..."

"A short version please? I'm very busy," Vidya interrupted him.

"Okay. Long story short – Saleem Afzal has come out of retirement."

Sandy paused, as if hoping for a theatrical gasp followed by hearty applause. All he got was a raised eyebrow.

"How much did you bribe Suresh out there to let you in?"

Typical publisher snob.

"You can call Saleem to check if you want!"

"I don't have his number." Her face remained expressionless.

"Well..." Sandy realised then that he didn't have Saleem's number either. "All I can tell you is that he's writing one last book... with me. He says he can't write stories any longer unless someone writes them with him. So he asked me to collaborate on half-stories. You know, one of us writes the first half, and the other one finishes it. Why don't you read what we've written so far and maybe you'll realize that I'm not lying!"

Something about what Sandy said must have touched a

chord in Vidya. She leaned back into her chair, folded her hands in front of her face, and stared at nothing in particular on her table.

"Typical Saleem. You can trust him to pull a stunt like this... writing a book after so many years with a complete nobody."

Sandy's face fell. *I maybe a nobody, but not after this book! And did she have to call me that to my face?*

Vidya Shankar had an air of confidence around her. Her hair was more white than black, the eyes behind her spectacles sharp, and her skin was touched by a stray wrinkle here and there. But none of that could hide the fact that she must have been breathtakingly beautiful in her time. Sandy sensed that there was some sort of history between her and Saleem.

"Well... uhh... so Saleem wanted me to come down and speak to you about publishing the book," Sandy said and fell silent again, not quite sure what to say.

"Do you have the manuscript?" asked Vidya.

"No. We're still working on it."

"Do you have a synopsis of the book?"

"Umm... no."

"Then how can I help you, Mr Gupta?" she said, looking exasperated.

Sandy was at a loss of words again.

Vidya finally decided to cut him some slack. *What happened is not his fault, after all.*

"Listen," she sighed, "once you guys are done with it, or are about to be through with it, come back to me with either a manuscript or the synopsis, and we'll take it from there. Here, take my card. It has my number."

Sandy decided to take advantage of her softening, and tentatively broached his other agenda.

"Ummm... I'm sorry if I sound like I'm prying, but were

you and Saleem friends? He spoke quite fondly of you."

"Did he now?" said Vidya sardonically, confirming Sandy's doubts.

"Yes... it's just that he is so reclusive. Doesn't talk much about himself, about his life before or after the accident. Or even the accident. Look, I'm just asking out of curiosity. It's always good to know the person you're working with."

Vidya looked at Sandy long and hard. Saleem was in her past, and she had convinced herself to forget all about him. She never spoke of him, and very few people knew about her and Saleem to begin with. Her involvement in Saleem's life and work had faded to obscurity with time, and she had made her peace with it. She had *learned* to be okay with it.

The sudden resurgence of Saleem had startled her, but she had kept her composure. But she felt strangely drawn to this kid. She knew he was genuine in his intentions, wanting to know only to learn more about the man he idolized, rather than for some ulterior motive.

"Do you know about Saleem's accident?" asked Vidya.

Sandy nodded his head.

"How?" she shot back.

"Well... from this gentleman called Ashok Jain. He is the son of..."

"Brijnath Jain. Yes. I know those two bloodsucking leeches. If it had been up to them, they would have turned Saleem into an assembly line of books. He must have said that they were very close to Saleem...?"

"Yes, he did. Said his father was very close to Saleem. And that Saleem told him everything," Sandy said.

"And did you believe that?"

"Well... I didn't have any reason not to."

"Then let me correct you. Brijnath Jain was a slimy bastard!

And there's quite a bit that he did not know about Saleem!" she almost shouted. Vidya then made a visible effort to compose herself.

"Unfortunately, Saleem cut off relations with everyone after the accident. In my case, of course, Saleem and I had grown apart a long time before it happened. The accident pretty much sealed the deal."

Sandy guessed that asking about the nature of their relationship would be a tad too personal. So he decided to steer the conversation in another direction.

"I found this photograph in Saleem's house. Could you tell me who these people are?"

"Does Saleem know you have this photograph?"

"Well... uh, no," said Sandy sheepishly. He showed her the photograph with the four people. Vidya took the photograph from him and stared at it for a while. To Sandy's surprise, her face broke into a wide smile.

Wow! She knows how to do that!

She held up the photograph with her left hand, and placed her finger one by one on each person in the photo.

"Vishaal, Guru, Saleem and Vineet. They called themselves the Injustice League of Delhi University. Jokers, the four of them!" she said.

"The Injustice League of Delhi University? Saleem was into comics?"

"Oh yes! They bored me to death with their 'Who is better? Batman or Superman' discussions."

"You were with them in college?" Sandy asked.

"No... I met Saleem much later. Their bond lasted beyond college, and luckily, all of them worked here in Delhi. So that helped too. Guru and Vineet moved to the United States. But Vishaal is still in Delhi. Retired now... stays with his children."

Vidya leaned back, presumably reminiscing about old times.

"You know... if you want to find out what Saleem was like... you should go and meet Vishaal. He stays in Vasant Kunj," she said.

"That's not too far from my place! Do you have an address?"

Sandy almost jumped out of his chair. Vidya gave him a stern look, and he quietened down. She browsed through her phone, and then extended it to him.

"Here. This is his number."

"I have this other photograph too," Sandy checked his pockets, but could not locate the other photograph.

"Damn, I must have left it at home." Sandy took Vidya's phone dejectedly and copied the number.

As he noted it down, he heard her speak in an oddly cautious voice, "How is he now? Saleem?"

"He is in hospital. He suffered a heart attack last week," he said almost casually. Sandy then saw the look of horror on Vidya's face and added immediately "...but he's out of danger now. Would you like to come and see him? I'm sure he'll like..."

"No!" said Vidya sternly, looking very angry all of a sudden. "Get one thing straight. Anything to do with this book, I deal with you. Not Saleem. I don't even want to see his face."

"Oh... all right ma'am," said Sandy, taken aback.

"Look – I'm sorry I shouted at you. But I don't want to see him. Now if you don't mind, I'd like to get back to work."

"One last question," Sandy said.

Vidya sighed with exasperation. *The kid has tenacity... have to give him that.*

She raised his eyebrows at him through her spectacles.

"You said you met Saleem later... after his college days."

"Yes."

"How did you guys meet? Professionally? When Sandy began his career?"

"No. We met at something we both loved doing. Or rather – something I loved doing. Eventually, he came to love it too,"

"What was that?"

Vidya smiled. "Dancing," she said, leaving Sandy with his mouth agape.

CHAPTER 5
Love at First Sight

"New story. You're going to like it," said Saleem by way of greeting.

Sandy sat down on a chair in Saleem's room at the hospital, where Sandy had convinced the doctor to let Saleem have some biryani, passionately arguing that Saleem was so sick of the hospital food that he might just lose the will to live, which would be a shame considering how remarkable his recovery had been.

Sandy had thought it was a good joke, but the doctor had not been amused. Nevertheless, he allowed Saleem to eat some of the biryani Sandy had sent for him. Saleem had been in a fairly good mood since.

"I like all the stories we've done so far, sir," said Sandy earnestly.

"This one is even better," said Saleem, ignoring the blatant, yet earnest, attempt to flatter him. "Where do you get this Biryani from, by the way? It's fantastic!"

"Tara makes it," said Sandy with a lot of pride.

Saleem was taken by surprise. "Really? I must meet her… superb biryani. Now you know why you must never let go of her…"

Sandy laughed. "Yes! The biryani alone makes it worthwhile, doesn't it? But jokes apart, she really is something special."

Sandy looked pointedly at Saleem, hoping to get him started about Vidya. Apart from generally asking how she was, Saleem had not been curious about Vidya at all. He did not even want her phone number when Sandy had offered it, muttering something that sounded like, *'It's of no use'*.

"I'm sure she is, kid. Now read."

Sandy's disappointment was evident, but Saleem chose to ignore it. Sandy began to read.

Perched atop the glowing neon sign on top of Hotel Empire, Morgan looked down upon the city. It looked innocent enough from there, even if it was anything but that. *My city*, thought Morgan, and then snorted with laughter, almost losing his balance and falling off the building.

"Not that it would make any difference, except add another crater to the road. It would give more matter to the media to crib about. If they went after the MCD with the same fervour, maybe the city would have had better roads," he said to himself.

Morgan was a superhero. He had been quite kicked about it, at least in the beginning. He first discovered his powers four days after being discharged from the hospital. He was brought to the hospital two days before that, from the Morgue. On a white water rafting trip to Rishikesh, Morgan had fallen in the river and drowned. He had been leaning too far from the edge of a cliff, and had lost his balance, plunging head-first into The Ganga. He was pronounced dead, but miraculously came back to life, coughing out a whole lot of water at the feet of a morgue employee – Murali – who had been struck with the kind of fear that would grip a man who sees a dead come back to life in the middle of the morgue. When Murali realized that his legs were still attached to his torso, he decided to put them to good use for one last time and made a run for it, screaming bloody murder, but was run over by a bus. Murali survived, but never used his legs again.

Poor sod. On hindsight, I should have seen that incident as an omen for things to come, Morgan thought to himself.

Four days later, Morgan realized he could fly. Or rather, leap over very large distances. *No one can escape gravity... sooner or later, everyone must fall.* Morgan had been very pleased with himself for having come up with that line. He indexed it for future use, depending on the persona he chose.

If I go the Spiderman way, I'll use it in a patronizing, wise-cracking tone while I beat up goons, but if I go the Batman way, it will probably have to be used as a serious, baritone punchline delivered after silently listening to a villain's overdrawn lunatic rant.

Once he realized that he had something special going for him, Morgan went on a comic-book buying spree. After all, who would know the business of being a super-hero more than actual super-heros, even if they weren't real. Thanks to the comic books, Morgan realized very early the error in the ways of using god-gifted superpowers for personal gratification.

'With great power comes great responsibility' was the motto Morgan settled on, even if it was repeated at a very irritating frequency in Spider-man comics.

What he didn't realize was that with great power come even greater problems.

Atop Hotel Empire, Morgan decided to get down to business. He tuned his ears to the police radio frequency, hoping to pick up information of some crime, not that it would be of much use. Most of the time, they were called to the crime scene *after* the crime had been committed. In some cases, he even found them assisting in the criminal activity. These Morgan steered clear of, at least for now. He had decided to not take on the corruption in the police department till he had made friends with an honest cop that he could work with.

"AEEEEEEEEEEEEEEEEEEEEEEEEEEE!!!"

Morgan looked up. The scream, 13 km south-west from his location was blood-curdling.

Someone is in need of some saving.

Morgan removed the hood of his jacket from his head and took off in the direction of the scream.

The hood was a major problem when he leapt. It often blocked his vision, and once he had gone crashing into the 14th floor of an office building. That had led television channels to speculate whether he was a corporate espionage agent for hire, stealing company secrets for rivals.

The superhero costume was a matter of great importance and deliberation, and his comic book counterparts had been largely unhelpful in figuring out a practical solution for him. He wasn't a reclusive billionaire like Tony Stark or Bruce Wayne, or a genius like Peter Parker or Reed Richards. And Superman only confused him. *How could no one tell that Superman and Clarke Kent were the same, in spite of Kent making absolutely no attempt to hide his face?*

When he saw no other solution, Morgan dejectedly decided

to stick to everyday clothing, using a balaclava to hide his face. The solution, however, turned out to be a source of great consternation during a daring attempt to stop an armed bank robbery in the middle of the day, in which the robbers were using similar balaclavas. At first they had taken him to be one of their gang and had handed him a bag full of cash... something that the dastardly television reporters had publicised widely, *even after he had prevented the robbery from being a success.* Of course, the fact that a bullet deflected from his body and hit a cowering civilian during the ensuing shootout after he had revealed his intentions had not helped revive his image.

Morgan had switched to hoods since then, and feared the day he would run into hooded criminals.

He heard police sirens. He zoomed in with his hyper-vision and saw eight police jeeps with armed personnel making their way towards the source of the screams. Morgan, his heart racing now, landed on a building overlooking a large crowd which had gathered outside the building at the centre of all the commotion. It was the office of a major corporation. Suddenly, a bomb ripped through the sixth floor of the office, sending the crowd running for their lives in all directions like headless chicken.

Morgan waited, trying to locate the actual source of all the chaos, when his phone started ringing.

He took one look at his flashing phone and groaned. It was his boss. He contemplated not taking the call, but then decided against it to avoid any grief that would follow the next morning.

"Hello?"

"Morgan! Where are your projections? I made it abundantly clear that I needed them this evening."

"I'm so sorry, sir! I'm almost done with them... you'll have them before you come in to work tomorrow."

The fat slob won't come in before lunch. More than enough time for me to get through those damned projections.

Morgan heard gunfire below. He saw the policemen engaged in a fierce shootout with about fifteen armed men who had emerged from the office building.

"What's all that noise, Morgan? Where the hell are you?" his boss shouted.

"N... nothing sir. Just a movie."

"Wow! Just great! First you don't meet your deadlines, and then you have the audacity to leave office early so you can watch a movie!"

"It's 11.30 PM sir. Way past office timings," Morgan said.

"Shut up! Office timings are till work gets done. And your work is not done."

Morgan didn't say anything. He kept his rising anger under check.

I'm a goddamned superhero. And here I am, listening to a sorry fat degenerate giving me hell.

"We'll have a word about this tomorrow, Morgan." His boss hung up.

The battle continued below. The armed men seemed to have an upper hand on the police. This was the moment when Morgan could more than even the odds.

But what's the point? Fighting petty criminals and watching the thankless media make a mockery of me. Stuck in a painful job, with no semblance of a life. It's almost as though everyone is happier without me. I should just walk away and get on with my life. There's no one worth fighting for, anyway... at least no one the police can't handle. No crafty mastermind, or a super-villain. This city is no place for a super-hero.

A bullet struck a police officer in the leg, who was taking cover behind a jeep. He cried out in pain and fell down.

Fuck it. Just one last time.

Morgan leapt up into the air and dropped right into the middle of the armed men, the road below him cracking with the impact. For a moment, the firing stopped. The terrorists looked at him, astonished. Then one of them opened fire at him.

The bullets bounced off Morgan, as he walked calmly towards the man who had opened fire at him. He grabbed him by the throat and threw him violently at the wall behind him. The man crumpled to the floor, and the image of his boss flashed in his mind. He could hear the cops cheering for him in the background.

Morgan turned around and sent two more terrorists flying. Seeing the battle tip in their favour, the cops began to advance on the terrorists.

Atleast I'll go out with a bang. That was the last thought that flashed through Morgan's mind before he was suddenly wheeled around by brute force. Something hit his stomach with an intensity well beyond his imagination and a normal's man endurance. Morgan looked up and saw a man dressed in a suit, oblivious to all the gunfire around him.

Before Morgan could react, the man punched him again. He went flying across the road and crashed into a building. The remaining terrorists and the cops both stopped firing in that moment, and there was complete silence.

131

Morgan shakily got back on his feet. His heart was beating fast, and he was bleeding from his mouth. He looked at the man in the suit, who was calmly walking towards him from across the street. Morgan walked towards him. His pace quickened. The grin on his face widened. In that moment, more than ever, Morgan felt like a super-hero.

"What made you think of writing a superhero story?" asked Sandy.

Because I can't remember where I've kept the key. Saleem almost surprised himself by saying that out loud. Outside the window, the last remnants of daylight were fighting a losing battle against the approaching night. Saleem never quite liked dusk.

"Well," he said, "I told you I've always been a big comic book fan. It's surprising that I've never written a superhero story before. Considering this is my final book, it's only fair that I put one in it."

"Oh... I thought it had something to do with the *Injustice League of Delhi University*."

Saleem looked up, evidently surprised. Sandy was smiling, finally sensing victory over the Saleem's reticence about anything to do with his personal life.

"So, Vidya told you about that," said Saleem. He picked up the glass of water on the side table and drank it down in a gulp.

"Yes. She told me quite a bit actu—" Sandy began excitedly.

"I'm tired," said Saleem, all of a sudden. It was a obvious attempt to kill the discussion. "When do you plan to start work on this?" he asked.

"Tomorrow. I'm going out with Tara tonight. She has

something important to talk to me about."

"Thank her from me for the biryani. And tell her I'd like to meet her."

Sandy smiled. "I will."

In that moment, more than ever, Morgan felt like a superhero. He felt as though his moment in the sun was finally here. This mysterious suit clad villain was someone who was quite obviously superior in strength to the other regular thugs he had trounced—at times, quite literally, by merely lifting a finger. He briefly fantasized about a future in which he would engage in never-ending, cleverly crafted battles with this super villain and, of course, eventually emerge victorious. He had felt the strength of this man's arms in the last punch that had landed on him and sent him flying. Images of superheroes and their arch enemies flashed through his mind – Batman and the Joker, Superman and Lex Luthor, Spiderman and the Green Goblin, and now Morgan and this yet-unnamed super villain.

Morgan stood two feet from this man who, surprisingly, did not make a move. They stood there, sizing each other up, as all the commotion around them came to a complete standstill. Cops and robbers alike, everybody lowered their weapons and forgot what they were doing as they surrounded Morgan and the man. From afar, the gathering may have looked like a circle that school-kids form when a much anticipated fight finally breaks out during recess.

The man in the suit was about two inches taller than the five foot, ten inch tall Morgan. He appeared to be fitter than Morgan, with broader shoulders and greater girth. His arms were thicker than Morgan's thighs. Morgan figured he must have firmer thighs as well. He was fair and square jawed. Morgan thought the man looked handsome enough to be in the movies and felt a sudden uneasiness stir up his heart. He realized he was having a classic case of butterflies in the stomach. Surely, he had not felt like this in a long time. Morgan felt extremely aroused.

Morgan was a closet homosexual and had been so ever since an episode with a senior in college. He had enjoyed it so much that he had seen no point in reporting what his friends (and even the senior himself) had thought was molestation and a crime. In fact, Morgan had repeatedly tried to get into more trouble with the guy until the day the senior had graduated out of college. He had then realised that he was a homosexual, and had gradually also discovered that he liked to be dominated and roughed up by his partners. The fear of social taboo, however, had prevented him from ever admitting it publicly or even attempting to find suitable partners.

Morgan wondered what it would be like to be wrestled into submission by this man back in his bedroom.

Damn it. This is the worst time to have such thoughts. Morgan quickly pulled himself together, dismissed such thoughts that had cropped up at such an inopportune moment, and decided that he had to get back into the super hero game.

"Who are you, stranger?" Morgan had not made a conscious decision about it, but realized that he had just spoken in a Batman-like baritone. He remembered his college days when he would try to act all tough and cocky just to annoy his senior who might have then 'punished' him.

"Who's asking?"

The reply had been calm but immediate and in a deeper baritone than Morgan had mustered.

At that moment, Morgan kicked himself for not having

come up with a name. He thought hard but could only come up with clichés from his comic books. He had never been the brightest student in any of his classes. He had been pretty much at the bottom of the list and had, on two occasions, been politely but firmly requested to repeat the ninth and the tenth standards in school. The life altering accident had given him the gift of agility and strength but had not added even a fraction of a point to his IQ which still languished at 61. He knew. *He had checked.*

Desperate to make a good impression on the expectant crowds and the handsome villain in front of him, Morgan decided to go with the buying-time-by-talking- clichés strategy.

"I am asking. The hero of this city. The hero this city needs. The hero this city deserves. The hero who's here to—"

"Cut the crap," the other man cut him off.

Morgan had not even been given a chance to finish the sentence. "You're not the first fool I've met. You're nothing but a freak that's read too many comic books and now suffers from extreme delusional fantasies of grandeur. If you ask me honestly, I think between you and me, these guys should lock you up first." The man waved his right hand towards the cops and then pointed at Morgan.

Morgan, however, had barely heard what the man said. His concentration had been focussed on the man's lips, which hardly moved when he spoke. He had been fantasizing about kissing them when he suddenly heard the eerie silence around him, and realized that the man had stopped talking. It was now his turn to speak.

"I'm sorry. Could you repeat that?"

The man raised his left eyebrow and tried to fathom what this hooded man was trying to accomplish with this charade. The spectators had begun to murmur, having been joined, by then, by eager crime reporters who had reached the spot accompanied with their cameramen.

The man looked annoyed, unable to understand where Morgan was taking this.

"I said, I don't have time for nutcases like you. Now, scram, or I'll smack you to the next town."

Did he just say he'd smack me?

Images of comic strips where the hero kisses the damsel with a big bubble that read 'SMACK' flashed in Morgan's mind.

"Ha! I would love to see you try that," he said, hoping that man in the suit would take him seriously.

The man was now completely baffled. He had met these freaks of nature before. Anomalies who, by some random accident, had developed extreme muscular strength and thought they could become crime fighters. He too had been a result of a similar accident; but he had decided to put his gifts to a more profitable use; and crime had always paid more than crime-fighting. What surprised him now was the fact that none of the idiots he had encountered in the past had ever invited him for a confrontation like this. Hoping to end this standoff soon, he decided to deploy the second most popular tactic of evasion from the Criminal's Handbook (the first being – 'run like hell.')

With lighting speed, the man grabbed one of the female reporters standing around them and held her delicate neck in his massive hands, threatening to break it at the slightest provocation.

"I'm giving you your last warning. Back off or I'll break her neck like a potato wafer."

Morgan was heartbroken. Like a teenager in love who reads too much into every action of their object of infatuation, he assumed that this man was not a homosexual because of the way he was holding the woman.

The man was becoming impatient and tightened his grip around the woman's neck. She squealed.

A voice said, "Hey! You hood-man! Are you going to save her or not?"

Morgan snapped back to reality and turned to see where the comment had come from. He saw a cop flanked by other cops and reporters.

Right. I have to save her.

He felt his calf muscles contract as his super-human reflexes came back to him. In one quick swoop, which most of the spectators didn't see, he got behind the suited super villain and locked his arm around his neck tightening his elbow just under the man's chin.

"Let her go."

The man had truly been caught by surprise. He had lowered his guard in the last few seconds of the confusing standoff with Morgan. Morgan had been quick. And as the arm around his neck began to tighten and block the blood flow to his brain, he realised how strong Morgan was too.

"Okay. Okay." The woman was let off and she scampered back to the crowds, who began to cheer.

The man brought his hands up to Morgan's arm and tried to pry it from around his neck. He was writhing as the lack of air began to take its toll. Morgan felt the man's strong, bulky body rub against his own. He loosened the grip just a little so as not to suffocate him. He was not a murderer after all. The man continued to move against Morgan while his hands still tried to pull away Morgan's arm.

Morgan was beginning to get aroused now.

This was just the kind of bedroom action that he liked,

even though he was the one delivering the pain here. Morgan's breathing began to get faster. A couple of seconds passed and Morgan could not take it anymore. He realized he wanted to have the man right there.

In one quick action, he freed the man from his grip and spun him around like a ballerina spun by her partner in the middle of a routine. He embraced the man around his back, took off his hood, leaned into him and planted a long, wet kiss on his lips, forcing his tongue in.

The crowd gasped audibly in surprise. Camera flashes went off like a thousand lights, blinding both of them. The man struggled and waved his arms helplessly while Morgan used all his strength to hold him in the kiss. This was a form of combat that the man was not prepared to handle.

For Morgan, time had slowed. Years of sexual frustration had eventually burst out like molten lava does from a volcano that has been holding it all in for centuries. The unusual circumstances, coupled with his new-found unusual powers had taken their toll and in a moment of arousal, he had shed his inhibitions and decided to take what had been deprived to him for so long.

Finally, when he opened his eyes, he saw fear and disgust in the eyes of the man who was still locked in a kiss with him. He let go and looked at the man who now looked as helpless and confused as a baby. He felt a wave of love and kindness sweep over him as the big man in the suit crumpled and swooned in his arms.

The activity around Morgan had changed drastically while he had been entranced in the kiss. Seeing their leader fall – to a kiss – the rest of the thugs had made a run for it, and some of the policemen were now fast on their tail. A group of four policemen were waiting to handcuff the man in the suit.

As soon as Morgan eased his grip on the man, he got up and ran to the cops. He fell down on his knees and begged to be handcuffed. He kept pointing at Morgan and pleading with the cops to keep him as far away from him as possible. The policemen looked amused.

The magnitude of what he had done dawned upon Morgan. He had encountered and overpowered a Super Villain, and kissed him. He had saved the city! Like all superheroes in comic books, he decided to vanish from the scene, hoping that the reporters would be abuzz with tales of his heroics. More than anything, the kiss lingered on his lips, and he felt relieved.

He reached home, brushed his teeth and set the alarm for the morning. He went to sleep with an immense sense of satisfaction and relief.

The alarm clock rang sharp and loud and interrupted a dream in which he was 'interrogating' the man in the suit in a locked cell. Morgan turned off the alarm and lazily climbed out of bed. He had never felt the sense of excitement that he did that day as he got out of bed, especially on a working day. It was not his work that he was excited about, though. He wanted to read the tales of his heroics from the previous night that should be all over the newspapers this morning. He knew it had arrived.

He rushed out of his bedroom and grabbed the newspaper that lay on his doorstep. He looked at the front page and rubbed his eyes. He looked at it again.

There was no mention of what had happened the previous night.

This can't be true. I'm sure the papers can't have not gone to press that early last night.

He began flipping through the pages in a hurry, scanning each news article. Finally, on the eighth page, he found a mention of the events of the previous night in the bottom right corner, next to an article about a man who had tried to commit suicide by jumping off a building, but had failed because his belt had got stuck in the sharp projections on the railing when he had jumped.

Morgan froze and his heart skipped a beat. He stared at a picture of him kissing the man in the suit, as policemen and reporters watched with amused expressions on their faces. The events of the last night replayed in his head. He dropped to his knees while still holding the news paper.

"FUCK" was all he could say, as he fainted, falling face first on the newspaper.

The headline read 'Stunned Cops Arrest Blast Suspect' and then in a smaller typeface below it, 'Suspect Alleges Molestation.'

"You will need the key. That is the only way."

"You look disturbed," said Saleem calmly.

"I am disturbed!" barked Sandy.

He looked more than disturbed. He looked like a bomb that could go off any minute. Sandy had entered Saleem's hospital room an hour ago, and had not sat down since. Instead, he had spent approximately two-third of the time sulking and staring out of the window, and the rest of it pacing the floor like a caged tiger.

"Could you please sit down? It's stressful watching you march all over the bloody room."

Sandy sat down.

"Good. Now – what is the problem?"

"Why should I tell you? You never tell me anything!" shouted Sandy.

Saleem was equal parts concerned and annoyed. The kid had no business throwing a tantrum at him. But at the same time, Saleem could sense that this was something serious.

"All right. I'll cut you a deal. Why don't you tell me what happened, and I will answer your questions without the usual attempts to change the topic."

Sandy buried his face in his palms. He muttered something inaudible.

"Excuse me?"

"I said Tara is leaving!" Sandy yelled.

"What do you mean *leaving?*"

"Going away! Her father's getting transferred to Singapore, so she's moving away as well."

"I'm really sorry," said Saleem.

"I mean... how can she just throw away these years we've been together? I even told her that we'll make it work long distance till I can move there too. I'm going to be writer, after all... It won't matter if I work out of Delhi or Singapore."

"What did she say to that?"

"She said that if that happens, we can always look at things as they stand then. What is that even supposed to mean?" Sandy said.

"It means that life isn't something that is entirely in your control. Neither of you know how things will be in the future. I'm sure neither of you ever thought that one of you would have to move away. Now, did you?"

Sandy shook his head.

"The future is also a story, kid. Since we don't know it, we let our imagination create it. But then stories and the real world often go their own separate ways."

"I was in such a bad mood, I think I totally wrecked the story."

There was silence for a moment, and then Saleem began to laugh loudly, startling Sandy. He wanted to say something, but he couldn't stop laughing long enough. The old man's laughter was infectious, but he didn't want to laugh, and it left him with an expression half-way between a scowl and a smile.

"You didn't wreck the story," said Saleem, once he had stopped laughing. "I like it."

"You're kidding me."

"I think this is my favourite story so far."

Sandy smiled weakly. The compliment had worked, and Sandy felt a little better. "You said you'll answer my questions..." he said.

"Yes I did. Fire away."

"What's the deal wth you and Ms Shankar?"

Saleem smiled. "It's complicated. As you might have guessed, it was more than just friendship. But we were never quite together either. We just loved the time we spent together... all that time..."

"Dancing?"

Saleem had a strange expression on his face... as if he had never heard that word before. He seemed to be in a trance, staring blankly into space. He snapped out of it as suddenly as it had come over him.

"Yes," he said matter-of-factly, "Dancing. That's where we met for the first time. I was working on a book where the protagonist was a dancer and I wanted to experience it for myself. So I took up dance classes, and Vidya was an instructor there. Since I didn't have a partner, she used to dance with me. The irony of it all is that I never got around to finishing that book."

Saleem leaned on his pillow.

"You see, I was really bad at it, except when I danced with her. Not that I magically knew the steps when I danced with her, mind you. It's just that I didn't care when I danced with her... and that somehow allowed me to shed my inhibitions. It felt like we were transported to a whole other world every time we danced together."

A memory from years ago assailed Saleem. A cold night. The air carried the smell of rain. They walked together to the bus stop. She raised her hands and twirled her fingers. *Abracadabra.* It began to rain at that exact moment. Saleem was astonished. She took his hand, and they began to dance.

If heaven exists, this has got to be it, he had thought. And they had danced as if there was going to be no tomorrow.

"Sir?"

Sandy's voice brought him back to the present.

"Let's talk about it some other time, kid. I think I'll go to bed now"

Sandy packed up his things and left without saying anything else. He was getting used to people ending conversations with him because they were either too tired or too busy. He wasn't sure, but he thought he saw Saleem wipe a tear from the corner of his eye with the back of his hand.

As he was walking out of the hospital, he noticed a familiar figure from the corner of his eye. He whirled around just in time to spot a woman getting into a taxi. Before he could figure out who she was, he was distracted by his phone buzzing in his pocket.

It was Tara. Sandy disconnected the call, and started walked slowly to the bus stop. There was no one else there.

"Don't feel so sad, Sandy. We don't need her," he heard a voice whisper to him. He felt the hair at the back of his neck stand up. Sandy looked both inside and outside the bus stop. There was no one there.

Five minutes later, he climbed into a bus, still not sure if what he heard was real or a figment of his imagination.

Saleem stood in front of the locked door. He had a plan.

"Come on. Where are you?" he said out loud.

There was a deafening roar, as something crashed through the roof of the living room. The whole apartment shook, and a man emerged from the dust and rubble, holding his head and walking gingerly.

"Sorry about your roof... and your table," said Morgan.

Saleem smiled. He was finally taking control.

"We have work to do," said Saleem, and turned to look at the locked door, "I need you to break that down for me."

"How?" asked Morgan.

"You're a superhero, right? Do your thing."

Morgan hung his head. "Some superhero. You guys made a fool of me. You know, if you had given me a girlfriend to begin with, none of that nonsense would have happened."

"You don't know that. We writers can twist things around quite well. I mean, look at what's going on here."

Morgan nodded dejectedly. "What's in there?" he asked.

"The Lost Story."

"That sounds ominous."

"Only one way to find out."

Morgan took a deep breath, and charged at the door. He took it down with no difficulty. As he stood back and admired his handiwork, Saleem rushed past him into the room. He looked confused. It looked too familiar.

It was then that Saleem realized that he was in his living room again. He could see the locked door on the other side. He whirled around to find a solid wall behind him. The table in from of him was intact.

"Damn," he said.

Saleem walked up to the door and shouted out, "Morga ! Come back! We need to try something else."

"It won't work, Sandy. You'll need the key." It wasn't Morgan. It was Vidya.

"I'm Saleem... not Sandy."

"Really? But you look like Sandy to me."

Saleem rushed into his bedroom to look in the mirror. It was Sandy staring out of the mirror at him.

"You will need the key. That is the only way," said Vidya. She had followed him into the bedroom.

"What's going on?"

Saleem was staring at his arms, and touching his face. It felt like him. But the mirror said otherwise.

"That doesn't matter. You know what has to be done."

"Why is The Lost Story so important, Vidya?"

"Because it's the only way out."

"Out of what?"

Vidya remained silent.

"You have to use the key," Vidya said again.

"But where is it?"

She raised an eyebrow, and pointed to the mirror. Saleem looked at the mirror, and saw Sandy again. That's when it hit him.

"Sandy? What does he have to do with the key?"

"He IS the key, Saleem."

CHAPTER 6

Re-entry

"Come on, kid. Look a little alive."

The usual cheer and brightness on Sandy's face had been replaced with a sombre expression. The spark in his eyes was gone, and it seemed like he had forgotten how to smile.

"How long are you going to pine for her?"

It's easy for you say! The thought almost exploded out of Sandy's lips, but even through the gloom that pervaded him, he realized that that would be crossing the line. Instead he just shrugged.

"All right, let's try something here," said Saleem. He was obviously uncomfortable with the way Sandy was behaving. He knew he would be fine with time, but he had come to be fond of the cheer that Sandy brought to his otherwise dreary existence. The voices, the constant feeling of moving towards imminent doom, and the realization that he was just a frail old man who's time was almost up often filled his mind with uncertainty. In stark contrast, this kid represented everything that was lacking in his life.

"There's always a way out, Sandy. There's always hope," said Saleem, turning his laptop so the screen could face Sandy, "So, I wrote this. It may seem like there's no way out of this...

but that's the challenge. You know the rules... so finish this for me."

Sandy didn't say anything. He just picked up the laptop and began reading.

Recon ID: 198SG423XC672
Day 74
Survivor Index: 1,52,657

Class ref: Incident Recon

>Nigeria is now silent. Reported Population: 0
>Last known human occurrence: Ikire City Centre
>Hideout inadvertently discovered on sighting a child (female, estimated age: 8 years)
>Apparent reason for emerging from hideout: unknown
>Notes: The child was heard requesting permission to watch <quote>the angels come down from the sky.</quote> Permission denied.
>Alien Scouting Party Strength : 25. Equipment: Standard oval exoskeleton pod. Able to transform into basic shapes. Capable of firing disintegrator ray
>Alien Scouting Party Leader approached by the child.
>Child hands Leader a crayon drawing of alien exoskeleton pods. Mostly accurate depiction, augmented with halo and wings
>Child executed via disintegrator ray. Illustration cached. Population in hideout exterminated.
>First recorded instance of interest in human assets
>Anomaly Registered.

Recon ID: 1C5D765F290VG
Day 96
Survivor Index: 37,021

Class ref: Global Recon

>First alien contact with species Loxodonta Africana (common name: African Savannah Elephant)
>Highest recorded loss of alien life in a single battle
>Elephant herd exterminated
>Species Loxodonta Africana extinct in the following 37 hours
>Loss to Alien Life: 0
>Advanced adaptability indexed
>Post Anomaly 1 (*Recon ID: 198SG423XC672*) escalated interest in human culture recorded.
>Synchronous global raids across major cultural centers of the world. Incidents registered at Istanbul, Glasgow, Alexandria, Paris, Osaka and Madurai
>Human Aggregation (Survivor Index: 1523) on board luxury liner *Queen Mary II* discovered in the Pacific Ocean and exterminated
>Extensive use of ground forces result in eradication of surviving pockets of human life
>Lingering human perceptions of alien invasion: Religious Leaders recorded event as the coming of Armageddon/*ragnarok*/*pralay*. Followers perceive aliens as 'divine beings' and make offerings
>Apparent reason for offering: Appeasement of 'divine beings' (aliens)
>Many surviving human groups discovered and executed

on account of this misplaced belief

>Most attempts to remain undiscovered rendered ineffective

>Inference: Initial assumption authenticated. Aliens possess technology for precise detection, classification and mapping of carbon-based life-forms

Recon ID: 743HAA45IH34E
Day 104
Survivor Index: 12,032

Class ref: Internal systems check

>System check initialized
>Cloaking Module... operating at optimal levels... *check*
>Receiver Module... all receptors operational... *check*
>Transmitter Module... last transmission log: 342 hours 13 minutes ago...
>Operational at 100% power... *check*
>Memory Banks scan initialized
>'History' Module... 100%... *check*
>'Fine Arts' Module... 100%... *check*
>'Science & Tech' Module... 100%... *check*
>'Geology' Module... 100%... *check*
>'Medicine & Psychology' Module... 100%... *check*
>'Astronomical Data' Module... 100%... *check*
>'Language' Module... 100%... *check*
>'Genetic Information' Module... 100%... *check*
> 'Miscellaneous' Module... 100%... check
>Zero bad sectors in all memory banks... scan completed
>Critical operating systems scan... operating at optimal levels... *check*

>Proximity Sensor scan... operating @100% power... *check*
>Core Reactor... operating @75% power... *check*
>Thrusters... operating @0%power... *check*
>Energy Harvesters... operational @0% power... *check*
>Scheduled runtime initialization: 7 hours 14 minutes
>System check concluded

Recon ID: FG5617G5KK892
Day 108
Survivor Index: 9,782

Class ref: Outbound distress transmission

>Initialized
'My name is Dr Sudhir Langer, and I belong to a surface-dwelling species on the planet Earth known as *homo sapiens*. The species evolved to its modern form about 200,000 solar years ago, and until recently, was the most evolved and dominant species on Earth. Earth is a planet that revolves around a yellow-dwarf star which we call the Sun. Our solar system is located on the inner edge of the *Orion-Cygnus Arm* of the Milky Way Galaxy.

This *Recon Drone* is our final and mostly hopeless attempt at preservation. Over the last few months, humanity has come under attack by a hostile space-faring alien species, with technology far beyond our understanding and capability. No attempt was made to establish communication... They just attacked... And their strategy suggests that they have been studying us for years. They came prepared and they hit us where it hurt. From then on, we did not stand a chance.

This distress signal is a secondary objective of the Recon Drone. We do not expect to be heard... atleast not in time to be saved. Like I said earlier, the primary objective of this Drone is preservation. The extensive data-banks of the Drone contain comprehensive information about the human species, our journey through time and history, our culture and art, and our knowledge. Its other function is to record the final moments of humanity, and the ruthlessness with which we have been eradicated. Let this serve as a warning to any other evolved life-form about these aliens that we know so little about, so that you may not meet the same fate as we did. This message has been programmed to play in all known human languages, to assist comprehension. An extensive image bank that accompanies the data should also help. We hope it will be understood.

They attacked without warning at 0:00 Greenwich Mean Time (GMT) on 21st December, 2012. It's rather ironic, because the date was prophesied to be the end of the World… the last day of the Mayan calendar. The world did not on end that day, but it was certainly the beginning.

The attack was two-pronged. The first wave was a co-ordinated strike on the 50 biggest cities of Earth and their surrounding areas. Bustling centers like Tokyo, New York, Shanghai, Moscow, Mumbai, Paris, Seoul and Mexico City were reduced to ghost towns by an incredibly powerful biological agent, which disintegrated all carbon-based life form in these cities to dust in mere moments. From human beings to the tiniest single-celled organisms, everyone perished before they knew what was going on.

Along with the cities, the other targets were critical planetary resources. They destroyed mineral and crude oil sources, and refineries using what we have come to call – disintegrator beams. This weapon had the same impact as the biological agent, except that it disintegrated all matter. Africa, the Middle-East, and Canada were the most severely hit by this attack. All military bases and weapon manufacturing facilities across the globe were also targeted and annihilated. No matter how secret the bases were, the aliens seemed to know exactly where to find them. And as if that wasn't enough, major agricultural belts, storage and food processing units across India, China and Europe were also destroyed. Within three minutes, the population of Earth had been reduced by 45%. We lost 95% of our critical resources, and were left without elected leaders and any military prowess. We had been brought down to our knees with no way to get back up.

Then, they left. For two months.

In those two months, what remained of the world tore itself apart. With global shortages of food and fuel, riots broke out across the globe. Their plan appeared to be simple, and economical. Why waste their resources on eradicating us, when we were more than capable of doing the job ourselves?

After two months, they arrived in greater numbers, to finish what they had started. We got the first glimpse of the aliens when their ground forces descended to the ground, Or so it seemed.

We don't know what they look like, because we believe that the oval exterior is an exoskeleton or shield of some sort that they use to protect themselves against our environment. These exoskeletons appear to be able to seamlessly transform into various shapes, and fire disintegrator rays through two slits on what we believe is their front side. They also appear to have some sort of a propulsion device at their base, which enables them to float about a metre above level ground, and even water. These exoskeletons are extremely strong, and can only be brought down by heavy weapons such as rocket launchers. Unfortunately, we don't have too many of those left.

Even though we have managed to bring down a few of these

aliens, it has not been possible to procure its body to study, since they appear to possess some self-destructive mechanism that makes the alien fire the disintegrator gun upon itself reducing it to dust. Even if they have a weakness, we have not been able to discover it.

They are also very good at locating hidden human groups, which is quite a feat, considering how few of us are left. We have come to the conclusion that they possess an incredibly advanced tracking technology. Truth be told, compared to the kind of weapons they have, it doesn't come as a surprise.

I, and my team of scientists, have acknowledged that we have been completely outclassed in this scenario, and accept that we are witnessing the end of humanity. With what can be construed as a misplaced sense of bravado – and possible blind faith in some kind of divine intervention – we have created this Recon Drone and launched it into space. It has prototype power cells and stealth systems to evade detection, and tracking technology that may not be as advanced as the aliens, but allows us to effectively log every remaining human being on Earth. The drastically reduced population density helped a lot in perfecting it. It has been programmed to stay in orbit till the human population reaches zero, after which it will launch into space and, hopefully, find you.

By the time you find this, we will probably all be dead. It's an insignificant event within the unending scope of the universe, yet it's a damned pity. We are a remarkable species, capable of beauty beyond measure, destruction beyond remorse, and stories, some real and most imaginary, but all extraordinary. Stories of love, and triumph, of heroes and dragons, of times long gone and times yet to come. Such wonderful stories... and they will all be lost. That is one module

I cannot create within the data banks. Our stories are in us, and they will fade away with us... *like tears in the rain.*
>End of Transmission

Recon ID: BG56K9R8Z234M
Day 114
Survivor Index: 782

Class ref: Global Recon

>Largest human collective aboard the prototype submarine *New Ark* (Survivor Index: 3689) discovered during alien operations around the Marina Trench in the Pacific Ocean
>Caching of items and monuments of cultural significance intensified across the world by alien forces
>Statue of Liberty, Eiffel Tower and Gateway of India are the latest in the series of monuments to be transported into the mother ship from the surface of the planet
>Activities suggest no interest in the natural resources of the planet
>Surviving pockets of humanity survive by scavenging and in some cases, cannibalism
>Latest incident classified as religious fanaticism
>Aliens led to surviving cluster by a defector as a <quote>sacrifice to appease the agents of the *shaitaan*</unquote> in the outskirts of Islamabad, Pakistan
>No survivors, including defector

Recon ID: HJ78OP31GHUY4
Day 131
Survivor Index: 0

>Survivor Index parameter executed
>Power Thrusters @0% power
>Thrusters @50% power
>Thrusters @100% power
>Launch sequence initialized

Sandy got up from his chair.

"I've emailed it to myself," he said to Saleem, who's eyes had not left him since Sandy had begun reading. "I have a thought... I'll finish this and send it across by tonight. And I won't be coming tomorrow... I have to go somewhere."

"Sandy, cheer up for God's sake!" said Saleem, raising his voice in an attempt to shake Sandy out of his depression."

"I know it's going to be all right, sir," said Sandy with the same dead voice. "But right now, it just isn't."

For once, Saleem did not know what to say.

The green letters stopped scrolling as the details of the last recon glowed ominously on the black screen in the dark, over-crowded hall. Silence hung heavily in the air like carcasses in an abattoir. The General stood behind the tall podium, placed at the bottom right corner of the large 25 by 25 foot screen. He scanned the silhouettes of the 80 odd occupants in the hall and waited for a response – any response. When none was forthcoming, he motioned for the lights to be turned on.

The French president bent over the mike in front of him and broke the silence in his heavily accented English.

"General, is this a joke?"

A few murmurs began to be heard in the hall.

The General spoke sternly.

"Mr President, that was one of the possibilities we considered when our military base near the south-pole reported the crash of the Drone 3 days ago. But I'm afraid we now have conclusive evidence that the Drone – and by extension, its content – is genuine."

The Chinese premier waved his arms and muttered something as the General waited for the interpreter to translate.

The interpreter paused for a few seconds before he spoke. "Bollocks," he said.

The General pushed a button on a panel in front of him, and a photograph of mangled and burnt metal in a icy crater appeared on the screen.

"The 'Recon Drone' as we have discovered it is called, was discovered at 13:47 hours at 89.2 degrees South, 0.56 degrees west by one of out aerial patrol vehicles. A recovery team was dispatched immediately. Prima facie analysis of the outer layer of the object suggests without a doubt that it has been subjected to extremely high temperatures and has crashed at a phenomenally high speed, very similar to a re-entry crash landing. The temperature of the metal indicates it crashed about 7 or 8 hours before it was discovered. It was immediately taken in for further analysis."

He pushed the button again and a close up of the outer surface of the object appeared on the screen. The bottom right quarter of the screen showed a graph with abbreviations under the lines. One of those lines was highlighted in a red circle.

"We then conducted extensive tests on the composition of the outer layer, and you can see the results at the bottom right of the screen. The elements we found are all common elements that are found in abundance on our planet. All but one."

He clicked another button and the visual on the screen zoomed in on the highlighted line on the graph. The letters 'Fe' were printed below it.

"The line that you see on the graph, the one encircled in red, is that of the element iron. But there's one important difference. This element was identified as a new and very different form of iron than we have ever seen before. Scientifically, it is known as an isotope of iron. Such an isotope has never been found on the planet."

The image changed to a very complex graph with multiple curves intersecting each other.

"Our scientists have been trying to isolate this isotope. What you see here is a graphical representation of the elements in this Drone. Essentially, we believe that the isotope was formed by a complex chemical process, involving extreme conditions of gravity, pressure, and temperature. We are talking extremes tending towards infinity... something like singularity... that has been thought to exist in... black holes."

The German Chancellor interrupted the General's monologue with a raised hand. She almost whispered into the mike.

"So you are saying that this... object... is from outer space. Is it?"

There were no murmurs in the hall. All eyes were on the General.

"No... and yes."

Chairs creaked as they scratched the floor. People picked themselves up from their chairs and sank back into them. Water glasses were refilled. Pages shuffled and turned. A ripple of disbelief seemed to go through the room.

"Ladies and gentlemen, leaders of the World, trust me when

I say this because time is of the essence here. We have run enough double checks before having called all of you here. Had we been unsure, we would not have invited heads of India and Pakistan, South Korea and North Korea and all of Africa and the Arab world for instance, to be here in one room, without prior information about members of the gathering and the modalities of the meeting. Now, if you would allow me to finish…"

The General's words had the desired effect, and no questions were asked and everyone did their best to remain calm. He pressed another button and an image of an orange metallic box appeared on the screen.

"What we see here is a regular black box, the kind that are found in airplanes to record and retrieve data in case of a calamity to help investigate causes. This particular black box was found at the heart of the Drone. The box is made up of the same isotope, but surprisingly the data was almost completely intact. Some sectors within the data banks have been corrupted, but an estimated 96.5% of the data has been recovered."

The screen behind the general turned black as images started flying into the screen.

The Great Pyramid of Giza. The Stonehenge formations. The Taj Mahal. The Great Wall of China. The Leaning Tower of Pisa. Images of monuments and buildings flew into the screen from all sides, stayed for a few brief moments and then faded.

The General spoke.

"The black box contains a vast and detailed record of the history of our planet and our species. From the first record of humans originating in Africa about 200,000 years ago to the first recorded civilizations roughly 15,000 years ago to a supposed 'alien attack' on 21st December 2012. Unfortunately, the details of the attack and many of the subsequent details is the very data that has been corrupted, save for some bits and pieces of information here and there. But that is hardly useful in determining what is about to happen. The record ends on 3rd May 2013, a hundred and thirty one days after the 'attack' when, it says, the last of the humans have been wiped out."

The images on the screen now changed to works of art. Images of the sculpture of Pharaoh Khafre, over 5000 year old. Bronze sculptures of Riace Warriors that were discovered on the seabed dating back to the Fifth Century BC. Over 9000 statues of the Chinese Terracotta Army unearthed from the Third Century B.C. The Nasca Earthworks created 2000 years ago. The Mosaics in Damascus. Ajanta Ellora caves in India. The Mona Lisa. Works of Picasso and Michelangelo.

"The data contained in the black box is so large in quantity that we are still assimilating and assessing the scope of it. Its creators evidently went through… or, as the Drone seems to suggest, *will* go through great pains to capture every possible detail of mankind's achievements. The box also contains some music scores and books, and scripts."

Breathtaking landscapes, animals, birds, graphs, equations and data now began appearing on the screen.

"Every recorded detail of the most complex and finely balanced system known to man – our planet Earth, has apparently been squeezed into the black box here. Blueprints of our greatest inventions and discoveries, including the blueprint of our very own existence – DNA are in here."

The General paused for a moment to catch his breath. He drank a sip of water from the glass placed in front of him. He knew that the people in the room were finding it hard to believe all that he was telling them, exactly like he had. At that moment, he wished he was back home with his wife as she tended to the roses in their garden.

The British Prime Minister tapped on the mike in front of him.

"So let me get this straight. What you're saying is that this Drone is not just from outer space, but actually from the future. A future in which you expect us all to be annihilated by aliens. And in the face of this calamity, some scientists *will* send this... encyclopedia of Earth, into space. And you are basing this fantastic conclusion on an isotope you can't explain. Is that right? It seems to me, General, that you have been a victim of a well-planned, elaborate prank."

The General sighed.

"It is not merely an isotope that we can't explain. The last test that was performed on the material was radio-carbon dating, a foolproof method to determine the approximate age of a substance. Carbon dating tests on the Drone revealed, to our shock and dismay, that this substance is more than 60 billion years old. That's four times older than what we believe is the age of the universe. Obviously, much older than just our planet."

Everyone was silent.

"What we believe is that the Drone was launched successfully into space and that it has travelled for over 47 billion years. Further, we believe that somewhere in its flight, the Drone may have been pulled into a black hole or a wormhole, the mysteries of which are completely unknown to us. The Drone might then have travelled in time, and crashed on planet earth again, three days ago."

Everyone was still silent.

"Ladies and gentlemen, leaders of the world, I am not here to convince you of anything. It is my job to inform you of these developments. You are free to believe or disbelieve, and do as you please with this information. Even as we speak, over three thousand healthy human beings from various professions, races, and religions are being brought together from around the world to be launched in a secret submarine from a secret location as early as tomorrow. It would obviously be advisable to not let this information out in the public domain in order to prevent worldwide panic and paranoia. In the fortunate event that this Drone – and the information contained in it – turns out to be a hoax, the world will live on and the release of this information will prove to be unnecessary and foolish. And in the unfortunate event that the Drone is real, I suppose it would be better if we do not spend our last moments in abject fear and panic. This way, hopefully, half of the world's people will die peacefully in their sleep."

"Whatever the case may be, we will all know for sure in less than 52 hours."

The General nodded to the perplexed audience, left the podium and walked out of a door near the screen. The image on the screen now displayed the current date and time.

'9:34 PM : 18th December 2012 (GMT)'

Saleem shut his laptop down and buried his face in his hands. A million thoughts ran through his head as he contemplated how the story had ended.

No hope.

Saleem was afraid for Sandy. Time heals all wounds, but not if you let them turn into obsession.

And you know better than anyone what obsession can turn a man into.

Saleem thought of his life before the accident. He had had friends. He had had a career. He had had a life. It had been near perfect.

Except for the obsession you harboured within you.

And where had that taken him? He looked back at his life after the accident. There was nothing there. Nothing worth remembering. Nothing worth being called a life. Except the last few days.

But what happened, Saleem? What happened in that accident that made you give up on your deepest obsession?

Saleem realized that he had no answer.

What is The Lost Story, Saleem?

"I don't know," said Saleem out loud. "Maybe it's the answer to all these questions."

"These are not my memories."

Sandy opened the gate that led to the front door of Vishaal Mathur's house through a garden. It was a single storey house in one of the more affluent localities of Delhi that allowed the luxury of having a driveway and a garden in front of the house. A black BMW stood in the driveway. There was a small swing set in the garden and obviously expensive toys lay scattered around the garden.

Sandy had spoken to Vishaal the previous day, telling him that he was Saleem's friend, and that he wanted to talk about him. Vishaal had sounded wary over the phone, but had invited him over nonetheless.

Sandy rang the doorbell which was answered by an old man.

"Mr Vishaal Mathur?"

"Yes. Are you the boy who called yesterday?"

"That's right, sir. My name is Sandeep Gupta. I am a friend of..."

"Saleem. Yes. Come in," Vishaal said.

Sandy followed Vishaal to a dining table, where Vishaal gestured for him to sit down.

"Would you like something to drink? I can only offer water or a cold-drink. My daughter-in-law is not home right now and the servants are on leave for the day."

"That's all right, sir. I'm not thirsty."

Vishaal nodded and sat down.

"I don't want to take up too much of your time, sir. I'm trying to find out more about Saleem's past. I spoke to Ms Vidya Shankar, and she asked me to speak to you."

"And what makes you think I will be forthcoming about

Saleem? He is a private man, Mr Gupta. If he is such a good friend of yours, why don't you ask him?"

"Because he won't tell me. And honestly, I think something isn't quite right with him," Sandy said.

Ordinarily, Sandy wouldn't have been so direct, but he didn't care any longer. He had a feeling that this old man wanted to talk. *Otherwise he wouldn't have invited me over,* Sandy had reasoned. He was about the same age as Saleem Afzal, but appeared to be much healthier. He was tall, with a hairline that had not receded with age. His hair was snow white, but his face still looked young. The exquisite paintings hung around the house and the air about him gave away the fact that life had been good to him.

"What do you mean, Mr Gupta?" Vishaal asked.

"Please call me Sandy."

"All right, Sandy. What's wrong with Saleem?"

"He seems to phase out a lot, and I think he hallucinates. I suspect it has something to do with his past, and more specifically, his accident. I've heard many strange things about it, but I believe there was something more to it… something that Saleem has not been able to let go of."

Vishaal just stared at him.

"Does the term 'The Lost Story' mean something to you?" asked Sandy.

Vishaal slowly shook his head and said, "It could be the book Saleem was working on back then."

"*The Lighthouse* was published… that can't be it."

"There was another book."

"Another book?" Sandy sat up, feeling like a detective who had stumbled upon a vital clue to an otherwise murky mystery.

"Yes… Saleem was working on another book. He was driving to his uncle's place in Bhimtal to finish it… as was his ritual."

"Ritual?" Sandy asked.

"You have to know something about Saleem. He didn't just write stories, he was obsessed with them. When Saleem was writing, it was as if he was transported to another world all together. He shared the same physical space as the rest of us, but he was never really there. He became uncommunicative, bordering on rude. When he was close to finishing a book, he would pack his bags and go to his uncle's place to finish it. 'Away from all the things that don't matter,' he'd say. That's probably what cost him his relationship with Vidya... or whatever it was."

"What do you mean?"

"I think, deep down we all realised that nothing could matter more to Saleem than the world of make-believe that he lived in. Stories are dangerous that way. When you live long enough with them, the real world feels bland and inconsequential in comparison to the fantastical world of your creation. And Vidya could not bear to be inconsequential... not even for a moment," Vishaal said.

"I know that feeling... you know... of getting lost in stories."

"Don't go down that road, Mr Gupta. It is tempting, yes. But it takes everything away from you. I have seen that happen."

Sandy did not say anything. Vishaal was rubbing his knuckles together, probably out of habit.

"So anyway," he went on. "Saleem had been working on this book for years. He did not show it to anyone or even talk about it, which was uncharacteristic... because he usually bounced off his ideas on us. One day, he just packed up and left for Bhimtal without telling anyone. Next thing I heard was about the accident."

"So maybe this incomplete book could be The Lost Story."

"Could be. But there's no way of knowing what became of it."

"I might have a clue." Sandy told Vishaal about the locked door in Saleem's house. He told him of his suspicions that Saleem spoke to it as if it were a person. Vishaal listened carefully without interrupting him. When Sandy was done, he was silent for about five whole minutes.

"It's not the first time he's behaved like that with that room. But if that manuscript is in there, there's no easy way of opening it," Vishaal said.

"Why?"

"Because I was the one who locked that door one final time. I remember that day… It was a few months after the accident. Saleem had cut himself off completely from all of us. Guru had already gone to the US by then. So imagine by surprise, when I received a call from Saleem at 11 at night. He sounded very scared. He asked me to come immediately.

I rushed to his house to find the door ajar. Inside, Saleem was sitting on the floor with his back to the farthest wall from that door. I asked him what was wrong. He handed me a key to a lock, and told me to lock that door immediately. Then he said something very strange."

"What?"

"He said 'Do not go in, even if the voices call out to you.' I thought it was some kind of post-accident trauma finally kicking in. I went up to the door and took a quick look inside. There were a lot of old books, newspapers, and a whole bunch of papers strewn around. I was afraid Saleem might go ballistic if I went in, so I just locked the door and went back to him. He looked much calmer, but what he said next made my heart sink.

'I'm done, Vishaal. Never again.' I knew he was talking about writing. Writing was everything to him... his whole life and existence. So you can well imagine the kind of psychological trauma he must be going through."

"He's writing again," said Sandy.

The words shocked Vishaal enough for him to stand up. "What?"

"Yes. One last time. He's collaborating on a book... with me."

"How does he know you?"

"I am a fan. I wrote to him with a story I had written. He liked it so much that he decided to come out of retirement." Sandy would normally have been bursting with pride at this. But right now, the words came out mechanically. Something about the tone disturbed Vishaal.

"Are you all right, Sandy?"

"Yes," he said, forcing a smile to his lips. "What happened next with Saleem?"

"Well... I drove him down to Bhimtal the next morning. He said he wanted to leave the keys with his uncle. We stayed there for a day, and then we came back. Meeting him became more and more infrequent after that."

"Can you tell me his uncle's address in Bhimtal?"

"You are going to go there for the key?" Vishaal asked.

"Yes."

"In that case, I can't give you the address. Saleem wanted that room locked for good, and I will respect his wish. I think you should leave now."

Vishaal stood up and started walking towards the door, but Sandy stayed in the chair.

"Whatever this is, sir, it needs to come out and Saleem needs to deal with it. I don't know what's in this Lost Story, and why Saleem abandoned it, but he needs to finish it. That's the only way out."

"Out of what?"

Sandy was silent, and sat there with a vacant look in his eyes. He did not know why he had said that. After about a minute or so, Sandy snapped out of his reverie and looked at Vishaal, who had a concerned look on his face. "I don't know, sir. I'm just going by my gut."

Vishaal looked indecisive. Sandy decided to press the advantage.

"All right, look – I won't open the door without Saleem's permission. That's a promise."

Sandy walked up to Vishaal and extended his hand. Vishaal did not take it.

"Mr Mathur, I will go to Bhimtal anyway. So all you can do is stall me for a few days... because I am going to find that key."

Vishaal finally relented. "Ask for Ahmed Sultan's house. I don't remember where exactly it is, but the locals will be able to tell you."

"Thanks for your time, sir," said Sandy, and left.

Saleem stood on the balcony of his uncle's house. It would have been a serene sight of the river gently meandering along the path created by the sloping hills, but for a gigantic spaceship looming over the hills.

Saleem watched as smaller spaceships emerged from the larger one in the sky. The segment of the road that was visible from the balcony was packed with people and cars. No one was going anywhere.

Saleem went back inside. He realized that there was no point in running. There was nowhere to go. He stood in front of the mirror and stared at his reflection. He noticed the dark circles under his eyes, the sagging skin under his chin and the thick lines etched upon his forehead. He agreed with himself that the years had not been kind to him.

All of a sudden, his reflection walked out of view inside the mirror. Before Saleem could make anything of it, flashes from his past began to play out on the mirror like a highlight reel. He saw Vishaal, Vineet, Guru and himself posing for a picture outside the fine arts department. He saw himself dancing with Vidya… it was one of the earlier classes; he was shuffling uncomfortably around a confident and elegant Vidya. He saw her again… raising her hands and twirling them. 'Abracadabra' she said.

Tears welled up in Saleem's eyes. 'NO! Don't come near me!' he saw himself shout at his friends, as they stood in the middle of the road in the dead of night. They were all drenched from head to toe. He saw a truck approaching his car head on at high speed. He instinctively raised his arms in front of his face to protect himself.

When Saleem looked in the mirror again, he saw Sandy sitting in front of him. 'The fact that they end, sir,' he said. Suddenly he saw Sandy standing in front of a crowd, delivering a speech with remarkable eloquence. He saw Sandy walking with a girl on a broad road at night. They had their backs to him and they walked slowly, like they had all the time in the World. Saleem could see India Gate in a distance. Slowly, Sandy took the girl's hand. Her fingers closed around his fingers one by one.

"These are not my memories," said Saleem out loud.

"Are you sure?" said a voice behind him. Saleem did not try to locate its source. He had grown used to it.

"Yes."

"The world is ending, Saleem. We're trying to save all its stories in the recon Drone. This mirror is the gateway, and you and Sandy get priority."

"Why is that?"

The voice did not say anything. Saleem looked in the mirror again. The flashes were gone. His reflection stared back at him.

"Done saving our stories?" asked Saleem, almost sarcastically.

"All but one. The Lost Story is stilled locked up."

It was Saleem's turn to not say anything. The voice, however, continued speaking after a pause.

"But not for long. He will be on his way soon to retrieve the key. He knows where it is."

Anger exploded inside Saleem. He rolled his hands up into fists, and smashed his right fist into the mirror. The mirror cracked.

"I told you to stay away from him," said Saleem through gritted teeth.

"Do you even know who I am?" said the voice, mockingly.

Saleem could only fume silently. The voice cackled with laughter.

"He's as much a part of this now as you, Saleem," said the voice. "Besides, you started it."

"Excuse me?"

"The Lost Story. You started it. He's going to have to finish it. Just like all the others."

Vishaal watched the boy walk to the end of the lane, where he turned left and disappeared behind the building. He stood there for a while, staring at nothing in particular.

A car stopped outside the gate, and two kids ran out of it, and bounded towards him with joy on their faces. Vishaal spread open his arms for them.

Sandy stared at the phone's flashing screen phone. It was Tara. He contemplated whether he should pick up the call, but it stopped ringing before he could decide. He pushed away the thought of calling her back.

I have more pressing matters at hand, like figuring out how to get to Bhimtal as soon as possible.

All of a sudden, Tara's words echoed in his mind. *You sound obsessed.*

Am I obsessed? thought Sandy, his feet rooted to the ground in the middle of the road. *Why am I doing this? Am I intruding into Saleem Afzal's life? I snooped around his house without his permission and literally stole things, asked about his personal life behind his back, and now I'm going to Bhimtal to retrieve something that he clearly does not want. It certainly sounds like obsession… but then, why does it feel like the right thing to do?*

A car honked loudly behind him before he could arrive at an answer. Sandy walked to the side of the road. He concluded that he would trust his instincts and wait for the answers to come to him. He decided to leave for Bhimtal early the next morning.

Saleem woke up with a start in his hospital bed. He checked the clock on the far wall. It was 11 PM. He picked up his phone from the side table and called Sandy.

"Hello?" Sandy spoke into the phone.

"Sandy… where are you?"

"I'm going out of town for a couple of days."

"Are you going to Bhimtal?"

There was silence on the other end. "I will speak to you when I get back, sir," he said finally.

"Listen Sandy... you don't have to..."

"I do, sir. And not just for you. Something tells me that both of us are tied to the contents of that room. For our sake, I'm going to get the key. You can then decide what to do with it."

Sandy did not wait for Saleem to say anything. He disconnected the call.

CHAPTER 7
The Broken Bottle

Sandy was having a really, really long day. And not a good one at that.

He had left for Bhimtal in a cab at 6 in the morning. They had made good progress till about 8 AM, when they were just about to reach a village called Gajraula. The way ahead of there was blocked due to an accident. Sandy waited on the road in frustration but finally decided that they would be better off taking a detour.

With interior roads being what they are, the detour turned out to be a bumpy ride. A large part of that detour was spent driving patiently behind a bullock-cart at an excruciating speed of 10 kmph, till the road became wide enough to safely overtake. Moreover, they got lost twice on the detour. Sandy took out all his frustration on the driver who did not react at all to his fretting. This only served to aggravate Sandy further.

By the time they got back on the road to Bhimtal, it was already one in the afternoon. The view on the way was not particularly spectacular but enough to give Sandy a sense of awe. The hills always did that to him. They brought a sense of perspective with their magnificence and seemed to display a sense of rock-steady resolve, something he felt he could use.

However, because of a few landslides over the past few days, they encountered another problem. When they were about 10 km from Bhimtal, they found out that the direct road was closed. They had to drive all the way to Nanital and then come back to Bhimtal. By the time he reached his hotel, a picturesque little place called *The Fisherman's Lodge*, it was already 6 PM.

Sandy decided to email the story he had written along the way to Saleem and go to sleep.

Hemant was having a really, really long day. To describe it more accurately, he was having the longest day of his life, and it was still far from over. The sound of glass breaking on metal had sealed it irrevocably. But more on that later.

Hemant hadn't exactly been having the most spectacular time of his life for a while now. His boss was killing him with assignments that were impossible to complete even if the days were 48 hours long and stacked up to 14 in a week. His landlord had served him a notice of a month to vacate the house, because they had apparently not appreciated the drunken argument he had pursued one night with their dog about noise discipline around the house. His parents were breathing down his neck for him to get married and *settle down*. He virtually had no social life but for his girlfriend, Kavita, who had also been issuing ultimatums of marriage. It had become crystal clear to Hemant that nobody cared about what he wanted; and he had resigned himself to the fact that he had ceased to live his life for himself. He was only following orders and trying to meet the expectations set upon him by others.

This particular day had begun the previous night, when he had received a call from his distant uncle. He had been arm-twisted into agreeing to spend the day with his uncle, since he was visiting after what his uncle called 'a lifetime'. After many valiant attempts to wriggle out, Hemant had finally given in and agreed to travel from his Gurgaon home, which was in one corner of his universe, to Noida, which lay in the other extreme corner of his cosmos. Moreover, to be able to make it in time for breakfast, he had to cancel his usual drinking session with his friends. The only upside to the whole thing was that he got to take a day off from the drudgery of office.

The fateful day had commenced with Hemant being woken up at 7:30 AM by a disappointed uncle who was already lecturing him on the phone about becoming 'a little more responsible.'

The bus ride to his uncle's house was a long one, with 2 changeovers in between. Hemant hated the thought of travelling by buses. He also hated the fact that he was always so broke that he had no other option.

The hot summer day did nothing to add to Hemant's comfort as he tried to ignore the nauseating smell of sweat all around him by falling asleep, only to be woken up by the annoying feeling of his own sweat-soaked collar sticking to the back of his neck again and again.

Finally, after a very long two-and-a-half hours, Hemant stumbled out of the bus. His uncle greeted him with a warm hug and then immediately began a lecture on responsibility, punctuality and how they were important to sustain a good marriage, something that Hemant had delayed for long enough already. After that had been dealt with, they left for Chandni Chowk.

Travelling for four hours in the sun in Delhi buses to have a heavy breakfast that had to be eaten standing in a cramped and stuffy shop in Chandni Chowk, while listening to a discourse on the importance of a wife, was not really Hemant's idea of a rejuvenating weekend. He, however, did not really have a choice.

Next item on the itinerary, Hemant realised with dismay, was a visit to the zoo.

Who goes to the fucking zoo anymore?

His uncle would not have any of 'mall and movies' nonsense because he believed that it was "one of the main factors in creating the current degenerate generation which didn't care for family and simple living."

In the zoo, standing under the relentless, blazing sun, Hemant couldn't help but stare at the monkeys in a cage and wonder who was actually living in cages like animals. *They or I?*

Somewhere around the snake enclosure his phone rang. It was Kavita and she was weeping uncontrollably.

What now? Hemant groaned to himself and to Kavita.

Between her sobs he figured out that Varun, Kavita's colleague, had spread some nasty rumour about her in the office.

"Calm down, Kavita. Listen I'm out with my uncle right now. Let me call you in some time."

She was inconsolable.

"Babe, I'm having a really long day as it is. I understand that you are upset. Please just calm down, have some water, and wait till evening. I'll sort this out."

She called him insensitive.

"Kavita, God dammit! What do you expect me to do? Just leave my uncle and fly like superman to your place?"

She called him incompetent and a coward. Hemant blew his top.

"Don't you dare talk to me like that! And what was it that Varun said, anyway?"

Varun had apparently spread a rumour in the office that she was sleeping with her boss, and his boss as well, to climb up the corporate ladder. She told him that Hemant's attitude disappointed her and disconnected the call.

Hemant put the phone in his pocket and looked down at the pavement as his heart let out a scream. He was angry now. Angry at his uncle, for dragging him all around Delhi while lecturing him on marriage. At Kavita, for not understanding his predicament and calling him insensitive, incompetent and cowardly. At Varun (*that pig!*), for doing what he did and putting Kavita in this position. Angry at the monkeys, for mocking him from within their cages. He decided to head back and take care of business.

"I'm really tired now, uncle. Can we go home? I have to meet a few friends in the evening in Gurgaon as well…"

His uncle agreed but did expect to 'at least' be accompanied back to Noida where he could finally leave.

By now Hemant was so numb with rage that the next few hours of bus rides and his uncle's unending tirade went over him like water around a big rock. After dropping off his uncle, he took out his cellphone and considered his options. He was still extremely ticked with Kavita and decided against calling her. He wanted to call Varun and shoot him through the phone but he decided to hold it for a bit later. There was only one other person left to call – Himanshu, his drinking companion.

"Hey. I'm coming over in two hours. Keep the booze ready."

Himanshu asked him what he wanted to drink.

"Anything. I've had a very long day and I don't care. As long as it has alcohol in it."

On his last bus ride for the day, Hemant's anger coagulated and concentrated into hatred towards Varun. He could not put any blame on any of the others. Varun was a stranger who seemed like he had no business messing up Hemant's life anymore than it already was.

He reached Himanshu's house by nightfall, did not waste any time, and got straight down to downing one whiskey after another. The alcohol was now acting as fuel for his anger.

He narrated the day's events to Himanshu as they opened a second bottle of whiskey.

"Really. I don't get it. What right does that Varun have to say anything like that about Kavita?"

"...and thanks to him we're fighting as well..."

"...he needs to be taught a lesson..."

Finally, intoxicated by frustration mixed with alcohol, Hemant picked up the phone and dialled Varun.

"Where are you?"

Varun, it turned out, was drinking at a common friend's place. He told Hemant to calm down and cursorily told him to not raise his voice with him.

"Yeah. I'll teach you how to talk, alright. I'm coming over and if you have the balls to match your tongue, you'll stay there."

The two of them were at the house in 10 minutes. They rang the bell and clenched their fists. The moment Varun opened the door, Hemant barged inside and pushed him on to a couch that was just behind him. Things had started to move really fast.... And loud.

Himanshu tried to hold Varun down as he and Hemant yelled at each other. The others in the room stood quietly trying to make sense of what was happening.

"How dare you talk about my girlfriend like that? I'll show you!" Hemant screamed furiously at Varun, even as Varun kept insisting that he had not said anything to warrant such a reaction. Himanshu kept trying to tell Varun to be quiet or he was going to get badly beaten up.

Finally, Hemant channelled his rage and frustration into physical energy and started raining down punches on Varun. Himanshu watched in horror as Varun's face began to get bruised. Hemant was proving difficult to pin down.

Finally, on hearing the commotion, the owner of the house, Anil, had come down from the first floor and intervened. He took charge of the situation and told the two that they would have to take this outside. He told them both to get out, and that they could settle whatever it was outside.

Hemant turned towards the door and started to walk.

Himanshu walked behind Hemant.

Varun, beaten and vengeful, followed.

Hemant stood outside the house on the road and waited for Varun to emerge. The rush of adrenaline had finally given him the high that the whiskey had been unable to. He'd had a very long day and he felt perfectly justified to want to beat Varun to pulp. But he had begun to feel a little giddy and decided that he should probably just lay a few more punches on Varun and leave.

However, Hemant's long day was about to get longer.

He saw Varun walking up with a bottle of vodka in his hand. He smashed the bottle on the wall and swung its jagged edge at Hemant's head.

Hemant was stunned, as was everybody else.

He felt the warm, wet blood trickle down from the side of his head, onto his ear and cheek.

Then came the pain. A sharp, piercing, cold pain.

He saw Varun swing again…

Saleem was in a spot of bother. He had woken up in the morning with a mild pain in his chest. He decided not to tell the doctor about it, for the fear of having his stay in the hospital extended.

If I have to sit and stare at a wall, I'd rather do it at home.

By afternoon, the pain had intensified, and he had no choice but to inform the doctor. But before he could ring the bell, he fainted.

When he came to, he saw an extremely sombre doctor.

"Your heart is very weak, Mr Afzal. I'm afraid there isn't much we can do for you now. Your recovery was quite remarkable, but there seems to have been a relapse. The next attack, I'm afraid, might be fatal."

Saleem did not know what to say. He didn't even know what to feel at the prospect of an imminent end. He had always feared death. Not the dying itself, but what lay after – a forever of nothingness. But faced with death for the very first time, he was surprised that he had not been gripped by fear. Oddly enough, it almost felt like relief, but Saleem wasn't sure. Maybe he liked the fact that stories ended as well.

"Can I go home?" he asked the doctor.

The doctor considered his request for a few moments. "I suppose so," he said. "We are going to keep you here for another day or two. If your condition improves, I guess you can be discharged."

The doctor left the room. Saleem opened his laptop. There was an e-mail from Sandy.

Hi sir,

I have reached Bhimtal. Will get in touch with your uncle soon for the key. Call me intrusive if you must, but something tells me that you want to unlock what's behind the door. Like I said, you can decide whether you want to go through with it or not. In the

meantime, here's another story. Inspired by some real life events.
Cheers,
Sandy

PS – I can see why you liked coming here to finish your books. This town is so peaceful. I'm feeling better just being here.

Saleem had mixed feelings after reading the e-mail. He felt a hint of anger at the intrusion into his private life.

But you already knew that, didn't you?

He also felt a tingling sense of adventure. But everything was wiped clean from his mind as he read through the story Sandy had sent him. His eyes widened as *deja vu* gripped him.

Saleem finished reading and closed his laptop. He was shivering. Motives and a few details here and there aside, he had been transported to a night twenty-six years ago.

How could he know?

Saleem deduced that maybe Vineet had told him about it. The kid did mention it was inspired by real life. He let out a laugh. The kid had managed to spook him. *Considering everything that has been going on around me, not the best of times.*

"Damn cheeky of him to do this," he said out loud. He opened his laptop and began writing.

Varun was having a really, really long day. To put it more accurately, Varun was having one of the longest days of his life, and it was far from over. When he heard the sound of glass breaking on metal, he felt a combination of disbelief and empowerment. He could never have imagined himself attacking someone, much less with a weapon. But holding it in his hand sent a surge through his body that purged the feeling he had had since morning of being powerless.

He was far from horrified at the sight of blood gushing from Hemant's head. In fact, he felt invincible as he advanced towards Hemant ready to swing his weapon again.

That'll show them. Drunken bullies. The world has walked all over me long enough. Now it's time to turn the tables, starting with these two...

But more on that later.

Varun had reached office that morning with his heart ablaze with the prospects of going through a full week of work. He yawned as he sat down on his chair and turned on his computer. Preeti, his girlfriend, had talked his ear off for three hours last night.

If only she spent her time in bed indulging in activities other than just talking.

Varun sighed to himself and glumly pondered his forced celibacy, as the Windows icon popped up on his monitor. Just then, the familiar whiff of J'adore perfume filled his senses. He swirled around to see Kavita walk by. She was wearing a white satin shirt, with the top two buttons open providing a tormenting peek at her cleavage. Her skirt ended just above her knee. Varun couldn't stop staring as she walked by, legs flashing and her perfect figure swaying seductively in her tight business clothes.

Varun spent the time it took for Outlook to load to undress Kavita in his mind. A slight smile played around his lips and he checked the couple of emails in his inbox.

However, it was wiped right off his face when he saw the email from the Region Head. The position of Senior Manager, that had opened up a week ago, had been offered to Kavita.

His heart burst into furious flames. He had put his blood,

sweat, and tears into this company for five years. Then Kavita had cat-walked into the company from a business school, and had now risen above him in hierarchy in two short years.

"What the hell!" thought Varun, as he stormed into Anirudh's — the regional manager — office.

"How could you, Anirudh?"

"Calm down, Varun!"

"How could you? You told me last week that this promotion was as good as mine! And then you do this to me?"

"Varun, shut the door," Anirudh said.

He turned around to see curious heads pop out of cubicles. They had their gossip for the lunch hour now. He decided to give them just a bit more to talk about by slamming the door shut.

"Was that necessary?" asked Anirudh. He was calm in the face of this fury.

"Yes! And I need you to start talking... why?"

"Listen, Varun. I've been under pressure from the top honchos to promote Kavita. Next time a position opens up, I promise you, it's yours."

"Bullshit! You are just giving me another one of your carrots! I gave my life to this company for five years and this is how I am repaid."

"Varun..."

"NO! This is enough. I want you to retract this promotion and offer it to me!"

Anirudh stood up.

"SHUT UP AND SIT DOWN! While we do share a good relationship, I would like to remind you that I am your superior and I will not tolerate you or anyone who reports to me, talking back to me like that."

Varun sat down, shocked. Anirudh had never looked angrier, and he had done worse.

"I've been telling you for years now. Being good out there on the field isn't good enough. You have to make a better impression not just to the customers but internally as well. Look at your communication skills, you still fumble when you're speaking English. Look at how you dress sometimes. I told you to go out and get better clothes, but you haven't listened once."

Varun opened his mouth to speak. He wanted to point out that Kavita had trained under him for a year. But he seemed to have lost his voice. Anirudh carried on.

"A Senior Manager has to make presentations to the board, and even interface with international clients. Kavita is much better than you in that respect. And frankly, I don't think you have it in you to rise to her level."

Varun was shocked. He had always been one of the company's top performers. The reputation he had in the market was unprecedented, and here he was being told that he did not have the calibre to rise up in the hierarchy.

As the person he had always looked up to stomped all over him with his words, Varun felt powerless. To speak. To act.

"Varun, I want you to go back to your cubicle and think about this. I don't want to see your face for the rest of the day."

He got up and left, avoiding the eyes that he knew were trained on him. He spent the rest of the morning in silence, contemplating what Anirudh had said. In the lunchroom, he decided to eat alone.

"Hey buddy!"

Varun looked up to see Sameer sitting across him.

"I heard about what happened. And then I heard about what Anirudh said to you. I bet you must be feeling totally down and out right now."

"Good guess."

"Listen Varun... you're my friend. And I've learnt a lot from you... So I'm gonna level with you..."

Sameer looked sombre. He was from the same batch as Kavita, and had joined at the same time as her. Varun and Sameer had struck up a good friendship, and he had met what had now become his drinking gang through Sameer. Ironically, an occasional inclusion to this little group was Hemant – Kavita's boyfriend.

"Kavita has been sleeping with Anirudh for a couple of months now," whispered Sameer.

"WHAT?"

"Keep it down. Listen... she was always a bit of a slut even during college. Almost broke up with Hemant once because he suspected she was sleeping with his friend Himanshu..."

"The same Himanshu?"

"Yes... the one who often joins us with Hemant. Well... Hemant's suspicions were correct. She's like that... gives in to temptation very easily. And here the stakes were high as it is. So don't beat yourself up, okay."

"Okay," Varun was still shocked at these revelations. *What a fucked up world we live in*, he thought.

"And listen – keep it to yourself."

"Yeah... sure!"

Sameer watched Varun go. He had seen revenge in his eyes since morning as if it was stamped across his forehead. He knew that everyone in office would hear of it by the end of the day.

That will teach her for not putting out, he thought.

Varun was startled by the ringing phone. He had nodded off on the cab ride to Sameer's house for a marathon drinking session. He had confirmed with Sameer that Hemant and Himanshu would not be joining in today.

He saw the number and groaned. It was his mother.

After the usual pleasantries, the conversation inevitably moved to the topic of the promotion. His mom wanted to know if there was any news.

"I didn't get it, ma."

"Why?"

"There's this girl in office – Kavita. I told you about her, right? She got it. She is an MBA... and it is needed to qualify."

"Didn't she train under you?"

Varun closed his eyes and let out a sigh. "Yes," he said.

There was silence on the other end.

"Hello? Ma? Are you still there?"

"Yes, yes. I was just thinking. If you had seen the sense in doing an MBA after your graduation like your younger brother, you wouldn't have seen this day," his mom said.

And now she's going to tell me how awesome Karan is.

"I mean – look at Karan. He is already earning more than you. Did you know what he bought your father for his birthday? A Tissot watch. We are so proud."

Anger, which had already been simmering all day, exploded once more inside Varun. He decided he did not have to take this anymore.

"Ma, I'll talk to you later," he said and disconnected.

He drank in silence at Sameer's while the others laughed and joked. He reflected on the day's event and the rest of his life.

Am I a failure?

These thoughts were rudely interrupted by the phone. It was Hemant. He was drunk. He was pissed. He knew Varun had been talking about Kavita in the office. He was coming over.

After the initial incoherent shouting match between the two, Varun had only tried to protect himself as Hemant punched him repeatedly. It was life's cruel joke, the physical ones just underscoring the real punches that life had been raining down on him since morning.

The commotion had woken up Anil, the landlord who lived on the first floor. He had rushed downstairs and told them to take their problems outside his house. Hemant and Himanshu walked out. They were not done.

Varun got up.

Maybe I deserve this. I'm going nowhere in life. A failure to everyone... even my mother. I should probably roll over and die.

NO! A voice screamed inside Varun. *You don't have to take this. The only person holding you back is yourself.*

This voice was forceful and commanding, and it gripped Varun from head to toe. He decided in that moment to finally act... to finally stop letting life happen to him and taking things in his own hands.

He picked up the bottle of Smirnoff just as he walked out the door.

Varun swung the broken bottle at Hemant's face again. Hemant raised his hands to protect himself, and the edge of the glass caught his finger. Hemant screamed, dropping to his knees, holding his left hand with his right. His little finger was dangling at an impossible angle, attached to his hand only by skin and tendons.

Varun felt two arms pin him to the wall. It was Himanshu. But he was unstoppable. He sank his teeth into Himanshu's right arm, as he screamed in pain. Himanshu let go, and watched in horror the missing chunk of flesh from his arm lodged in Varun's teeth.

Varun spat it out and shouted, "Come on, you assholes! I'll take on both of you!"

It was a stand-off as Himanshu and Varun stared each other down. Hemant was still on his knees, dazed. His shirt was drenched in blood.

The rush of adrenaline made Himanshu's head spin. The silence was finally broken by the distant sound of sirens.

Himanshu was having a really bad day. As the sound of sirens got louder, he realized that it could only get worse from here on.

Let's rewind one last time.

No one could have imagined that Himanshu was having a rough patch. After all, he had everything. A high paying job, a house of his own, an active social life, and a way with women. How could a life filled to the brim feel hollow?

But that morning, Himanshu did, as he woke up with a hangover. He had gone to the opening of a new club in town.

Damn these clubs. They suck.

Himanshu was disillusioned with everything around him. He had a great job that he hated, but couldn't quit because he needed the money to maintain his lifestyle, which mostly included clubbing, expensive designer clothes, expensive food and alcohol, and a home loan for a flat he didn't want to live in.

What's the point of it all? Earn lots of money, get married, have kids, watch and suffer as they grow up while you grow old, pay for their luxuries, get them married, and slowly fade away to oblivion? The Earth will keep turning. The universe will keep expanding. Life will go on till it evolves into something else and I'll be forgotten as a nobody who did nothing worthwhile.

His mind wandered to last night. The club was full of socialites who were there mostly because they were expected to be there; rather than to enjoy the music. Girls looking hot, guys trying to stick their tongues in their mouth, because that is the only thing they ultimately cared about. Everybody wore what he imagined were their best masks, covering their hollow selves.

And I spent ten grand on that.

He was having that kind of a day. He had called in sick and then decided to go get some coffee and spend the day reading a book. He saw the crazy old man who would frequently come and stand outside the coffee shop. He would stand there for hours, quietly, unless he saw a cat. On those occasions, he would squat on the floor at some distance from the cat and proceed to have a conversation with it for as long as the cat would stay.

Is that what I'm going to turn into one day?

His phone rang. It was Hemant. He seemed irate, and wanted to come over to drink. Himanshu invited him over and headed home. He was a very close friend.

As he waited for Hemant, Himanshu realized how strongly despair had gripped him. He had no idea where he was heading. He had no idea where he wanted to go. No amount of sleeping around could distract him anymore from the fact that he had serious commitment issues. He imagined himself old and dying, alone and friendless. He was almost in the throes of fear when the doorbell rang.

It was Hemant.

Himanshu looked on, horrified as Hemant punched Varun repeatedly. Not by the act itself, but the morbid fascination it evoked inside him. In his made-up life, the sight of a man's hand making firm contact with another man's cheek felt real.

It felt primal and he didn't want Hemant to stop.

Even as the sirens got louder, Himanshu could see the bloodlust in Varun's eyes.

He really wants to kill us.

As the realization struck, Himanshu grasped something far more terrifying. He wanted Varun to try. Himanshu balled his hands into fists, ready to charge into Varun. The moment felt real, in stark contrast to his plastic life. After many months, he felt alive, and he was in no mood to let go of this feeling.

And just then, the police interceptor van turned into view.

Madness knows no bounds, but sitting in the back of a police van can bring anyone crashing back to reality. It hit Hemant, Varun and Himanshu in almost the same moment, as they stole glances at each other. No words were needed.

Himanshu looked around and decided that the policeman sitting in the front was the most senior among them. He cleared his throat.

"Excuse me, sir, we realize that we were extremely stupid. Don't know what had gotten into us. Isn't there any way we can work this out among ourselves without going to the Police Station?"

The policeman turned around with a look of disgust on his face.

"Shut up."

"Come on sir… there must be something that can be done."

"I said, shut up," he growled. "Or I swear I will break every bone in your body.

The policeman turned around again to look at the road. "As it is, I'm having a really bad day," he mumbled to himself.

"Are you here to steal from my house?"

"Excuse me, would you be able to tell me where Ahmed Sultan lives? He's a local... has been living around here for a long time."

Sandy was standing at the reception of the Fisherman's Lodge. The weather was beautiful outside, and a small cloud was floating over the lake. Simon & Garfunkel's *The Sound of Silence* played from the speakers installed all over the hotel. The manager at the front desk thought about the name for a few moments, and then shook his head.

"No sir," he said. "I've only recently been transferred here from our property in Shimla, so I don't really know too many locals. If you want, I can ask one of the bell boys."

"No, that's all right. I think I'll go take a walk. The weather is very nice."

"Indeed sir. Walk towards the temple along the lake. Once you cross the primary school and the foot bridge, you'll reach the main market area. I'm sure the shop owners would know the person if he is a local. It is a very small town, everyone knows everyone else."

Sandy surveyed the lake as he walked towards the temple. *So this is the setting of the legendary battle between Sujit and The One.* He stopped in front of the primary school and faced the lake. The bank below him looked like the setting for the battle in the first story that he and Saleem had worked on.

"How far we've come from there... We are almost done, aren't we, Saleem?" he murmured to himself. Sandy was leaning on the railing on the side of the road and watching the lake. A solitary paddle-boat was moving towards a small bunch of ducks floating idly some distance away. The child in the boat was visibly excited as they got closer to the ducks. The ducks sensed the approaching threat, and began paddling away. After a few moments, the boat gave up the chase. Sandy could not see the child's face from the distance, but he could imagine his disappointment.

He stayed there for a few more minutes before moving on.

"Why do you want to meet Ahmed?" asked the clerk at the shop. He hadn't shown much interest in entertaining Sandy till he dropped Ahmed Sultan's name. Then suddenly, the clerk got up and hurriedly led Sandy under a tree in front of his shop.

Now he looked at Sandy carefully as he waited for an answer.

"I have some personal business with him. Do you know where he lives?"

"Yes, I do. But what do you want from him?"

Sandy felt annoyed at the clerk. "I don't think that is any of your business. Will you tell me where he lives or should I ask someone else?"

The clerk laughed. He called out to the tea vendor close by. "*Arre* Bheem *bhai*, this saheb from the city wants to meet *Bhu-baba*."

The tea vendor left his stall and came half running to join them. He had a silly grin on his face.

"Why do you want to meet *Bhu-baba,* saheb? He is mad. He doesn't let anyone enter his premises, and if any of the local kids trespass, he runs after them with a stick shouting *bhu bhu bhu*. God knows what that means... but that's how he got his name."

Just Great, thought Sandy, *as if pesky locals were not enough, now I have to deal with a crazy old man.*

"He has something that belonged to my father," lied Sandy. "So can you tell me where he lives so I can go to his house before it gets any darker."

"Yes saheb, do not go to his house in the night. They say it is haunted."

"It's haunted only at night?" asked Sandy sarcastically.

"Come on saheb, everyone knows ghosts only come out at night."

Misinformed even in superstition, Sandy thought. He decided not to indulge these two idiots any longer. He pulled out two fifty rupee notes.

"Listen… these can be yours if you tell me the address and absolutely nothing else."

Sandy knew he had hit the jackpot when he saw the greedy look in both their eyes. The tea vendor almost snatched the money out of Sandy's hand, and then handed one note to the clerk almost grudgingly.

"Just go up this road. Take a left when the road ends. The third house on the left is *Bhu-baba's* house. A word of warning – he'll probably be working in his garden right now. Keep a safe distance and call out to him till he hears you. Do not sneak up on him under any circumstances."

"Why not?" said Sandy, feeling extremely bewildered.

"He might attack you," said the tea vendor simply, and they both left.

Saleem, Vineet, Vishaal and Guru sat in the back of the police van. Their shirts were torn, and Saleem's head was bleeding. Guru was holding his arm and grimacing in pain. There was complete silence except for the steady drone of the wipers and the pitter-patter of the rain outside. Vineet finally decided to speak up.

"*Sir... we are really sorry! Isn't there any way we can work this out among ourselves without going to the Police Station?*"

The van screeched to a halt.

"*Why Saleem?*" *asked Guru. The pain in his arm had reduced considerably, and he had finally found his voice*

Saleem looked at him. He looked calm, almost lost, but Guru had known him long enough to know that he was hurting.

"*There were nine of them, and four of us,*" *said Vishaal through gritted teeth. He was still fuming over the completely unnecessary turn of events.* "*They just wanted to intimidate us... they had no intention of actually fighting... why, Saleem? Why did you have to attack him with the bottle? If you had just waited it out, they would have left.*"

"*Not to mention,*" *said Guru,* "*that we are completely drunk. We weren't exactly going to paint a rosy picture in front of the cops, even if it was those guys who provoked us. We should be thanking our stars... you almost sliced that guy's finger off. If they hadn't run away at the sight of the cops, we probably wouldn't have gotten off this easy! Do you have a good reason for picking the fight.*"

"*Yes, I do,*" *said Saleem. He got up and began walking back towards the cinema hall where their car was parked.*

"*Care to enlighten us?*" *shouted Guru after him.*

Saleem stopped, but did not say anything. Finally, he turned around to face his friends. They were all staring at him.

"*Because I needed to feel something. When he screamed in pain, it felt real. When he smashed the brick on my head, the pain was real. I needed to feel something to know that I'm still alive."* His voice was laced with desperation and agony. Vishaal, Vineet and Guru were taken aback by his answer.

It had started to rain harder. Guru walked up to Saleem and put his arm around his shoulder. Saleem buried his face in his palms.

"What's wrong, Saleem?" whispered Guru.

"I'm trapped," said Saleem, and Guru was taken aback by the suffering he saw in his eyes. He mentally rebuked himself for not noticing it earlier.

"I'm trapped, Guru. In this world of make believe. Reality just feels bland compared to the things I write and imagine. I just want to stay in my own world... where everything comes to life with a mere thought. The power, Guru... the power of it is intoxicating... and that's all I want... even though I know that with each passing moment... I'm losing my connection to reality and to you guys. To everything. And you know what the scary part is? I like it!"

Saleem began to move away from Guru. He was getting hysterical. His friends began to move towards him.

"NO! Don't come near me! Or you'll get sucked into my world too... you won't be real either! You'll just be stories in a sea of stories, as inconsequential in my mind as we all are in the real world."

Saleem did not wait to hear what his friends wanted to say. He didn't know what he wanted them to say. He turned around and began to run. He ran till he could not run anymore. It had stopped raining. The pain was unbearable. Saleem squeezed his eyes shut and let out a gut-wrenching scream.

When he opened his eyes, he was back in his house, standing in front of the locked door. There was a sign in front of it that said – *"All roads end here."*

Saleem was staring at the sign when the electricity went out. In the silence, Saleem could hear heavy breathing behind him, as if *someone had been running after him. He turned around to see Sandy standing at the other end of the room. His eyes were glowing in the dark.*

"Almost time, Saleem," he said.
He raised his hands and twirled his fingers.
"Abracadabra," he whispered.

"Excuse me, sir," Sandy called out to the old man with his back to him from outside the gate.

The old man was engrossed in watering a rather robust growth of red dahlias in his garden, humming an old Kishore Kumar song. He either did not notice Sandy, or pretended not to, out of habit of ignoring pesky by-passers.

"Sir? Can I have a couple of minutes of your time, please?" said Sandy, this time a little loudly. That caught the old man's attention. He gingerly straightened his back and turned around to look at him. The man looked irritated. He was short, with a slight stoop and wore clothes that were two sizes too big for him. His hair was pure-white and stood up in odd places as if from a bad haircut. Judging by his pale skin and shaky walk, Sandy estimated that he must be about eighty five years old.

He saw Sandy and shuffled slowly towards him. Sandy instinctively took a step backward to stay out of his grasp across the gate. The old man paused behind his garden's gate, and Sandy immediately recognized him as an older version of the man in the other photograph he had taken from Saleem's house.

"What do you want? Are you here to steal from my house?" growled the old man. The house in question was the most dilapidated house Sandy had ever seen. Most windows were missing panes, and the ones on which the glass had managed to last were covered with a thick layer of dust. Next to the entry, there was a huge pile of old, broken furniture. Sandy also noticed some vines growing out of the cracks in the stepped roof.

He shifted his attention back to the old man in front of him who has peering at him with owlish eyes.

"No sir. I am not here to steal anything from your house. I am actually a friend of Saleem Afzal."

"Who?"

"Saleem Afzal? Your nephew?"

Ahmed's face twisted into something that vaguely resembled an amused expression.

"You are a friend of Saleem's, eh?" he asked in a mocking voice.

"Yes sir, I am."

"That's a new one."

"I don't understand," said Sandy, genuinely confused.

"Never mind," said the old man, opening the gate. "Come on in. I would offer you something, but my maid has not come in today. In fact, I don't think she will be coming again."

"That's perfectly all right, sir," said Sandy with a sigh of relief. He couldn't imagine eating or drinking anything that was made inside this house.

"Do you mind sitting in the garden? It's too dark inside and I don't have electricity."

"I'd actually prefer it, sir."

Ahmed stopped and began to stare at Sandy. "You are a polite lad. Don't remember the last time anyone called me 'sir.' Do you know what the people here call me?"

"No I don't," lied Sandy.

"Bhu-baba! But I don't mind. As long as my antics convince them that I am a raving lunatic and that my house is haunted, I'm happy."

Sandy did not know what to say to that. So he just nodded, hoping that his facial expression communicated that he empathized with the old man.

"So, friend-of-Saleem, are you here for stories?"

"Stories?"

"Stories of Saleem. He was a good kid. Quite a famous author in his day. He used to come here to finish his books. Said it gave him the much needed insulation from the noise and the hum-drum of the city that he required to finish his books. He used to say that this was his escape from reality."

"Saleem needed to escape from reality to finish his books?"

"He was never a big fan of our everyday lives and world. It just wasn't good enough for him. Even as a kid, he had the most vivid imagination. I remember how he used to lay in this very garden for hours when he was ten years old. He would cook up the most fantastic stories about the clouds that would pass. A fire-breathing dragon locked in combat with a starship from the future. An unknown race of magicians, overseeing us and controlling the tiniest details of our lives. I didn't even know ten year olds could imagine such things."

Sandy! SANDY! What are you doing lying down in the balcony at 2 in the morning! It's freezing outside! You'll catch a cold!

Mom... imagine if there's another kid like me living on a planet that revolves around that star, and looking up at our sun and imagining the same thing!

I'm putting you to bed, mister! You and your silly fantasies!

"HEY KID!" Sandy snapped out of his childhood memory.

"Sorry... I was wondering the same thing... how could a kid so young have an imagination like that."

"Saleem was a special kid. He wasn't big on talk. He didn't like meeting people, or even going to school. His parents were always concerned that he would never have friends. But Saleem didn't need friends. He had his stories to keep him company. When he needed friends, he would just imagine them and have a sandwich party with them in the garden. Many years later, when he had finished a book and was back from the place where he went to when he wrote, he told me that reality only held him back. He said that one day he'll write a story worth losing himself over. I never quite figured out what that meant."

The Lost Story, Sandy almost said out loud, but stopped himself.

Sandy was fascinated by the stories of the young Saleem Afzal. He decided to stay on for an extra day to spend some more time with Ahmed Sultan, so he could learn more about Saleem. But right now, he had the matter of the key to attend to.

"Sir, I actually came to meet you with a specific agenda. I was wondering…"

"DAMN THOSE PESTS! YOU BOYS! GET AWAY FROM THOSE FLOWERS!"

Sandy was startled by the sudden burst of anger. He saw two boys trying to pluck some flowers from across the fence. Sandy reckoned this was a usual routine to irk the old man. Sandy felt irritated at the boys. *How can they be so inconsiderate towards a poor old man.*

Ahmed hobbled towards the fence shouting "Bhu! Bhu! Bhu!" Sandy reckoned he wanted to say *bhaag*, but the shortness of breath reduced it to *Bhu*. Right on cue, the boys squealed with laughter and made a run for it as they sang at him, "*Bhu-baba aaya! Bhu-baba aaya!*"

The effort had knocked the wind out of Ahmed. Sandy rushed to him.

"Can I get you some water?"

"No... I'm going to be... all right... come back... tomorrow, all right...? Come in a little early... when these irritating brats... are at school..."

Sandy stuck around till Ahmed caught his breath. He then left, closing the garden gate behind him. He turned around to look at Ahmed Sultan after walking down the road a bit. The old man had gone back to watering his Dahlias, looking exactly as he was when Sandy had walked up to his house.

CHAPTER 8

The Annoying Old Man

"So did you find that Ahmed Sultan you were looking for?"

It was 8 PM. Sandy was sitting outside on the deck of the hotel. It was a chilly night, but the deck offered an experience unlike any other. There was a gentle breeze about, and he could make out the silhouette of the surrounding mountains in the moonless night by the light of the countless stars in the sky. The polluted skies of Delhi never offered such a beautiful view. The music of Pink Floyd that played on the speakers made everything other-worldly. Sandy felt disconnected from everything – from the burden of matching the steps of the great Saleem Afzal, from the pain of losing the love of his life. His life in Delhi felt like a dream, and he could almost feel himself slowly fading away into an entirely different world before he was rudely dragged back by the manager.

Sandy felt a wave of irritation, but he controlled his urge to tell off the manager. Instead, he smiled.

"Yes, I did. Thank You."

"I asked the chef about him. He told me that the old man has grown senile with age, and is known to ambush and beat young children that pass his house."

Sandy could not control his anger this time.

"Did he also tell you that the same kids harass him by trying to uproot his garden? Just because he's old and different, you will accept any outlandish nonsense about a harmless old man."

The manager was taken aback by the backlash. He murmured an apology and excused himself. Sandy took a deep breath to calm himself down. He wondered if he had overreacted, but came to the conclusion that the manager had deserved the verbal lashing.

Sandy stared at the shimmering lights from Nanital on the distant hill beyond the lake. The sight had a calming effect on him. He leaned back in his chair and looked up. The sky was draped in a blanket of stars. Sandy's mind drifted to Tara.

'How I wish she was here.'

Sandy immediately pushed the thought away, and began to imagine how his life would change after this book. Would he become a celebrity overnight? Or would he be forgotten in the ripples that the return of Saleem Afzal would create in the litary world? Would Tara come back to him?

'You sound obsessed,' she had said.

Annoyed by recurring thoughts of her, Sandy looked around and caught the manager talking to a young couple sitting on the other end of the deck. He went back to thinking about what the manager had said.

'Poor Ahmed... old people have it tough,' he thought.

He suddenly had an idea for a story. Sandy turned on his laptop and began to type.

I think it would be safe to say that I am a regular at this café near my house, since I spend about one-tenth of my waking hours there. When you spend so much time at a public place,

I suppose you become part of the furniture. You start interacting with the other, similar pieces of furniture and notice the odd, quirky guests who land up every now and then.

About a couple of months ago, an old man started visiting the café. He was short, with a slight stoop and wore clothes which were probably two sizes too big for him. His hair was pure-white and stood up in odd places, as if from a bad haircut. Judging by his pale skin and shaky walk, I estimated that he must have been about seventy years old.

In the beginning, he would walk into the café and straight to the counter. The boys behind the counter would smile uncomfortably at him, as they made conversation with the old man. He would then shuffle over to the newspaper stand in the corner by the glass wall and almost ransack the shelf. It was a little amusing to watch as he would clumsily and noisily fold the papers and stuff them back into the stand as while the staff sniggered at quiet jokes they cracked to each other. Then, he would stand near the door with his hands behind his back and scan the café through squinted eyes from behind white-bushy eyebrows. Finally, then, he would leave.

The ritual continued for about two or three weeks until one day, when I was sitting alone, he came up to me and said "Hi." I greeted him back in my usual friendly way and shook his extended hand. He asked me if I was having coffee and how many cups of coffee I had in a day. Before I could answer his previous questions, he told me that having too much coffee was bad for the heart. He chit-chatted for five minutes and left. All the while, he held on to my hand. It had started as a handshake, but he just didn't let go the whole time.

Soon, this became another ritual. He would come in around the same time every day, hold my hand and have the same conversation. *Was I having coffee? How many cups did I have in a day? Having too much coffee is bad for the heart.*

Once you're furniture, you start noticing small things about other pieces of furniture. I noticed how he would squint hard to look at me and then how his eyes would suddenly dart left and right. I noticed how he would still hold on to my hand even when I would try to wriggle out of it. To be very honest, it started to get very, *very annoying.*

One day, I went up to the boys behind the counter and inquired about the old man. They told me that he lived just around the corner and laughed at the fact that he was completely cuckoo in the head. I considered that in my assessment of him and agreed with them.

The ritual went on, annoyingly. Soon, I began adapting, and came up with ways to avoid him. Like an ostrich, I would try to avoid eye contact with him, hoping that he would not notice me and just walk by. Other times, I would pick up my phone and pretend to be on a call when he was around so that he would not disturb me. Sometimes he walked by, sometimes he still interrupted. I could also see the growing frustration of the café staff towards the old man. They had started worrying that he would soon start having a negative impact on their business as their other regular customers had also started complaining about the annoying old man.

Finally, about a couple of weeks ago, I was standing outside the café, talking on the phone, when I noticed the old man standing patiently behind me. I tried to stretch the conversation as much as I could, hoping that he would go away. He persisted and stood there. I disconnected the call and put the phone in my pocket and looked at him with a surprised expression. I acted as if I had not even seen him there, even as I began thinking of ways to wriggle out quickly.

We started the never ending handshake and the standard coffee conversation. He reminded me that too much coffee was bad for the heart. He complained to me that the café staff had started calling him names like 'mental' and 'nutcase.' I gave him friendly advice that he should not pay heed to such juvenile antics and simply ignore them. He squinted further into my eyes and said he would take my advice. He then started asking me about what I did, where I lived and how I felt about my country. I tried to keep my answers short and to the point, so as not to give him any new hooks to start another thread of conversation. The handshake had now gone on for more than ten minutes. I was becoming more and more annoyed. Finally, I told him that I had some work and that I had to go back inside. I don't remember, but I may have been a little rude.

Just before I forcefully pulled my hand from his grip, he told me that he was happy he had made friends with me, and then he left. I went back inside and joked to the café staff that the nutcase had really caught hold of me that time. The next couple of days, I completely avoided him with the fake phone call trick.

A few days later, I went back to the café. I walked in and had just settled down when one of the boys on the staff came up to me with a big grin on his face and declared that the old man would not be bothering 'us' anymore. They had apparently bribed a cop to teach him a lesson. The cop had pushed the old man around, and told him not to come to the café anymore.

I felt a little sad for the old man. His comment about how glad he was to have made friends with me came back to me.

A couple of weeks passed and we didn't see the old man.

The emotion of feeling sorry for the old man grew into a feeling of guilt. I imagined a burly cop roughing up the frail old man. I kept thinking to myself that the old man had probably just been looking for someone to talk to. I wondered if his kids were nice to him... Maybe they didn't even speak to him, which is why he tried talking to strangers just to be able to talk to someone. I thought about the handshake and realized that maybe he just wanted to feel a warm human touch, even if it was that of a stranger. I concluded that maybe he wasn't really insane. He was just desperate. Desperate to talk to someone. Desperate for human touch.

Even now, every now and then, I look up when the door opens hoping it will be the old man and I can shake his hand again and talk to him about coffee and how bad it is for the heart.

Sandy woke up in the morning and picked up his watch from the side table. It was 9 AM. He sat up in his bed and stretched out his arms. He had not slept so peacefully since the day he found out about Tara leaving.

He got up and walked to his laptop. He was surprised to see an email from Saleem Afzal.

"Wow!" he said to himself. "That was fast!" Sandy opened the email.

Sandy,
Here's the rest of the story. I'll probably be back home by the time you return to Delhi. See you then. Did you meet Ahmed?
Have you got it?

" *Saleem*

Sandy opened the attached word document and began reading.

"You expecting somebody?"

"Huh?"

"You keep looking at the door every 30 seconds as if you expect somebody to walk in."

"No... no... nothing like that."

Ajay went back to reading his book. He seemed lost today and was not his usual wise-cracking, arrogant self. I could tell that he wasn't really reading the book he had in his hands. I decided to persist.

"Dude. Seriously... what's up?"

"I... nothing... it's just..."

"Come on. I know you enough to be able to tell something isn't quite right. Is Payal giving you hell?"

Payal was Ajay's girlfriend. Hot like the devil, but with the personality to match. I couldn't imagine anyone other than Ajay being able to stand her, mostly because he was as intent on protecting his independence as she was on obliterating it. It was a recipe for disaster, and maybe it had started taking its toll on Ajay.

"No dude. Payal isn't the problem. At least not for now. And when she decides to be a problem... I know how to handle it."

"And how do you intend to handle it?"

"Adios Senorita," Ajay grinned. But whatever was nagging him lingered in his eyes. He stole another quick glance at the door.

"So what's the problem, then?"

"Well... all right."

I sat back and listened as Ajay told me about the old man.

I recalled seeing him once when I was sitting here with Ajay. He had told me to avoid eye contact, and pretend to talk on my phone to ensure he doesn't come over and start picking our brain.

I felt anger rise up to my throat when I heard how he had been manhandled by the policeman. Nutcase or not, no one deserves that. Certainly not a frail old man.

"I can't believe this! These guys did that?"

"Yes."

"Did you say anything to them?"

"About what?"

"About generally acting like insensitive idiots. If they know where he lives, they should go and apologize."

"I went there. The house has been locked for years. No one seemed to know about an old man... it seems these guys were wrong about his address."

I could see guilt in Ajay's eyes, even though he didn't have anything to do with it. And I could see he wasn't taking it very well. I decided to ease up on him.

"Maybe he was a ghost... like the done-to-death movie plot. This intriguing character that doesn't seem to exist, or died some 30 years ago. Usually it's a hot chick, but we'll roll with the old dude for lack of better options."

Ajay smiled weakly and fell silent. He decided to continue staring at his book as the waiter brought our cappuccinos. I looked around... the coffee shop was mostly empty, except for the usual crowd. There were the two guys in the corner, lost in their game of chess, as if nothing else in the world mattered. The couple who met every evening were probably having an affair outside their marriage; and for some strange reason, they felt compelled to exchange their halting vows of love in English, even when they were clearly not comfortable with the language. It was good for kicks.

"Maybe he was an assassin."

"What?" I was shaken out of my reverie by Ajay.

"The old man... maybe he was an assassin. Or a serial killer... he seemed zany enough to be one. Maybe he came down to scope out targets, the coffee-offenders of the world who promoted it by having too much of it."

Ajay was smiling, playing out the theatre of his imagination. It's something we both liked to do to pass time – create stories around people based on how they behaved while they hung out in the coffee shop. Like the two men in the corner, who controlled the global economy with their elaborate game of chess. Or how the group of Korean students, who would talk in hushed voices, were actually a delegation of aliens trying to figure out how to get past the bureaucracy and red-tapism to warn the government of an imminent collision of a comet with Earth.

"Maybe..." I replied. "Maybe he was a wizard... on an important mission to stop an evil wizard who's finally discovered that the vital ingredient for his potion to control the world was coffee beans."

"Yeah? Well then why did he need them from this particular coffee house? Maybe he was God himself."

"Well... if that's the case, we didn't make much of an impression, did we?"

Ajay fell silent, the smile wiped clean off his face. He opened his mouth to say something, but decided against it. I imagined a frail old man being beaten up by a burly cop. I imagined him being pushed outside the glass door, surprise in his eyes as he lost his balance and fell down the three steps, tears welling up in his eyes and a sharp pain he felt in his hip. I imagined him getting back up to his feet, slowly and groggily, as the policeman and the coffee shop staff stared him down. No remorse. No kindness. Only cruel smiles to go around. The aliens turned around to see what the commotion was all about, and then returned to the more pressing problems at hand. After all, there was a planet to be saved. The men controlling the global economy didn't even bother looking. Such things are trivial in the grand scheme at every turn of their game.

The anger rose in me again.

"What the hell. This is not even fair! An old man getting pushed around by those burly cops. And all we can do about it is sip coffee? He was probably lonely... just looking for a friend to talk to... someone to tell his stories to... and look at what he got! Seriously man. What's the point of coming up with these imaginary stories about people if we can't even bother with a real one?"

Ajay looked shocked at my sudden outburst. I was too angry to care.

"I mean – he's been around a long time. Who's to say he didn't have some fantastic tales to tell? But because he is old and different, we just choose to brand him a nutcase. And that's just a damn shame."

I decided I could not be in that place anymore. I picked my bag and stood up.

"Dude, I'm outta here. Let's pick a different place to meet next time. See you!"

Ajay did not utter a word. I strode out of the coffee shop to my car, threw the bag on to the back seat and decided to have a smoke before leaving to calm my nerves.

As I lit the cigarette, I could see, from the corner of my eye, someone looking at me intently. I turned to look in that direction, and found myself face to face with the old man. It was definitely him. He had taken me by surprise.

"Hi," he said.

"Uhh... hi."

"My name is Kailash," he said, with a wide smile on his face.

He offered me his hand.

"Hi, Kailash."

I shook his hand. He didn't seem to be in a hurry to let go of mine.

"Do you know what Kailash means? My dad would tell me every name means something..."

"No... not really..." I said.

"Do you come to this coffee house often? Do you like drinking coffee? How many cups do you drink every day?"

He was relentless, and I felt weird... as if I was being cross examined. I needed to get out of this. Especially the handshake.

"Umm... no... I don't drink coffee at all."

"Okay... do you live close by?" the old man asked.

"No."

"Where do you live? Can you give me your address? Your phone number?"

"Umm... I don't live in Delhi... just visiting a friend here," I lied.

"Can you give me your phone number?"

"Ahh... I don't carry a cell phone... I've heard it gives you brain tumour."

"Really? I will research this on the internet. My son got internet installed at home a week before he died."

I felt a pang of sympathy. He still wouldn't let go of my hand.

"Have you ever been abroad?" the old man continued without a break.

Paris. Monte Carlo. Salsburg. Munich. Vienna. Zurich. Bonn.

"No," I said. "I've never been outside India."

"My father had once gone to the USA. Have you been to the USA?"

"No." I decided to stick to speaking the fewest possible words.

"My father told me that USA is beautiful. Clean, organized... not like India. There are no traffic jams in USA, you know?"

"I didn't know that."

"Can you give me your email address? I will write an email to you so we can discuss this more."

I decided to give him my old hotmail ID... the one I didn't use anymore. He finally let go of my hand to take out a notepad and a pen from the front pocket of his shirt. I quickly put my hands in my pocket.

"Next time when you come to Delhi, will you meet me?"

"Sure," I lied.

"How will you find me?"

"I took your phone number down," I lied again.

"Oh... I gave you my phone number?"

"Yes," I lied. "Listen – I really need to go now, Kailash. It was... uhh... nice meeting you."

He smiled. I got into my car and turned on the ignition.

"You didn't tell me your name."

"Mayur," I lied.

And then I drove off.

"You love playing God, don't you?"

Saleem woke up with a sharp pain in his chest. On impulse, his hand moved to the bell on the side table that would call the nurse. But he stopped himself at the last moment, and forced himself to breathe heavily. The pain soon subsided to occasional dull throbs.

"This is not good," said Saleem softly, gently rubbing his chest.

"Do you have coffee?"

The voice had come from directly across the bed. Saleem squinted to make out a silhoutte of a man standing there.

"How many cups do you have in a day? Do you know coffee is bad for your heart?"

"Okay... so this is not real," said Saleem.

"What is not real?" asked the silhouette.

"This whole thing. It's another one of those dreams I have after we finish a story. I'm not sure how they come about. But this definitely is not real."

"What's real and what's not is a matter of perspective, Saleem. To me, this is the only reality. What you and that boy wrote for me."

"Then why are you here? We did not write this."

"True. But someone else did, right?"

"I do not understand." Saleem was groping for the switch of the table lamp, hoping to get a glimpse of the man's face. He found it and pressed the switch, but the light did not turn on.

"It won't work," said the old man. The voice was closer to Saleem now. He felt a little uneasy.

"Who are you?"

"I am anything you imagine me to be... an assassin, or a serial *killer, or a wizard from a secret order, or even God!"*

The voice was getting louder and coming closer. Saleem tried to move out of the bed, but for some inexplicable reason, he couldn't. When the voice spoke next, it was agitated.

"I mean... you could have made me anything! Anything at all! But you had to make me old... and fragile... and crazy... and helpless. I was ridiculed. I was insulted. I was lied to!"

The voice was getting angrier.

"You fucking writers! You and your world of make believe. You love playing God, don't you? But Gods fall too, you know...? And closer to the ground, you come to terms with the reality of your imagination. Do you want to know what it is, Saleem?"

"N... no, I don't," Saleem was terrified.

"It is not a pretty place. I'M GOING TO KILL YOU, SALEEM!"

Two hands gripped Saleem's neck tightly. Saleem grabbed the wrists and tried to loosen the grip, but he realized it was a losing battle. He struggled to break free, even as he felt the life trickle out of him.

Saleem woke up with a start. He immediately turned on the lamp on the side table and looked around. There was no one there.

"Just a nightmare," he murmured.

He went back to sleep. But he left the light on.

"You see that window there? On the far left of the house? That is the window to Saleem's study. He used to come here to finish his books. Did I tell you that?"

Ahmed continued without waiting for Sandy to answer.

"He used to say that this place was the portal to his world of make believe. And I could see it in his eyes that he really believed that. His eyes... they always seemed to be looking into another world, even when he was here. He was a different person altogether when he was writing. I could never quite figure out if it was a good thing or not. You remind me of him, you know."

Sandy looked up at Ahmed's face. He was gazing steadily at him with a smile on his face.

"How so?" asked Sandy.

"The look in your eyes. You have that same distant look in your eyes, like you are not entirely here."

Ahmed and Sandy were sitting in Ahmed's garden again. It had taken Sandy a few minutes to remind the old man who he was, and that they had met the previous day. But once he had remembered the meeting, Ahmed did not seem to have much trouble recollecting the details of their meeting.

Ahmed had talked at length about how the villagers harassed him, just because he never mixed with them. *There are rumours about me*, he had said, *both me and my house. That I am mad. And that my house is haunted by spirits. It is just something I encourage. Don't believe any of it.* Sandy did not intend to. Apart from the odd peculiarity, Ahmed Sultan came across an intelligent person.

"So, what do you do?" asked Ahmed.

"I am a writer, actually. Working on my first book." Sandy wasn't sure how Ahmed would react to the fact that Sandy was working with his nephew. For some unknown reason, he was strangely reluctant to divulge this to Ahmed.

"Oh yes, no wonder you are a friend of Saleem's." Ahmed

winked jovially at Sandy. Sandy had no clue why.

"So Mr Writer, do I get to see your first book in my lifetime?"

"Yes you, will sir. In fact, I will personally come and give you a copy."

Ahmed looked at him for a long time with an impassive face. Sandy was startled to see tears forming at the corner of his eyes.

"That's very nice of you," said Ahmed.

"It's not a big deal, sir. However, I had come here to ask you for a favour. Many years ago, Saleem and his friend Vishaal had left a key for you. Saleem has sent me to you for that key. Can I have it?"

Ahmed stared at Sandy, who could feel his heartbeat go up a few notches. Slowly, almost painfully, Ahmed got up and started walking towards the gate of the garden. When he reached the gate, he opened it and looked at Sandy.

"Get out," he said, in a voice that was both hurt and angry.

Sandy was taken by surprise. "Excuse me?"

"Get out. I thought you were different from the others. Who come to make fun of me and my house and try to steal my things and run away. But you are worse. You insult the memory of my dead nephew."

Sandy wasn't quite sure he heard that correctly. Ahmed went on.

"When you told me you were a friend of my nephew's, I decided to indulge you simply because I felt you were some student here to learn about him. But now you act as if you know him and he's sent you when, in fact, he has been dead for twenty-three years!"

Sandy felt as if the ground had slid from beneath his feet. He did not know what to say. Tears had started streaming down Ahmed's face.

"He was driving up here, the poor lad when he was killed in

that awful accident. And you stand here in *his* house, and spit on his grave? Don't you have any shame? Just so you can steal things from his house in the city. But I will never give you the key. LEAVE!"

Sandy did not know how to deal with this situation. The townsfolk were right about Ahmed Sultan. He *was* mad. Or could it just be years of erosion upon a feeble mind? Maybe he just needed a reminder. Maybe a phone call.

But not right now. If I make him speak to Saleem right now he'll just assume it to be another part of my elaborate prank to steal his damned Dahlias. I better come back tomorrow.

As Sandy was walking towards the gate, he caught a glimpse of something glinting in the sunlight on Ahmed Sultan's chest. Sandy saw a key strung around Ahmed's next with a black thread. Something told him that this was the key.

Come on Sandy, said the voice inside his head, *what are you waiting for? End this now.*

Sandy walked past Ahmed to the gate. Just as Ahmed shut it, Sandy swirled around, reached out, and grabbed the key. The thread broke easily, and Sandy had the key. With a triumphant look on his face, Sandy turned and ran.

Saleem had just finished packing his bag when he heard a soft knock on the door. He turned around to see a young girl standing outside. She was about five feet and two inches tall, with sharp features and oval eyes. She was wearing a pink shirt over jeans. She acknowledged him with a wide smile, but that was not enough to mask the stress on her face and in her eyes.

"Hello Tara," he said, smiling at her. She was taken by surprise.

"How did you know? You've never met me!"

"Well… it's my superpower. Besides, Sandy's talked a lot about you. It wasn't so hard to guess."

The smile faded completely from Tara's face at the mention of Sandy's name.

"Do you know where he is?" she asked, looking desperate. "I've been trying to reach him on his cell and home, but he wouldn't answer. I went to his place, but his mother told me he's out with his friends. Only, I know he isn't, because his friends haven't seen him for days. He's been so occupied with the book you guys are working on… almost as if he's in a different world altogether. He talked to me on occasion, but that was hardly enough. And things haven't exactly been great over the last few days. I'm sure he must have told you."

Saleem nodded. His mind had drifted to a memory he had buried in the deepest recesses of his mind.

You are my last link, Vidya… the only one I can talk to. You are the only thing that's real in my life. But I'm not sure if that's what I want.

"Sir?" said Tara, interrupting his train of thought.

"I'm sorry," said Saleem. "We old people tend to get tangled in our own head sometimes."

He smiled at her, but she did not smile in return. She kept looking at him expectantly, which was when Saleem realized that she was waiting for an answer.

"Oh! He's in Bhimtal. It's this small town near Nanital, where my uncle lives. I've sent him there on an errand."

Tara looked relieved. She sat down on the chair next to the bed. "I had been so worried. Thanks for telling me. When will he be back?"

"Any day now. I'm not exactly sure. But the task I gave him

should not take too long," said Saleem, hoping that that would be the case.

"A word of advice though," said Saleem. "Let him have his time away. He might not be able to deal with seeing you… at least not right now. He was very distraught."

Tara looked sad. She opened her mouth to say something, but stopped. She seemed to be making her mind up about something. A few moments later, she got over her hesitancy and began to talk.

"Was I wrong?" she said, "I mean – my family is moving there. I've always wanted to go and study at NTU. This is important to me. And I honestly feel that it is better to go our seperate ways while we are here rather than hold on to the notion of a long-distance relationship that never really works. But then… I really love him, you know? And that always ends up confusing me. I don't even know why I am telling you all this."

'I love you, Vidya, I really do. But I belong there. To my world and my stories… I feel compelled to be with them, in that place where they are born out of nothing. They may be figments of imagination, but they are so real to me.'

'What is it about stories that fascinates you, Saleem?'

'How they bend, Vidya, at a mere thought. You can turn the world upside down with your mind. You can make the most fabulous and the most horrific things, and imagine places that you could never go to.'

'I appreciate them too, Saleem, but your obsession is not healthy. You have to realize, that stories end too. And beyond them, there is a whole world outside.'

'I know… and that world is not worth it.'

'Even with me in it?'

'Even with you in it.'

"Sir?"

Saleem was shaken out of the memory of that fateful day by the girl sitting in front of him.

"I tuned off again? I'm sorry."

"Maybe I should come some other time?"

"Yes... that would be a good idea. Maybe in a couple of days... Come to my house. If you leave your number, I'll call you when Sandy comes back. You can meet him."

"I'm going to Singapore tonight... to see the kind of courses the university has to offer. You're right... Maybe a few days away will give me the time to think things over again. He's really special, you know... and I've been lucky to know him."

"So have I," said Saleem.

Tara got up to leave.

"I'm glad to have finally met you, sir. It's an honour. It's great that you are on your way to a full recovery."

Tell that to my heart, he almost said. The pain in his heart was mild, but constant. He was almost getting used to it.

"Thank you," he said instead.

CHAPTER 9
Wish You Were Here

You insult the memory of my dead nephew!

The words still echoed in Sandy's ears, a hundred kilometers away from Bhimtal, much like the laboured "Bhu! Bhu! Bhu!" of Ahmed Sultan chasing the pesky kids away.

Sandy pulled out the key from his pocket and stared at it.

What's so important about that room? Does it have the manuscript of the other book Saleem was writing? Is that what has been haunting him ever since his accident?

The thought of the accident brought back Ahmed Sultan's words.

What if he was right? What if Saleem is really dead and the Saleem I know is just a ghost? Or maybe an impostor?

Sandy dismissed the thought as quickly as it came to him. He had talked to so many people who knew Saleem. *Saner people*. Surely, one of them would have brought up the fact that he's been dead for many years.

But Sandy knew that something wasn't quite right. This was something outside the realm of normal.

Is Saleem haunted by ghosts? Or is it some sort of paranoia? What is my role in all of this? Why am I doing this?

There were too many questions.

The answers will have to wait, thought Sandy, *there is a book waiting to be finished.* All this talk of ghosts and the dead coming back to life had given Sandy an idea for a story.

He held the letter typed on bond paper in his hands and read it again for the seventh time.

"DEAR MOYUK

IT GIVES US GREAT PLEASURE TO INFORM YOU THAT YOU ARE PROMOTED TO 'BRANCH MANAGER – GURGAON, PHASE – 1 BRANCH,' EFFECTIVE…"

He was overwhelmed with a sense of pride and accomplishment as he recalled the years of hard-work, months of successfully chasing targets, and hours of overtime that he had put in. For a small town boy like Moyuk, orphaned at the age of eleven, it was a very big achievement that he had risen to the role of a branch manager of a multinational bank almost as fast as management graduates from the best business schools did.

Life has finally started paying off, he thought to himself.

I wish my parents were alive. They would have been so happy to know of my achievement. They would have shared all the joys and sorrows of the last two decades with me, had that road accident not happened.

He folded the letter and put it back in his bag and shook off the sense of loss.

Moyuk had been given a week to move and was expected to take on the new role by the next Monday. He met his current landlords the same evening with a box of sweets and told them about the move, and offered them a month's rent in lieu of notice, an offer they cordially accepted.

Next, he called a property dealer in Gurgaon and told him requirements and expectations. *Ten thousand rupees rent, and not a penny more,* Moyuk had repeatedly impressed upon the property dealer. They agreed to meet on Saturday and go house hunting.

Moyuk smirked at the mind-set of the Indian landlord after answering the string of questions the property dealer had assailed him with.

Only married families with kids or single saints who have sworn to be celibate can get a house. A reclusive serial killer who doesn't smoke, drink or eat non-vegetarian food has a higher probability of being accepted as a tenant than a working professional with a girlfriend, who occasionally eats non-vegetarian food.

The next few days passed very quickly as he hurriedly tied up the loose ends at his present position. All the while, his excitement of the new role, new responsibilities and a better life kept growing. He saw himself sitting in his own cabin with a nameplate on the door.

On Saturday, Moyuk got up early and took the metro to Gurgaon to meet the broker who was waiting at the station. They exchanged greetings and were on their way to the first house. Moyuk felt that the broker was a little more chatty than normal.

But then they always are, he thought to himself.

"Sir, this first house is a very nice place. All managers live in this area. It's newly constructed, fully furnished and with a modular kitchen." The broker drove them to their first destination.

Moyuk spent about fifteen minutes inspecting the place and quite liked it. He finally inquired about the rent.

"Eighteen thousand per month, sir." The broker said with a big beaming smile on his face.

"I already told you... I have a specific budget and I would appreciate it, if you would show me houses within that budget."

"Sure, sir. Though I would like to inform you that houses within that budget are small squatty places where students stay. But if you insist..."

"Let's go and have a look." Moyuk was aware of his budget limitations and knew that he needed to be strict with property dealers.

The day progressed but all the houses that the broker showed Moyuk were either too small, too dirty, too noisy or too expensive. Some didn't even have a parking space for Moyuk's car.

Six hours passed and the June heat began taking its toll. Both of them knew that the possibility of the search ending in a successful result was getting weaker with every passing minute. Moyuk, however, knew that he had to persevere.

You only have to look hard enough and long enough to find the right bargain.

Eventually, the broker gave in.

"That's it, sir. That's the last of the places I had. I told you right in the beginning that you would not like any of them. And that's all you'll get in your budget."

Moyuk knew pressure tactics too well. Years of being in sales had taught him how to deal with them.

"Fine. I suppose I will pass on the right feedback to everybody else regarding your services."

The broker did not even try to establish eye contact.

"Just drop me back to the metro station," Moyuk told him coldly while looking the other way.

After about half a minute of silence, the broker finally replied.

"I just remembered, sir. There is this one more place. I'm not sure if it is taken. But I think it'll fit your budget and your requirements. It's just that the building is quite old. Would you like me to check?"

Moyuk sighed heavily.

"Well you've wasted most of my day, anyway. I suppose one more house would not really hurt. But make it quick."

He watched as the broker took out his phone and spoke into it.

"It's available, sir, and it's not too far from here."

"Fantastic, let's go check it out." Moyuk said as he smiled to himself.

You just have to look hard enough and long enough and you'll find the right bargain.

The two reached a peaceful apartment block that was lined around a square-shaped park. The apartment block looked as though well-to-do businessmen and professionals lived here. It had a tranquil and distinctly *rich* feel about it. Moyuk had a good feeling about the place.

He looked to his left as the broker pulled up in front of a two storey house, shorter than the newer three-storied and four-storied houses all around. A staircase to the right of the house led upstairs to the first floor. The dust clogging the mesh in the doors made it evident that both the floors were uninhabited.

"The place is actually owned by a family that is now settled in the United States. They come maybe once a year and stay on the ground floor. The first floor is empty."

The broker looked uneasily at his watch. "It would be great if we could hurry this up, sir. I am going to be late for another client I'm supposed to meet."

"You have some nerve telling me to hurry up, after wasting my day. Show me around." Moyuk smiled as he followed the broker up the stairs.

The door of the house opened into a hallway, three feet wide and about thirty feet long. There were four doors in the hallway, two on each side. The air in the house felt cold and stale.

"It's a two bedroom flat, sir. First door on your left is the living room and on the right is the toilet-bathroom. The second door on the left is the kitchen and on the right is the bedroom. You can have a look."

Moyuk looked into the toilet-bathroom. It looked satisfactorily big and equipped. He came back out into the hallway and heard the broker on the stairs outside, speaking to what sounded like another client. He then walked into the living room that was well furnished and even had a television. He opened a door in the living room that led to the balcony. The canopy of a big tree almost covered the balcony. He thought it gave the balcony a cozy, private feel.

Next, he looked at the kitchen. It was sufficient for the basic cooking he did on his own. Finally, he walked into the bedroom. It was a regular room with a double bed and a television on the wall. He opened the cupboards to check for storage space. Standing there, he felt just the sense of peace and calm he wanted in a house.

Just perfect.

He opened a door in the bedroom, and found that it led to a narrow, iron staircase leading down into a small unkempt garden. The grass was long and wild. He concluded there was no caretaker for the house.

After looking through the house one final time, he came out into the hallway to find the broker still standing in the staircase and talking on the phone. He tapped him on his shoulder and signalled for them to descend.

"So, sir? What do you say?"

"I like the place. How much is the rent?" Moyuk sensed a deal.

"The landlords have quoted twelve thousand, sir. But I'm sure they'll settle for ten. After all, they are settled in the US now earning in dollars. What is a few thousands in Indian rupees to them?" The broker wiped the sweat off his forehead with a handkerchief.

"Perfect. Bring the papers tomorrow and get the house cleaned, I'll move in around afternoon. Let's go."

The next day was a long hectic day for Moyuk – Packing, moving, monitoring the careless workmen to ensure that they don't break any fragile stuff, haggling with the transporters for price, finishing up the paperwork with the broker at his office… it seemed interminable.

Moyuk was completely spent by the end of the day. He was exhausted, both physically and mentally. He was happy too, with the job, the house, his life. He went to sleep with a sense of satisfaction and excitement for the life that lay ahead of him.

The next three weeks passed in a flash. Taking over a whole branch, its operations and employees is not easy work. He spent many extra hours in office to figure out the dynamics of the place and his work. He reminded himself that it was hard work that had got him so far in the first place, and hence must continue. His girlfriend, Alka, came home a few times on weekends and they shared some happy, intimate moments.

On Tuesday afternoon, Moyuk sat hunched on his table with the weekly reports spread out in front of him. Business seemed to be on the upswing, and the numbers were looking strong. He sipped his tea as he turned the pages. His cellphone began to vibrate making a rattling sound on the table. He mechanically unlocked his phone and read the new message he had received. He froze.

"DEAR CUSTOMER, YOUR ACCOUNT 871xxxxx041 HAS BEEN DEBITED ON 26/03/11 BY INR 50,000.00 TOWARDS ATM CASH WITHDRAWL – INTERNATIONAL DEVELOPMENT BANK"

He blinked as his brain tried to process the information that his eyes had sent it. He could not understand the numbers. He thought it must be a misprint or something as he read the automated ATM message from his bank about a cash withdrawal. If this was true, it meant that almost all the money that Moyuk had in his bank account had been withdrawn. He began to panic, as the realization sank in. He reached for his wallet and panicked even more to find that his ATM debit card was missing.

He immediately picked up the phone, and called his assistant branch manager, Aarushi, and asked her to come to his cabin. He was sweating profusely as he tried to explain the situation to her.

"I .. I don't understand this. I withdrew five thousand rupees in the morning. I've been a banker for the last nine years. I never make these errors. I am always very careful with these things. There's no way I could have left my card in the machine and walked off."

"Calm down, Moyuk. Let me ask Security to access the video feed at the ATM. We'll find out who did this, and we'll get your money back. Just relax," Aarushi tried to calm him down as she dialled a few numbers and walked out of the cabin.

Half an hour passed. Moyuk was pacing up and down restlessly in his small cabin. He tried very hard to remember how and why he had left the card in the machine. All he could remember was withdrawing five thousand rupees.

The panic subsided just a tad, as his phone rang again and Aarushi's name flashed on the screen.

"Did you find out who it was?" Moyuk said as soon as he picked up the phone.

"Uhh... why don't you come down to the monitor room?" Aaurshi said, sounding uncertain.

Moyuk almost ran to the monitor room, where about twenty screens were lined up – all monitoring feeds from ATMs in the vicinity and sections of the branch office.

"This is very strange, Moyuk. We're perplexed as to how this could happen. Take a look..."

Aarushi looked a little confused as she bit her upper lip and pointed to one of the screens.

Moyuk looked at the monitor as the video skipped and rewound to the time he was in the ATM. He watched as he saw himself tap on the machine and wait for the cash. He picked up the cash from the machine, counted it and put it in his wallet, and turned around.

Aaurshi spoke as she stood on his left, watching the video.

"So you did withdraw five thousand rupees, as is registered in our records. You then left your card in the machine and walked out. Three minutes after you walked out, another man walked in and continued the transaction and withdrew fifty thousand rupees from your account. What's strange, however, is that this man, looks exactly like you! Only in different clothes. We don't know what to make of it!"

Moyuk watched in absolute horror as he saw himself on the

screen again, withdrawing fifty thousand rupees. He noticed the Pink Floyd T-shrit the man was wearing.

"What's even stranger… is that not only does he look exactly like me, but the clothes he's wearing… are also mine!"

Aarushi and the technician turned and looked at Moyuk in shock as he stared at the screen, which was now frozen on a frame of what looked like Moyuk in a Pink Floyd T-shirt.

Two hours later, Moyuk was sitting in his chair in his office trying to figure out… or remember what had happened. It was clear to him that he could not go to the authorities and report it as theft. The video made that impossible. He strained and replayed every bit of the day's events in his head, but could not figure out the mystery.

Then struck him. The Pink Floyd T-shirt.

He picked up the phone and instructed Aarushi not to tell anyone about all this.

"Also, tell that engineer in the monitor room the same. I'm going home for the day."

Moyuk was sweating in the car in spite the air conditioning. He parked his car outside his house and darted upstairs. As he reached the door, he heard his heart thumping through the silence of the house.

Calm down Moyuk, he told himself as he unlocked the door.

He ran to his bedroom, opened the cupboard and began rifling through his clothes stacked up in three columns.

This is strange! It's not there!

Panic struck him as he began taking the clothes out of the cupboard and throwing them on the bed. He ran to the bathroom and did the same with the dirty clothes in the washing machine.

Where is it?

Moyuk went back to the bedroom, picking through the

clothes lying on the bed one more time. He sat down. He could hear his heart beating like it was going to burst through his chest any second. He tried to remember the last time he had worn that T-shirt. Blank.

Relax. Make some tea first and then try to think again.

He walked to the kitchen and put some water on boil and sprinkled some tea leaves in it. He leaned over on the slab in the kitchen as he watched the water boil. All of a sudden, he felt as if somebody was breathing down on his right shoulder. An image of a man standing right behind him and staring at him with angry bloodshot eyes flashed in his mind.

He turned.

Nothing.

Moyuk shook his head as he turned. The image of the man standing behind him flashed in his mind again as he added some sugar to his tea.

He took out the milk from the fridge and just as he began pouring it into a cup, he heard a scream.

"Aaaaaaaaaaaaaaaaaaaaaaahhh!"

It was a long, painful scream. Filled with anger.

Moyuk froze. He thought the scream had come from his bedroom. He placed the cup on the kitchen slab and looked out of the kitchen door towards the bedroom door.

The house was very quiet all of a sudden. There was no sound at all, not even the sound of traffic from the road outside. His legs felt heavy as he walked slowly towards the bedroom. He felt like his every move and every action was being watched.

He grabbed the door frame with his right fist and took a deep breath as he walked into the room. Nothing.

He felt extremely exposed, as if someone was watching him from behind the door he had just walked through. He tried not to think about the man with bloodshot eyes.

It's just nerves. He tried to reason.

He walked towards the other door in the bedroom, the one that led to the garden downstairs. It was locked from the inside. He had never opened the door since he had moved in. He opened it.

He stepped on the rusty staircase and looked down into the garden. A mountain of fear came crashing down on him.

There it was – his Pink Floyd T-shirt, lying spread out in the garden... shredded into pieces.

Saleem woke up with a piercing pain in his chest. His heart was protesting against the very notion of his existence. He had dozed off in his living room, where he had been reading Sandy's story.

Saleem clutched his chest and tried to breathe.

"Just hang on for a while, all right?" he said to the empty room. As if on cue, the pain dropped back to its usual level. Saleem leaned sideways to pick up his watch from the side table, when he noticed something unusual to his left. He turned to look, and his eyes widened with surprise. The door of the room was wide open.

Saleem stared at the door for a few minutes, but nothing happened. No monsters emerged.

"Sandy?" Saleem called out.

"He's not here, Saleem," spoke a voice that was everywhere and nowhere in the room.

"What's in there?" said Saleem.

"You'll have to go in and find out."

Saleem started to get up.

"Not so fast!" said the voice. "There's still one last story to finish."

Saleem looked at the glowing screen of his laptop.

"Can I go in after I finish it?"

"Yes. You can."

Saleem nodded. He picked up his laptop and began to write, stealing glances at the open door every now and then.

"OK STOP!"

"What? Come on, baby... You can't stop me right in the middle of it!"

"No! I'm too scared... You can't do this to me!"

Shruti jumped off the bed and sat on the chair adjacent to it. She stretched out and picked up the pack of smokes on the side-table next to the bed and lit one up. She took a deep drag, and then slowly exhaled the smoke, using the last bit of the spent smoke to make perfectly circular smoke rings.

"Wow! You have to teach me how to do that."

"Go away," said Shruti, ignoring Gopal's outstretched hand which signalled for the pack of smokes. "I'm not teaching you anything, and you're certainly not bumming any cigarettes off me, especially after nearly scaring me to death."

"Scaring you to death?!" Gopal imitated Shruti in an exaggerated manner, prompting her to reach out and slap his knee. "Shruti that was just a story! How can a simple story scare you to death?"

"For one, it is based in the same bloody house we're in right now... that too, alone! On top of that – you said it's a true story!"

Gopal snatched the cigarette out of Shruti's hand, and took a long drag.

"Shruti... it's just a story! I said it's real just to give it a touch of authenticity. There's no guy called Moyuk who lived in this house."

"Then why did you say so?"

"'Because that's how ghost stories are, right? They're spookier if they're set in the same place as the story-teller. That's why every time you go to an old palace or fort, the guide will take you to a specific room and tell you about the ghost of the long-dead beautiful queen who lived there and who still haunts the palace. It's for effect! Now let me finish!"

"NO!" protested Shruti, and got up to leave the room.

"Where are you going?"

"I need something to drink. Will you have something?"

"There must be some Pepsi in the fridge. Get some for me too!"

Gopal leaned on the headboard and took another drag at the cigarette. He was quite pleased with the way he had cooked up the story. It was much better than the way his neighbour had told it to him when he had first moved in. He could hear Shruti rummaging in the cupboard for glasses.

"I don't really get it, Shruti." Gopal called out to her. "What is it about ghost stories that scares you? I mean – they're all the same. Some evil spirit, or some tortured soul seeking peace or closure. They're so damn predictable all the time. So what's so scary about them, anyway?"

"The scary thing is Gopal…"

Gopal jumped. He turned to his left and saw Shruti sitting next to him, holding out the glass of Pepsi. She seemed unperturbed by him getting startled.

When did she come back into the room? I've been facing the door all this while. I didn't see her walk in.

"Do you want this or not, Gopal?" Shruti asked him.

"Y… yeah… of course!" stammered Gopal and took the glass.

"Anyway, it isn't the stupid idea of spirits or ghosts or monsters that's scary. I can deal with those just fine. It's the whole uncertainty… the whole… how do I put it…? The whole looking over your shoulder bit. Everything seems in place, and then all of sudden, something moves behind you. I see that, or imagine that, and I end up looking over my shoulder for a long time even after the story is done. That is the scary part."

Shruti continued to stare into Gopal's eyes, unblinkingly. Gopal felt queasy. Something wasn't right. He was still trying to figure when exactly Shruti entered the room when all of a sudden, he saw something move in the corridor, out of the corner of his eye.

"Hey! What was that?" he yelled.

"What?"

"I just saw someone move across the corridor outside the room."

"Now who's getting spooked?" Shruti teased.

"Shruti! I'm serious… it could be a burglar!"

"Gopal, you're scaring me!"

"Listen – stay here. I'll go check…" Gopal said.

"Gopal…"

"Shruti, I'm sure I saw something. It's probably nothing. But let me just check, all right?"

Gopal got out of the bed and moved slowly and cautiously out into the corridor. The movement had been towards the living room and the bathroom. He could see that the bathroom door was latched shut from the outside, but the living room door was open. Gopal tip-toed towards the living room. He could hear his heart beating.

The burglar might jump at me as soon as I enter the room. Okay, Gopal. Calm down. Step one – move your hand quickly to the wall on the left and switch on the light. And if someone's really there… well… those kick boxing lessons should come in handy.

The thought of his kick boxing classes made him feel braver. He moved to the door, and composed himself to spring the surprise. Gopal took a deep breath, and made his move. He turned on the light instantly, and got ready to attack.

There was no one there.

Gopal let out a sigh of relief. Just to be sure, he checked behind the sofa and the television. He heard a soft cough right behind him. The hair on the back of his neck stood up, and Gopal whirled around. Shruti was standing at the door, staring at him calmly, as if lost in the sight of him.

"Gopal."

There wasn't any panic or urgency in her voice, but something wasn't quite right. She had spoken in a flat monotone which was quite unlike her, and she continued to look at him right in the eyes without blinking.

"What Shruti?"

"Come with me."

She turned immediately and began walking towards the bedroom, without even waiting for him. Gopal followed her. The other door in the bedroom was open. Gopal looked at Shruti and raised an eyebrow.

"Look outside."

The same flat tone.

Gopal walked past Shruti, and noticed how her eyes never left him. He stepped outside on to the rusty staircase and saw something that knocked the wind out of him.

A Pink Floyd T-Shirt lay on the grass. It fluttered gently with the wind. Gopal could see that the front was shredded to pieces.

"Gopal."

The same voice. Dull. Monotonous.

Lifeless.

Gopal did not want to turn around.

"That's just a bucket of horse shit!"

Anirudh, Prakash, Jerry, and Kunal were leaning on the boundary wall of the garden. The grass had grown almost knee high. They could see a dirty old T-shirt lying in the middle of the park. The front was shredded.

At the far end, a flight of rusty old stairs led to the house on the first floor.

They had stepped out to play Cricket, but it was too hot. They were leaning against the wall and contemplating whose house they should go to. A visit to Jerry's house seemed most inviting, since he had recently discovered the location of his Dad's stash of *Playboy* magazines. They were almost ready to leave, when Anirudh noticed which house they were next to and decided to tell them the story.

"I'm not buying it!" said Kunal.

"It's true, dude!" protested Anirudh.

"So let me get this straight. One night, the guy who used to live here was telling his girlfriend a true story about how the previous tenant of the house was haunted. And then the couple got attacked by the ghost who haunts the house."

"Yes. Why do you think no one lives here? Because this house is haunted."

"C'mon dude! That's the problem with people these days – they see a house, or a building, or anything that's been abandoned for a while, and they decide to make a ghost story out of it. Give it a rest."

"I'm not saying every abandoned house is haunted. But there

are some pretty strange stories floating around about this one. Go to the RWA office and you'll see a notice that says that this house – even the garden – is strictly off-limits."

"Oh yeah? Well, watch this."

Kunal hauled himself over the wall, and jumped to the other side. His friends, shocked at this sudden move, stepped back.

"Come on, guys!" said Kunal in an exasperated tone, "Look – I'm right here! Do you see any paranormal activity? Don't be scared, you pansies! Besides, ghosts don't attack during the day."

"Kunal," Prakash spoke for the first time in a while, "I don't care whether this house is haunted or not. But please come back. I don't like this. Look around – there's absolutely no one here… What if something happens?"

"What if what happens?" shouted Kunal. He was very angry at his friends for being so unbelievably daft. "There. Are. No. Ghosts. People just like haunted house stories and make them up for every house that hasn't been lived in for a while. And you guys are stupid to believe them."

"There could be snakes in there," suggested Jerry.

"You know, Jerry, that actually makes sense. But just to teach these two a valuable lesson, I'm going to go down to the centre of the garden and bring back the infamous Pink Floyd T-Shirt."

"NO! Don't do that!" moaned Anirudh.

Kunal turned resolutely and began walking towards the T-shirt. He couldn't believe how stupid his friends had turned out to be.

What's with the infatuation with ghost stories? Why can't someone let ghosts live a little and go to more lively places? Like a nightclub, or a bowling alley, or a shopping mall. People just like to sit around fireplaces in the dead of the night and talk about ghosts in an abandoned wing of their college, or a forgotten construction site, or a lonely highway, or in this case, an empty house.

His train of thought was broken by a soft cough behind him. Kunal turned around to see if any of his friends had finally grown some balls and followed him in. They were all still hanging on the other side of the wall. None of them seemed to be breathing.

Gutless cowards. Dismissing the cough as a figment of his imagination, Kunal continued walking towards the T-shirt. He noticed for the first time how quiet it had become. He could hear himself breathing.

Kunal bent down to pick up the T-shirt. Had it not been shredded, it would have been a pretty cool T-shirt to have. He could see that the front of the T-shirt had been the album cover of *Wish You Were Here*. Just as he began to pick up the T-shirt, a drop of rain fell on it.

"Funny... there are no clouds..."

Kunal looked again and saw that it wasn't water at all. It was red in colour. Just then, another drop fell on the back of his hand.

He looked up, and saw a dead body hanging right above him.

Kunal yelled as he tried to back away, but fell down.

Where did this body come from? What the hell is going on?

Before Kunal could voice these thoughts, he realised, to his horror, that the body that had appeared out of thin air was *his own*. His neck was hanging through a noose, and its wrists were slashed and dripping blood.

"What the hell!" He shouted.

Kunal turned around, only to see that his friends weren't there anymore. He turned to look at the body (*his* body) hanging from the tree.

All of a sudden, it opened its eyes. Kunal opened his mouth to scream.

It was great weather for a summer night.

Mayank had stepped out for a smoke, making the excuse of needing a walk because of the excessive heat inside the house. There had been no electricity for four hours. It just added to his irritation. He was already annoyed that his room was going to be occupied by some distant relatives from out of town for three days. And they talked so much. Even now, after having exhausted all the possibilities of the bright future of some distant cousin who had snagged a nifty promotion in a reputed bank in Gurgaon, the conversation had turned to their supposed paranormal experiences. Mayank could not take it anymore.

It's funny how everyone likes telling ghost stories in situations that are most conducive to ghosts. In dark houses, around a fireplace, on a picnic in the lonely woods, or in a lone car on a deserted highway. Almost as if they were wishing for trouble.

Mayank's iPod was belting out Pink Floyd tracks. They went very well with the weather. As Mayank pulled a drag, he turned his head to the left.

"Aah. The Haunted House and its garden. Maybe I should bring all those guys here."

His Dad had been just regaling his wide-eyed relatives with the story of this haunted house, and how four boys had disappeared into it a few months ago. They had been last seen outside this house.

Mayank had chuckled at that. He remembered how his father had always told him to stay away from that house. It was a different story each time, once about some guy who was with his fiance in the house, another time about an unsuspecting tenant who got assailed by whatever it was that haunted the house.

Mayank never really gave it a thought. Tonight, partly due to all the conversation in the house and partly because he wanted to delay going back as much as he could, he came to a halt and turned to face the house, though from a respectable distance. Not that he believed in ghosts, but who knows for sure?

He thought about all the stories he had heard... What if the guy and girl had just run away because of their uncompromising families? What if those boys had been in the company of the wrong sort of crowd and one day they just disappeared? What if the bank manager had been siphoning off money from his bank, and finally got caught?

Sometimes, it is just easier to blame everything on ghosts and move on with life, thought Mayank.

All of a sudden, he heard a gentle cough behind him. The hair on the back of his head moved, as if the person who had coughed was standing right behind him. Mayank froze in his tracks, too afraid to turn around.

Finally it dawned on to him. Mayank began to laugh, and turned around. As expected, there was no one there. He pulled out his iPod to check the song.

He was right... it was *Wish You Were Here*. He remembered how there is a cough in the 26th second of the song by David Gilmour. And the breeze had chipped in to give him his own paranormal experience.

Mayank started walking back home.

In the gentle wind, the T-shirt moved slowly, as if someone was slowly turning it over. If you looked closely, you could still make out the lyrics of the titular song of the album on its mud-stained back.

We're just two lost souls swimming in a fish bowl
Year after year
Running over the same old ground
What have we found? The same old fears
Wish you were here

The wind sighed one last time.

"The fact that they end."

Sandy was in the middle of the strangest bus ride of his life.

It was unusually quiet in the bus. He had a lingering feeling that people were stealing glances at him when he was not looking. As if that wasn't enough, the bus had not stopped at all after picking him until he reached his stop... almost as if the driver was in a hurry to take him to Saleem.

He had received an email from Saleem the previous night, with the finished story.

Come to my house at 4 PM. It's time to end this.
Saleem

Sandy walked into the compound of Saleem's building. It was eerily empty... even the guard usually stationed at the gate was missing. Sandy's anxiety increased at this, but he walked on, regardless.

The door to Saleem's house was open. As soon as Sandy walked in, he was startled by the sight of so many people in the living room. There was Vidya, standing at Saleem's bedroom door, talking to Vishaal. Two men sat at the sofa, not doing anything. Sandy was pretty sure that they were Guru and Vineet. As soon as Sandy entered, they all turned to look at him.

They have been waiting for me.

"Hello Sandy," said Vidya.

"Where's Saleem?" asked Sandy in a shaky voice. "He told me to be here at four."

"Yes... It's finally time."

"Time for what?"

"To finish the Lost Story," Vidya said.

Sandy was getting increasingly bewildered. "Where is Saleem? Will someone tell me what's going on here?"

"It's not our place to tell you that, Sandy," said Vidya.

"Then who?" barked Sandy.

"You have the key; don't you?"

Sandy reached into his pocket, and pulled out the key he had taken from Ahmed Sultan in Bhimtal. He heard whispers in his ears. They drew him to the door.

Sandy slowly moved towards the locked door, feeling as if both his feet were chained to granite blocks. He did not have a good feeling about this. At the same time, he felt an acute sense of déjà vu.

"Have I been here before?" he thought out loud, looking around at everyone hoping for a response. He got none. Slowly, all the colours around him dissolved into shades of black, white and grey. Sandy was rooted to his spot, his heart beating fast and his eyes widening in fear as the bizarre events of the day reached their crescendo.

All of a sudden, everything around him seemed to dissolve into darkness. There was only Sandy, and the locked door.

"Come on, kid," said Saleem's voice. "I don't have all the time in the world."

Saleem's voice soothed Sandy's mind.

"Where are you?" he said.

"Come find me," said Saleem's voice, as if from a distance.

Sandy made up his mind. He was going to see this through to the end. He walked up to the door and turned the key in the lock. He dragged out the bolt and pushed the door open. He could only see darkness inside.

He hesitated again.

"What is it about stories that fascinates you?"

"The fact that they end."
"Then end this one."
Sandy walked into the darkness through the open door…

CHAPTER 10
The Lost Story

Sandy heard the door shut behind him just as he crossed the threshold. There was absolute silence as he stood in the opaque darkness. He felt it wrap itself around his skin. The absence of sight and sound completely disorientated Sandy, and he began to feel claustrophobic and nauseous. He felt his heart thumping in his chest, while he strained to catch a sensory stimulus of any kind.

Finally, after a few long seconds of panic, he began to be able to make out some vague outlines in the distance as his eyes adjusted to the darkness.

They looked like mountains at a distance surrounding a lake. It felt like he was standing on a balcony. He watched in fear and confusion as nature's sunrise orchestra began its performance all around him.

Where am I? And how the hell did I get here?

He heard what sounded like musicians softly striking the triangular chimes just as the sky over the mountain began to be illuminated with a soft, warm glow. The flutes joined in as the now orange glow filled the rest of the sky in front of him. The dark mountain ranges around him seemed to suddenly take shape as light fell on them. Violins and cellos added melody to the mesmerizing score as spectacular mixtures of yellow and fiery red lit up the sky behind the mountains in the east. The lake reflected the colours of the sky, creating an almost menacing effect – fire above, and fire below.

Where is this music coming from? What have I got myself into? Where's Saleem?

He heard the rising crescendo of the drums, snares and trumpets as the majestic sun rose in the east. He struggled to make sense of the torrent of thoughts in his head. The music played on as sunlight filled the valley, and a million ripples shimmered and glittered on the lake.

That's quite a sight! That looks like the lake from...

"Saheb, the cab is here. Are you ready to leave?"

Sandy froze.

Who could that be?

"Sandy Saheb..."

He turned around slowly to find an old man standing behind him. He was short, with a slight stoop and wore clothes that were two sizes big for him. His hair was pure-white, and stood up in odd places as if from a bad haircut. Judging by his pale skin and shaky walk, Sandy estimated that he must be about seventy years old.

"Who... Who are you?"

"Saheb it's me, Pratap. Shall I take your bags to the cab?" Pratap squinted as he hobbled towards the bags lying on the floor.

"Haven't I seen you somewhere? How did I get here? And where is the cab taking me?"

"It is *I* who should be asking *you* how we got here, Saheb... But I stopped thinking about it a long time ago." The old man shook his head slightly as he stared at his feet.

"Anyhow, don't you remember, Saheb? You booked a cab yesterday to go look for the Lost Story; and then to go meet your wife, Tara."

The old man, who called himself Pratap, picked up the bags and walked out of the guest house where a cab was waiting. Sandy, perplexed, followed him.

I don't understand any of this. Tara – My wife?

"I have kept yesterday's newspaper in the cab, Saheb. You should be heading out quickly or you might be too late. You don't have much time." The old man kept the luggage in the boot of the car and quickly scurried back into the guest house.

The driver walked up to Sandy and joined his palms in greeting.

"Good morning, Sandy Saheb. I am Ketu, Rahu's brother. He couldn't come today as he is in the hospital. He was drunk last night and got into a fight. Someone attacked him brutally with a broken bottle. But don't worry… I'll take you to Tara madam. Rahu told me he'll meet us there." Ketu was smiling.

Rahu? Ketu?

For a moment, Sandy abandoned his confusion as an inexplicable fear for Tara's life gripped his mind.

"No! I know what you guys do! I don't want you, or your brother, anywhere near Tara!"

Sandy was angry and terrified. Scenes of a murdered Tara flashed in front of his eyes as he imagined Rahu strangling her and laughing while he did so.

"Sandy, Saheb! You are digressing. Today we are going to find the Lost Story. Nothing else. I promise!"

Sandy, in an attempt to calm himself down, told himself that whatever this was could not be real. He was here, somehow, to find the lost story. He forced himself to believe it. But this brought with it a heavy sadness as he remembered that he wasn't actually married to Tara. On the contrary, she wasn't going to be around him anymore.

"Let's go." Sandy got into the car as Ketu drove out from

the guest house's porch and onto the hill road.

Sandy decided to rid himself of thoughts of Tara as he picked up the newspaper lying next to him.

He flipped through the boring article about national and state politics, accidents and local business news.

This is not yesterday's newspaper. I feel like I've read all this years ago.

Sandy flipped through the pages until an article on the eighth page caught his eye. It was a picture of a hooded man embraced in a kiss with another man wearing a suit while policemen and reporters stood in the background, looking amused. The headline read, 'Stunned Cops Arrest Blast Suspect' and then, in a smaller typeface below it, 'Suspect Alleges Molestation.'

Sandy smiled as he remembered what he had done to Morgan once Saleem had handed it over to him. He had derived a sinister satisfaction in turning Morgan's life over on its head.

"Sandy Saheb..."

Ketu interrupted his thoughts, and he looked up at the reflection of his eyes in the rear view mirror.

"What is it?"

"Remember, you have to find The Lost Story." Ketu's eyes had a mischievous but ominous glimmer in them.

"What do you mean by '*remember*'? I know what I have to do."

Ketu turned all the way around and looked at Sandy. He was grinning like a madman.

"Sandy, I'm just saying that you should try to not forget this time."

"Ketu, you should really be watching the ro... KETU, WATCH OUT!"

Ketu turned the wheel wildly to the left and the car swerved off the edge – into the drop. Sandy screamed in horror as he watched the road end and the view in the windscreen change to what looked like an endless fall. Ketu was not just smiling anymore. He was laughing hysterically as he turned and looked at Sandy again.

"Alright, Sandy. See you soon!"

With one last hysterical laugh he opened the door and jumped out of the plunging car.

The car crashed and tumbled along the wall of the cliff as Sandy was thrown and crushed along the inside walls of the car.

NO! THIS CANNOT BE HAPPENING. IF THIS IS A DREAM, IT NEEDS TO END NOW!

At that moment, as if on cue, the car stopped shaking and bouncing. It felt as if it was falling steadily into darkness. The mountains and the pit had disappeared.

Sandy was floating in the car now.

He pulled himself towards the wheel and tried to keep himself steady on the driver's seat, but was finding it hard to adjust to the sudden loss in gravity – something he had always taken for granted, *just like reality.*

He looked up in front of him and saw a rock that looked like images of Earth taken from outer space. The rock was quickly becoming larger and larger.

It looked beautiful.

"RECON DRONE APPROACHING PLANET EARTH."

The car radio kicked into life.

"RE-ENTRY SEQUENCE INITIALIZED."

Re-entry sequence? This can't be! I know exactly how this ends! We are going to crash!

"RE-ENTRY SHIELD AT ONE HUNDRED PERCENT."

Sandy tried to push open the car door, as the Earth became

bigger and bigger in front of him. The doors were locked.

"RE-ENTRY SPEED AT THIRTEEN THOUSAND AND FIFTY KNOTS. TRAJECTORY SET AT FOURTEEN DEGREES. SANDY, PUT ON YOUR SEATBELT."

Through his confusion and panic, Sandy realized that it was the sensible thing to do and he latched the belt around him. Scared out of his wits, he watched the earth speeding to embrace him at a bone crushing speed. The car shook violently and started to sound like it was being torn apart by brute force.

"TIME TO IMPACT – FIFTEEN SECONDS."

Sandy closed his eyes and cursed Saleem.

This is all your fault! You, and that stupid Lost Story of yours.

"TIME TO IMPACT – TEN SECONDS."

Sandy prayed to God to absolve him of all his sins and take care of his parents after he was gone.

"TIME TO IMPACT – SEVEN SECONDS."

Sandy squeezed his eyes shut and thought of Tara. His beautiful...Tara. Sandy hoped that Tara would remember and miss him when he was gone. He also hoped that his first and only book would become a bestseller, if only due to the mysterious death of one of the authors.

"TIME TO IMPACT – THREE SECONDS."

A tear slid out through Sandy's shut eyelids, and he clenched his fists as he braced himself for the impact.

"The poor guy had quite a fall."

"Yeah, I know. He went down screaming and shouting."

"I heard he was crying too," sniggered someone.

"Do you think there could be any brain damage?"

"You mean more than what's already there?"
"Hush... it looks like he's waking up."
"Is he?"
"The more pertinent question is *what* is he waking up to *now*?"
"SSssshhh!"

Sandy was in a strange state of consciousness. He was awake but he hadn't consciously realised that he was awake. It was a moment in which if he had been dreaming, he would have gone on dreaming knowing full well that this was a dream... It was a moment in which he heard everything, but nothing in particular.

He heard the hushed voices and the anxious shuffling of feet around him eventually cease. The only noise that remained around him was a constant and periodic beeping.

Must be the alarm. Sandy thought to himself.

Man! That was quiet a dream, Sandy!

He heard himself say it out loud in the peaceful and dark chamber of his own consciousness. He imagined himself standing in a dark and endless hall with a spotlight on himself.

I agree. It was all weird from the start. Ever since we opened that cursed door.

Ever since we opened the door?

Another Sandy appeared with a spotlight on him, questioning the Sandy who was already there. Slowly, he realised that a ring of Sandys stood surrounding the two, listening intently.

What door are you talking about?

You know... the door in Saleem's house.. the one that opens with that key.

Hahahahahahahaha!

The ring of Sandys laughed at the Sandy in the centre. The laughter echoed in his head.

So, you think that's when the weirdness started, is it? They all spoke together.

The laughter continued and grew louder while a thousand questions darted around piercing and slicing through the dark, invisible walls of Sandy's mind.

Oh my dear Sandy! I suppose you didn't find The Lost Story either, did you? Sandy asked Sandy as the ring of Sandys around them stopped laughing.

The Lost Story?

The ring of Sandys began whispering, repeating the same three words. The whispers grew louder and louder – a hum filling up the silence in the chamber until all that remained was a loud, piercing and blinding white noise.

"STOP IT!" Sandy screamed in his mind. The whispers ceased immediately and all the Sandys disappeared.

The persistent and regular beeping began again and made its way into Sandy's consciousness.

Sandy decided to open his eyes.

His vision was blurry at first but through the haze he could make out a number of people standing around him, looking down at him, waiting for him to wake up.

He turned his head to the right and through his now clearing vision he could make out the green bouncing line of a heartbeat monitor, probably the source of the beeping. Sandy's head hurt.

It dawned on Sandy that he was in a hospital.

"Mom? Dad? Tara?"

"Sorry, kid. Your parents don't know about this yet. I found out just a while ago. I'll call them soon." Saleem was sitting on a stool next to Sandy's bed.

"Wha... What happened?"

"They say you were in a car crash."

"A car crash?"

"Yes... and a pretty bad one at that. You were on your way to Bhimtal when your cab collided with a truck. Turns out the truck driver was drunk. He was going at 60. I hear your cab was going faster than that. By the way, who's Tara?"

The throbbing in Sandy's head was beginning to gather speed and momentum, becoming louder and more painful.

"Saleem. What the hell are you talking about? Have you gone mad? I was returning from Bhimtal, not going there. I met your uncle and got they key to that cursed door in your room... and then I opened it and walked into it. Remember? And Tara's my girlfriend... I keep telling you about her. And what's with this car accident story? Wasn't that the story of *your* accident?"

Sandy's voice rose steadily as he spoke.

"What am *I* talking about? Kid, They're saying it's a miracle that you got out of that crash without a scratch. But they're not ruling out brain damage or internal haemorrhage yet. You better rest. No need to stress that hyper-creative brain of yours."

Saleem smiled weakly at Sandy.

Ripples of déjà vu were hitting Sandy like electric shocks.

Calm down, Sandy. The old man's right. Let me get my bearings first.

"Yeah, Sandy. Better sleep it off for a few days. You're in it for the long haul, now. We'll take good care of you." Someone spoke from the far corner of the room.

Sandy turned his head to look. It was Morgan. Behind him stood Sujit, Fahid, Naina, Ketu and Moyuk.

"We got here as soon as we found out you had arrived. We are glad you're safe. The rest are on their way," Naina spoke jovially and smiled an eerie plastic smile as she tilted her head to her right. The rest of them followed suit.

Fear and panic gripped Sandy, paralyzing his limbs as he felt the power in body being drained out. He couldn't move.

"Who are the rest?" Sandy asked, not really wanting to know the answer to that question.

All the smiles disappeared.

"Don't you know? Rahu, Abhay, Hemant, Suresh and the rest of the *cast*," Moyuk said patiently with an extra emphasis on the last word.

"The rest of the *cast*?"

"Calm down, kid."

Saleem placed his hand over Sandy's now paralyzed right arm.

"Who are you talking to?"

"Them!"

Sandy jerked his head in the direction of the group.

Saleem looked up and then back at Sandy with pity. He spoke softly and sadly.

"There's nobody there, kid."

"What the fuck are you saying? I'm talking about Morgan, Sujit, Fahid and the rest of them… They're standing right there! Have you gone blind? We wrote them together, Saleem!"

"What are you guys doing here?" Sandy barked at the group but there was no response. They just stared back at him with blank expressions on their faces.

Sandy paused, and repeated the words in his head. *We wrote them together, Saleem!*

The invisible hands of panic gripped Sandy's neck and began to squeeze.

"Saleem! I think something's really wrong here. Probably wrong with me. I think I'm seeing things. What did you do to me? This is all thanks to that stupid Lost Story and that room of yours, isn't it? I want to see the doctor right now! And I want to see my parents!" Sandy was screaming louder now.

"Hey, will you relax? None of us had anything to do with this. We're in this together. Moreover, you shouldn't be getting so worked up in this condition right now. Let me go call the doctor and see if I can call your parents."

Saleem stood up and walked to the door.

Tears were trickling down Sandy's cheeks. He thought he noticed Saleem wink at Morgan. Sandy began to sob, feeling helpless and lost.

A warm sensation above his right elbow woke Sandy up. He opened his eyes and the ceiling reminded him that he was still in the hospital room and his heartbeat shot up. He immediately scanned the room to check for the *cast*. There was no one there except for a doctor on his right. Sandy dropped his head back on the pillow and swallowed, feeling a little relaxed.

I think they're gone now.

"Aah. Good to see you are awake, Sandy."

Sandy turned to look at the doctor, who had his back to him and was stooped over the table on his right, pumping a blood pressure machine. The warm sensation on his right arm was from the cuff of the blood pressure monitor.

"Oh thank God you are here, Doctor. How long have I been in?"

The doctor continued to pump the blood pressure machine, as if he hadn't heard Sandy.

"Doctor? What's the diagnosis? Have you contacted my parents?"

The doctor paused. The cuff around Sandy's arm was tight.

"Is it tight enough?"

"Yes. It is. Can you please give me some information now?"

Sandy saw the doctor's back bend further and he heard the clanking of some medical instruments on a steel tray. The pumping of the cuff resumed.

"Doctor! I think this is tight enough!"

"I decide when it is tight enough. And don't ask me questions you already know the answer to. You've been here forever, and there's nobody to contact."

The doctor turned as he spoke. Sandy was horrified. The doctor was old, short and had a slight stoop. His white lab coat was probably two sizes too big for him. His hair was pure white and stood up in odd places as if from a bad haircut. His skin was pale and he was squinting.

Sandy tried to move his limbs, but he was still paralyzed.

"It's you! Stay away from me!"

"Hold still, Sandy. I have to administer you your medicine."

The doctor was holding a syringe with a clear liquid in it in one hand, and a spoon with some white powder in the other. He squirted some of the liquid over the power with the syringe and placed it down on the tray. Next he picked up a Zippo, clicked it open and put the spoon over its flame. The white crystals began to melt into a liquid. Sandy continued to shake in the bed, trying to break free.

"I said hold still, Sandy. This won't take long."

He drew some of the white liquid into the syringe and held it up to make sure there were no air bubbles trapped inside. In a swift motion, he inserted the needle into Sandy's right arm and emptied its contents. Sandy could do nothing but watch.

Headrush.

Sandy looked at the old man as the walls behind him started to blur and become distant.

"Why do you keep doing this to yourself, Sandy? This is

not the first time. In fact, I'm quite tired of it. Don't you ever want to leave this room?"

The doctor's voice filled the room, as if it were coming from everywhere – the walls, the ceiling and the floor.

Sandy looked around as the white walls of the hospital room began to fade, revealing a crusty brown coloured room. The heartbeat monitor and the tray blurred into insignificance, and an old, dusty television took shape in front of him. He could move now. The hospital bed had disappeared and he was on the couch in Saleem's room. The door that he had opened with the key was directly in front of him.

The heroin in Sandy's system was now in full control as his head spun in a million different directions at the same time.

Sandy lay down on the couch and stared at the ceiling which appeared to be a twirling vortex directly above him.

He was enjoying this sensation.

He closed his eyes as he decided to let go... to be pulled into the vortex above.

Two men sat next to each other on the banks of the Crystal Lake and watched the reflection of the full moon sway gently in the water, as if inviting them to walk over and touch it.

The older of the two men would occasionally pick up small stones and throw them into the lake to watch the reflection of the stars dance in the ripples on the clear lake. No words were spoken.

"So we're back here. Again," the older man spoke, without looking at the other. There was a hint of sadness in his voice.

Sandy's head was much clearer now, much calmer. The

Crystal Lake always had that effect on him. He didn't respond to the question.

The older man threw another pebble into the lake. The sound of the stone hitting the water echoed as if from far away. They continued to look at the lake.

Finally Sandy spoke. His voice was devoid of all emotion.

"I'm sorry I couldn't find The Lost Story, Saleem."

Saleem sighed. "You don't need to apologize. After all, every try is worth it. Maybe we'll do better next time."

"Can I ask you a question?"

"Of course…"

"What is the Lost Story? What is it about? I can't seem to remember it."

Saleem picked up another stone. He held the stone in his palm, feeling its weight and shape, before throwing it into the lake. He wondered if a different shape would make a different sound on the water. In the end, it didn't matter. They all drowned.

"*This* is the lost story, Sandy. The story of *your life*. The story of *you* – Sandy in the real world. The one that you abandoned a long time ago, for your world of make believe. The Sandy who has locked in his room for the last 23 years"

Sandy continued to stare at the moon's reflection, not really surprised by the revelation. He felt as if a mountain had fallen on him, but for some strange reason, he had been expecting it… and was prepared for it. He had forgotten countless times. He had remembered countless times. But never once had he been surprised.

"For someone who likes stories for the fact that they end, you've never been able to finish your own story. You've got us all locked in your head, and yourself locked in that room for as long as I can remember. You have lost everything Sandy –

your friends, your family, Tara, your writing career… even your sanity."

"But I didn't leave Tara… It was she who left me."

Saleem laughed sadly and shook his head slowly.

"We've been over this so many times. Your idea of reality has always been a world standing precariously on the edge of your imagination, threatening to engulf everything that was real. Did she leave you? Did you push her out? Who can say? If I told you the truth, would you believe it? Or would you think of it to as another story? You're stuck in a story you think is real, Sandy. You are so far gone now that it just doesn't matter."

Sandy didn't speak. Saleem sighed.

"She left you because you made yourself believe that she was leaving you. It was right after you wrote *Lighthouse*. You were working on a story but seemed to have hit a road block. But you were too proud to admit that. '*How could the great Sandeep Gupta not finish what he started?*' you told yourself. You decided to lock yourself in your room and declared that you wouldn't emerge until you finished your story. Sadly, it took longer than you had planned. It was harder than you had imagined it would be. That's when, locked in that room, you created all of us and so much more… and erased all those who actually existed."

Sandy smiled sadly.

"A writer's block, you say…"

"It's not the block that was our, or rather *your* undoing, Sandy. It was our unrelenting obsession with make-believe that did us in. The obsession fed your hyper-creative mind and the self-imposed isolation made it worse. And now, all that is left in that room are your stories… a few broken memories of what was and some twisted interpretations of what might have been.

Everything and everyone – from Vidya to your parents to Vineet – are all just stories in your head. There's no Lost Story, anymore. There's just you. And you're lost."

Saleem picked up another stone, held it in the palm of his and for a few seconds, and threw it into the lake.

"What's behind the door, Saleem?"

"The real world."

Stone. Feel. Throw.

"Go back to the real world, kid."

Saleem got up. He stood beside Sandy and stretched his arms and back. When he was done, he bent down and put his right hand on Saleem's left shoulder.

Sandy didn't say anything. Saleem straighened up, turned around, and began walking away towards the woods around the Crystal Lake.

"Do you know what John Lennon said, Saleem?"

Saleem stopped and turned.

"What did he say?"

Sandy was still looking at the Crystal Lake.

"He said 'Reality is overrated. It leaves so much to the imagination anyway.'"

Saleem nodded.

"He was so right."

Saleem turned once more, and walked into the woods.

C.Koshman